MW01601187

LEATHER AND GRACE

MAGGIE RYAN

Leather and Grace

By

Maggie Ryan

Copyright ©2019 by Maggie Ryan

All Rights Reserved

Cover Design By: Jay Aheer@Simply Defined Art

1

"YOU KNOW, I don't remember any sponge bath I've ever gotten being given with such intimate relish," Quentin said as he let the door shut behind him. His presence caused Brody to chuckle, and what sounded suspiciously like a muffled giggle from the woman who had her hand wrapped around the root of his very impressive erection as her mouth engulfed half of his cock.

"Just ignore him," Brody said, moving a hand to the back of her blonde head. "Eyes to me."

Quentin could see the flush on her cheeks as she lifted her eyes to obey Brody's softly spoken command.

"That's my good girl. God, you are beautiful. Nice and deep, now."

Quentin leaned against the wall, his arms crossed as he unabashedly watched the woman perform fellatio. As her cheeks hollowed and luscious lips spread wider, blue eyes locked onto her patient's, she managed to take almost his entire length into her mouth, very effectively controlling her gag reflex as her throat accepted the invasion of his cockhead. It didn't take much longer before Brody's palms were cupping her face, his murmurs of approval accompanied by her soft mews as she prepared for his release. It came with a stiffening of his body and a bellow of pure bliss as he shot his seed down her throat.

Quentin had to admit the woman knew what she was doing, maintaining her position, her cheeks continuing to puff in and out, her hand gently squeezing as it slid up and down his length, milking every drop of his cum until Brody relaxed against his pillows, one hand dropping from her cheek to stroke across her top lip.

"Beautiful, simply beautiful, baby. You may release," Brody said, not taking his eyes from her as she slowly allowed his cock to slip free, only to swipe her tongue up, down, and around his shaft as if ensuring she left not a single drop of his essence behind.

"Thank you, sir," she said, sitting up and slipping off the bed. Quentin smiled as she pulled the thin sheet up and arranged it around Brody's body the best she could with his left leg hanging in the air, the cast that ran from his toes to his hip supported by the traction equipment. She moved to the head of the bed, squealing when he pulled her down to kiss her deeply at the same time as he swatted her behind. She was a bit breathless when he released her. "What was that for?" she asked, a hand moving to rub across the seat of her purple scrubs.

"Just because you've got the cutest little ass in the world." She smiled as he leaned forward a bit so she could fluff and rearrange the pillows behind his back.

"Okay, enough fussing. You may greet our guest."

Laurie immediately ran around the bed, and Quentin barely had time to push away from the wall before she launched herself at him.

"Oh my God, it's so great to see you again, Master Quentin."

Quentin stiffened for a moment and then tightened his arms, embracing the pretty blonde. "None of that. It's just Quentin to you. It's good to see you, Laurie. Though why you didn't take the chance to run when this fool busted his leg I'll never know."

"Even though he can't manage but a few swats now, I'm afraid my poor butt wouldn't like the price required when he heals," she said with a smile. Quentin grinned, remembering that the girl was not only committed to his best friend, she'd definitely enjoy whatever Brody deemed a proper price for any disobedience. The two had been inseparable since they'd met, and from the looks of it, they would remain so. Quentin felt a rare spark of jealousy, and yet wouldn't truly wish for them to be anything but happy together.

"I promise I'll make it up to you, baby," Brody said, pulling her down for another kiss.

"I'll hold you to that." Laurie brushed his hair back from his forehead to plant another kiss. "I'll let you two catch up while I run get your dinner." Turning to Quentin, she said, "I'm going to be bringing Brody's dinner and I'd be happy to pick you up some as well."

"Better take her up on the offer," Brody suggested. "I can't promise what you'll find in the fridge."

"We're not talking hospital food, are we?"

"No, Sammy's catfish special is on the menu for tonight. Of course, if you can't handle real Cajun food anymore, I suppose I can drop by the cafeteria..." She squealed when Quentin's hand connected with her backside.

"Still as saucy as ever, I see," he said, a bit amazed his hand seemed to have reacted without direction from his brain. Acting as if it hadn't been out of the norm, he continued. "I cut my teeth on Cajun food and no one can beat Sammy's."

"Good, then I'll be back in about an hour."

"Thanks, babe, and remind him that I'll need at least a double order of red beans and rice and extra gator balls. I have to keep my strength up," Brody said, giving an exaggerated sigh as he pushed up a bit, as if attempting to find a more comfortable position.

Quentin saw Laurie roll her eyes but she nodded. "I'll be sure to tell him you are withering away."

"Don't think I didn't see that," Brody said. "Add rolling eyes to your list."

"Yes, sir," Laurie said with yet another smile. "I'll be back soon. Try not to blow away until then."

"Speaking of blowing..."

"Lord, you are the most demanding patient I've

ever had." Giving a dismissive wave, she opened the door and then turned back, her teasing expression turning serious. "It's good to have you home, Quentin. It's been far too long," she said softly. "You've been missed."

After a moment's hesitation, he gave her a nod and watched as she slipped out of the room. Quentin just shook his head as he approached the hospital bed. "Still managing to deceive her into thinking you're a great guy, I see."

Brody shook his hand and grinned. "I know, it's rather amazing, isn't it?"

Quentin nodded and pulled the chair a bit closer and took a seat. He gestured toward the equipment hanging over the bed, "How's the leg?"

"Hurts like a son of a bitch," Brody admitted, "but it's the feeling of helplessness that's the real pain. Not only can't I give my girl a proper spanking, but with Dave on his honeymoon, I'm really short-handed. That's where you come in. I can't tell you how glad I am that you're back—"

"I'm not back," Quentin interrupted. "I can give you a few weeks, but that's it."

Brody took a moment then shrugged. "Well, that'll help. I've got a new class starting on Monday. You'll have the weekend to meet the staff and reacquaint yourself with the club. You know, the one you partially own?"

Quentin again ignored the dig. "What's the class?"

"Introduction into submission."

"Ah, fuck, Brody..."

"Before you say anything, you know it takes some women a long time to gather the courage to take that first step and, well, frankly, I don't have the heart to cancel. Look, I know this is a huge favor but I honestly can't think of a better man for the job." When Quentin didn't speak, he continued. "Besides, it's been almost two years. I've let it slide but, man, this was your dream as well as mine."

"I offered to let you buy me out."

"I'm not interested, and you can't sell unless I agree."

"That was a stupid clause—"

"And yet it's in our contract. Besides, Quentin, you can't hide forever. What happened—"

"Don't." The one word was snapped out in a tone that would have silenced almost anyone. But Brody just shook his head.

"You know I'm right. If Beth were here—"

"She's not!" Quentin snarled.

"But you are, damn it," Brody said, his own voice rising. "It's past time for you to pull your head out of your ass and rejoin the world. You can't keep blaming yourself. It was a tragedy, but you know that Beth wouldn't want to see you this way." Grimacing as he pushed himself back against the pillows, he spoke again. "Life is too damn short, and you aren't made out to be a hermit." When Quentin remained silent, his hand running across his face, Brody sighed. "Listen, forget it. I'll call the women and refund the fee."

"No." After a long pause, Quentin continued.

"You're right. If you cancel, some of the girls will see it as a kind of divine intervention that they shouldn't explore their needs. Society puts out enough of that crap. When is Dave due back?"

"A month from now."

"A month? Fuck, that's some honeymoon!"

"Yeah, well, nothing is too good for his bride." Brody chuckled. "Jen's a teacher so has the summer off. She even offered to forego the trip if Dave was needed here but—"

"I know; you didn't have the heart to cancel their honeymoon. Who's left if both you and Dave are out of commission?"

"Hand me that water, would you?" Brody asked, pointing to the insulated mug on the side table. After Quentin did and he took a sip, he answered the question. "Conner is a good man but he's not yet ready to fly solo, so he'll be your second. Adam is still manning the bar, Trent and Sloan are monitors and can handle the club. All three will be available to help with the training sessions, but they can't be expected to work 24/7. Membership has picked up considerably, which you'll know if you've been paying any attention."

"I have," Quentin reluctantly admitted. "You've done a great job, Brody. You could well afford to buy my share—"

"Again, I'm not interested," Brody said firmly. "I'm happy with the way things are even if we're short-handed. I'm expecting you to cover for me at least until Dave gets back." He paused and then said, "Look, if you still want to give it all up, we'll discuss it later." When Quentin opened his mouth, Brody quickly added, "But only if you give it your all while you are here. Our clients expect the best and won't be happy with you just going through the motions. I'd rather cancel the class if you can't promise—"

"I already said I'd do it," Quentin said, a little pissed at the inference that he would do some half-assed job. "A month for a honeymoon? You know, for a Dom, you are really a pushover."

"Let's keep that fact between us, okay?" Brody said, taking a sip of water. "And, as long as I'm being such a pussy, I've got one more favor to ask, but this is not really for me. It's for Laurie. She's got this friend..."

"I said I'd help at the club, but I didn't agree to being set up."

"It's not like that," Brody said. "I'm not asking you to date her. Her friend has her first art show tomorrow night. I'd promised to take Laurie but that's obviously out of the question, and I don't want her going alone. I'd really owe you if you'd be her escort."

"Gee, I'd love to, but I seem to have forgotten to pack my tux."

"No problem, it's not that kind of show. You might even enjoy it. Grace is a damn good artist. Speaking of art, you did bring my order with you, right?"

"Yes, but I haven't calculated your bill yet."

Brody chuckled and shook his head. "Don't tell me, the price of leather just skyrocketed?"

Quentin shrugged and then nodded. "Fine, I'll take Laurie and show her a good time."

"Not too good," Brody warned. "It's been a while since I've shared."

"I'll remember that," Quentin said, the memory of the sweet blonde kneeling at his feet, her mouth wrapped around his cock, flooding into his mind. It was just another pleasure he'd walked away from, and once again found he was very glad she'd had been there to help Brody when he'd simply been unable to stay.

"Thanks," Brody said. "I owe you one. Hell, I owe you more than one."

Quentin knew that was a lie. It was he who owed this man a great deal. Still, it was just like Brody to attempt to alleviate any sense of guilt Quentin felt over leaving his business partner to explain his walking away from a life they'd worked hard so hard to build together.

The two spent the next hour catching up and Quentin was more than ready to eat when Laurie pushed through the door. He stood and relieved her of the bags of food, his mouth watering at the aroma of Cajun spices. The daily special included blackened catfish, and fat, crunchy hushpuppies. The red beans and rice were every bit as good as he remembered. Between he and Brody, they managed to put away a dozen gator balls, which were a mixture of alligator, rice and boudin sausage in a cornmeal breading and deep fried to golden perfection. As Brody popped another jalapeno pepper into his mouth, Quentin grinned. The meal was definitely not the bland, healthier fare offered by the hospital but he didn't doubt it would go much further in keeping a patient's spirits up.

"Thanks, Laurie," Quentin said, gathering their trash and tossing it into the wastebasket.

"You're welcome," Laurie said. "Oh, and Sammy said to tell you that you better stop in to say hello."

"I'll do that."

Brody thanked her as well as she refilled his water glass. "Quentin has a nice surprise for you, babe," Brody said. When her eyes widened as she looked between the men, he chuckled. "Not that kind of surprise. He would love to escort you to Grace's show tomorrow night."

"Really? That's great!" Laurie kissed him and then jumped off the bed to hug Quentin and kiss his cheek. "You'll love it, I promise. Grace is fantastic!"

"I'm sure she is," Quentin said. "What time do I need to pick you up?"

"Eight sounds good, but you won't have to walk far," she said, lifting her left hand and wiggling her fingers. "Just down the hall, in fact."

Quentin didn't know how he could have missed the diamond on her finger. "Well, hell, when did that happen?"

"Just a few days ago," Laurie said, reaching down to entwine her fingers with Brody's. "If I'd known all it took was some rather spectacular drugs—"

"Hey, I proposed when in my right mind," Brody said. "Seeing my life flash before my eyes as I fell off that cliff, well, I realized that it wasn't worth..." he paused and then continued, "I knew that if I wanted the best medical care, I'd get it from my loving fiancée."

Quentin knew that hadn't been what Brody was about to say, but didn't call him on it. "Congratulations, I couldn't be happier for you both." When he saw her snuggle closer, he stood. "I'll leave you to tuck the big boy into bed."

"Wait. Honey, grab my keys, would you?" Brody asked, motioning to the rolling bed tray. She had it open when Quentin spoke.

"No need, unless you've changed the locks?"

Brody grinned and shook his head. "Nope. And, a man who keeps keys on his key ring isn't ready to shut those doors, my friend."

Quentin lifted his hand in a dismissive wave. "I'll talk to you tomorrow." Right before he stepped through the door, he turned back with a grin. "And, while I rarely can say this, you'd better be a good boy and do whatever Nurse Laurie commands." His words drew laughter from them both, and he managed to keep the smile on his face until he was out in the hall. He'd prepared himself for returning to the club but had not once considered that he'd have to be more involved than a simple overseer.

In the parking lot, he climbed into his truck and then sat without starting the ignition. He'd agreed to help and yet wasn't sure how much of a help he would be. Finding no answers, he turned the key and pulled away from the curb with a deep sigh. As much as he wanted to turn around and head back down I-10 to disappear into the Atchafalaya swamp, he had given his word. Weaving his way from the hospital through the labyrinth of streets, he couldn't help but admit that he could practically feel the blood in his veins begin to rush.

It had been a long time since he'd visited New Orleans proper and yet the scene remained the same. Tourists who had no idea which streets took them into the heart of the action clogged the roads, and horns blared, adding to the din of sound rolling through his window. Turning down a narrow side street, he maneuvered his way toward one of the oldest parts of the city. He left the truck in idle as he got out and unlocked the wrought iron gate that spanned the back driveway. He pulled through, jumped down once more to lock it behind him, and then drove to what had once been a carriage house but was now a garage. After parking, he climbed out of the truck for the last time, giving a whistle as he looked at the silver Jaguar that took up the other half of the garage. He grinned as he lowered the tailgate of his truck to maneuver the motorcycle down. Just as he loved vintage bikes, Brody loved vintage sports cars. The refurbished Indian Sport was his favored method of transportation in a city where traffic was often congested and parking spaces scarce.

Looking toward the house, he decided to leave the duffel bags for the time being. Now was as good a time as any to start paying back the debt he owed his friend. Returning to the truck's cab, he opened the glove compartment and retrieved a small jeweler's box. Opening it, he looked down at the ring that would gain him unlimited entrance even more so than his keys. Sliding it onto his finger, it felt both foreign and familiar. He unlocked the small gate and stepped through. If he were going to do this, he'd do it one step at a time.

Walking around the corner, he shook his head. It still amazed him that no one strolling outside the fence or eating in the restaurant would suspect what really happened above their heads. The house was located on a corner and took up more acreage than most of its counterparts. His first grin came as he imagined the tour bus narrator spouting how southern belles were once escorted around the grounds by the elite of New Orleans society and served mint juleps on any one of the large verandas that encircled the house. He and Brody had spent a great deal of money restoring every brick and stone after purchasing the house a decade earlier. Massive magnolia trees filled the courtyard, their blossoms sweetening the humid air and competing with the rich spices that wafted out when the door opened to allow an older couple to exit. Their smiles and the gift bag clutched in the woman's hand guaranteed they'd enjoyed their visit. He again had to smile at the irony. He'd been a bit unsure of Brody's plan to run more than one business and yet he couldn't deny the man's genius. Doing so allowed anyone who visited the city to enjoy great food in the front restaurant, and shop in the adjoining souvenir store to purchase anything from t-shirts and Mardi Gras beads to bottles of Sammy's special hot-sauce and packets of his spices to try to replicate the dishes they'd enjoyed. The address might well be one of the great old homes to see, the restaurant touted as one of the best for authentic Cajun cuisine, but only those who had been carefully vetted and who could afford the high price of privacy for their chosen play would ever make it above the first floor.

2

WALKING INTO THE RESTAURANT, he discovered every table was full, and people were chatting while patiently waiting to be seated. Waitresses scurried between tables, carrying trays full of red plastic baskets filled with mouthwatering dishes and tall glasses of tea, or any one of a wide variety of beers. The hostess gave him a big smile. "Welcome to Sammy's. I'm sorry, the wait is about a half-hour but I promise the food is worth it."

"That I know," Quentin said, "I'm not here to eat—"

"Quentin Doucet!"

A shrill voice had him looking up and breaking into the first real smile since he'd left his cabin.

"Hi, Miss Hannah."

"Don't you 'hi' me. Get yourself over here and give me a squeeze." The young hostess giggled as he obediently stepped around the stand, went to the older woman, and lifting her off her feet, he gave her not only a hug but a resounding smack full on her lips.

"Laws, put me down!" Hannah demanded, swatting at his arm and yet never once losing her ear to ear grin. "Oh, Sammy is gonna be thrilled to see you!" Before Quentin could speak, she turned toward the kitchen to bellow, "Sammy, you old coot. Come see who's kissin' your gal."

Quentin heard several people chuckle and a couple actually gasp as a man appeared, his body taking up most of the doorway. Sammy Breecher had been a beloved linebacker for the one season he'd played for the Saints before he blew his knee out. The tackle had averted the Falcon's from adding points to the scoreboard as well as earning bragging rights for the two cities age-old rivalry. Saints fans were grateful he'd kept the winning ball in New Orleans, but saddened that it had meant the end of a promising career. Sammy wasn't a man to be kept down. His positive attitude and commitment to giving back to his community had ensured his fans would praise him for his cooking just as they had for his ability on the field.

"Stop that hollerin', woman," he demanded, reaching the couple and bending to pop his wife's backside before he threw his arms around Quentin. "It's about time you got your skinny ass home, son."

"It's good to see you," Quentin said, barely flinching as the man's ham sized fist pounded him on the back. Though they were both about the same height, Sammy outweighed him by at least fifty pounds—none of it fat.

"Come on back," Sammy said. "You hungry?"

"With all that food you sent with Laurie?" Quentin said, rubbing his flat stomach. "You keep feeding Brody like that and we'll have to roll him out of that bed."

Sammy's laugh bounced around the room as they stepped through the door. "Just doing my part in keeping him happy. Not much else the fool can do."

"Oh, I'm sure he'll think of something," Hannah said, giving them both a look that had the men grinning. "You're too thin, Quentin. I don't want to hear another word. I'm bringing you a big piece of pie."

"Now that is something I would never refuse." It was the right thing to say as the woman would never admit it, but he knew she secretly adored the fact that her pies were famous.

"Make that two, and coffee," Sammy said, leading Quentin toward the small office at one side of the kitchen. "This good, or would you rather go into the other dining room?"

"This is fine," Quentin said, knowing the man referred to the private dining room that took up the back of the building. Taking a seat, he said, "I'd ask how business was going but from the waiting line you've got, I'm guessing it's good."

"Can't complain," Sammy said, rising to his feet when Hannah entered carrying a tray. "Thanks, darlin'." He took the tray and gave her a kiss on her cheek. Quentin smiled. The couple had met in kindergarten and had, in their own words, never given another soul a single glance.

After she left, the two men dug into the huge pieces of pecan pie, sipping on the chicory coffee between bites.

"Seriously, son, I'm glad to have you back. Brody will never admit it, but it's taken a toll on him, running the place on his own."

"I know," Quentin said with a sigh. "I never really expected him to refuse to buy me out or allow me to sell to another. It was almost too much for the two of us, and if the reports of the club's success aren't exaggerated, how he's managed is nothing short of a testament to his dedication."

"They're not," Sammy assured him. "You think the waiting line out front is long then you should ask to see the waiting list for membership. Brody refuses to allow the membership to become too large unless you two agree to expand the club or move it. That man has just been waiting for you."

Quentin was silent for several minutes as he finished his coffee. "I'll tell you what I told him. I'm here, but I'm not planning on staying. It's just too hard."

"Hell, son, life is fucking hard. You don't get to crawl into some hole like a mudbug. You grieve, then get up and move on. You've got an awful lot of living to do yet, and it would be a damned shame if you did that living alone. Hannah would tear you a new one if she thought you were going to take the easy way out."

"Easy? I promise, it hasn't been easy," Quentin said, a bit of anger coming through in his tone.

"We all lost Beth," Sammy said bluntly. Finishing his own coffee, he set his mug down. "I know it ain't easy but, Quentin, you can't keep blaming yourself. There wasn't a damn thing you could have done."

"I should have kept her safe," Quentin said softly.

"You couldn't have known she'd choose to ignore your request she either go with you or stay home. And she couldn't have known that by choosing not to do either, she was gonna pay with her life. Yes, it was horrid and yes, it hurts and will always be painful, but it wasn't your fault."

Quentin disagreed but kept his thoughts to himself. He'd never be able to stop wondering whether if he'd only taken the plunge and asked her to marry him, would she have said yes and agreed to go with him that weekend? Instead, he'd backed down, his gut telling him that while he thought he loved her, he wasn't completely positive she was as committed to him and their chosen lifestyle as she portrayed. Beth had gotten angry when the proposal she'd expected on their anniversary hadn't come. She'd informed him that he wasn't the only man in New Orleans and the moment he left town, she'd gone out, and had never come home. Her body hadn't been found for almost two months... months that had threatened to destroy Quentin.

He still wasn't sure what had been worse. Being suspected of murdering the woman he'd considered asking to become his wife, or being left to wonder what had happened to her. Records showed she'd been at the club that night but no one remembered seeing her. Their security checked people in by their use of the rings but, at the time, hadn't required a fingerprint as well. That had since been changed. Only the fact that several people testified that he'd been in Texas had kept Quentin out of jail, though he'd spent hours answering the same questions again and again.

A hunter stumbled across her body in the swamp and she'd only been identifiable through her dental records, her ring and the braided leather bracelet on her wrist. A bracelet that Quentin had made for her. Looking down, he realized he was twisting an almost identical ring around his finger. How could he move on when he felt such a weight of guilt that it threatened to smother him at times?

He wasn't aware that Sammy had moved until a hand descended on his shoulder. "I didn't say it will be easy, but the first steps never are. Just take it one step at a time, son. You've got people who love you and are here to help."

"I know," Quentin said, realizing his friend was echoing his own words of earlier. He reached up to cover Sammy's hand with his own. "Thanks, Sammy, thanks for being here."

"Never gonna go nowhere else," Sammy said. "This is where Hannah and I belong... where you belong."

Weariness descended on Quentin as he stood and Sammy seemed to know it. "You get settled in. Take another step tomorrow and another the day after that. I promise, one day you'll be walking into the light again."

Quentin managed a nod and went back out the front and around the building. It would have been faster to step through the door from the kitchen and take the elevator, but he wasn't in a great hurry and admitted he needed the time to gather his courage again. Grabbing his duffel bags from the truck, he went to a door at the back of the building. Draping the straps of the bags over his shoulder, he pressed the raised insignia of the ring into a depression and laid his right thumb onto the adjacent pad. The lock clicked and he pulled the heavy steel door open to take his first step back into a life he'd sworn he'd left behind forever.

AN HOUR LATER, he was out of excuses. After unpacking, which took him all of ten minutes, he'd walked around his suite of rooms, glad to see that while they hadn't changed, someone, most likely Laurie, had made sure nothing was left to remind him of the years he'd called this wing of the house home. There was fresh paint on the walls and new linens and towels. The color scheme was clean and the décor uncluttered. Anything that had belonged to Beth had been taken away, except for the one photo he'd found remaining on his nightstand. He wondered how many times it had been removed, only to be returned as Laurie fought to decide whether or not to keep it in place. He'd sat on the bed, the frame in his hands, for several long minutes. It was as if he were waiting for the smiling woman's expression to change into one of accusation, of betrayal. When she remained a frozen reminder of a woman whose life had been cut short, he took the frame with him. He wasn't ready to let go but couldn't imagine falling asleep with an actual memory so close. He had enough trouble with the memories in his head.

Placing the frame on one of the shelves holding books he'd read or had planned to read, he walked into the kitchen and opened the fridge. Smiling, he removed a beer and popped the cap with his ring. Holding the beer up, he said, "Thanks, Laurie." After taking the last sip, he took a shower, changed into a pair of black trousers and pulled on a leather vest over his black t-shirt. Out of excuses, he left his suite and walked to the elevator that was between his and the opposite suite that Brody called home. Brody and Laurie, he corrected himself as he entered the elevator. When the doors opened, he stepped into another world.

He stood for a moment, just looking around as if to acclimate himself to the environment. The hostess stood waiting, allowing him to approach her, though her puzzled look had him knowing she was wondering how he'd come upstairs. The elevator used by clients was at the other end of the hall. This one was reserved for only his and Brody's use.

"Hello," she said as he walked toward her.

"Welcome to *Plaisir*." He saw her eyes drop to his hand and widen as she saw his ring. "I'm sorry... I know I'm supposed to know everyone, but—"

"Relax, it's fine. You can't be expected to know me. I'm Quentin Doucet."

"Nice to meet you, I'm Ellen. What can I do for you, Master Doucet... or is it Master Quentin?"

Again he fought the urge to say it didn't matter. Protocol was protocol and he needed to remember that for the time he was here. "Master Doucet will do," he said, not really surprised when a little voice in his head asked when he'd become such a formal asshole.

"Ah, I might not recognize you but I know the name. Again, welcome to *Plaisir*, Master Doucet."

"You know, let's make it Master Quentin, all right?"

He had to give the woman credit as she didn't question his apparent indecisiveness.

"Of course, Master Quentin."

"Thank you, Ellen." He was about to explain his presence when he realized he wouldn't on any other night. Nodding to her, he stepped around the hostess station and pulled the open ledger from beneath the counter. "Busy tonight?"

"Yes, sir. Members are beginning to call earlier in the week to reserve space in one of the theme rooms and the private rooms. Saturday nights are busier but Fridays seem to be giving them a run for their money. I hate to disappoint those members who don't call early..." Her words broke off. "Forgive me, I'm usually not so chatty. I'm just a little nervous."

"Don't be," Quentin said, sliding the book back. "You're doing just fine. Meeting the clients' expectations is invaluable, and I appreciate your concerns."

"Thank you, sir."

Quentin managed a smile as he moved toward the door, his ring and thumbprint again giving him access. Turning the knob, he took another step back into what had been his past. They had gutted the entire third floor and the space was huge. A bar sat to his left and, from his quick glance, was doing a good business. There were several seating areas scattered around it and a large space behind, where a few couples were dancing. He grinned thinking he'd be able to hear the same music in a bar down the street and yet was quite positive the dancers would be wearing far more than some of these women were. Bourbon Street might see tourists who'd had one drink too many lifting up their shirts to flash their tits in hopes of having strings of beads showered upon them, but the women in his club were often totally topless and if they wore jewelry, it was quite often in the form of their master's collar around their throats or pretty little clamps swinging from tightly compressed nipples.

On his right toward the back, were several stations where public play took place. A few rooms had been set up for fetish and role-play. There were a half dozen rooms in the very back, available for booking for those who weren't into more than a little public display. He'd seen that every room had been booked for the entire weekend.

A shriek had him turning back to the bar only to see a blur of black hair and a flash of gold running toward him. "Master Quentin!" a woman squealed, breaking every protocol in the book by throwing her arms around him and jumping up and down. "It's really you! Oh, God, it's really you!"

"Hello, Jessica," Quentin said, giving the woman a hug and chuckling as her Dom approached at a much more sedate pace. "Hey, Keith."

"Quentin," Keith said, grinning and rolling his eyes. "She's just a little excited."

"So I see," Quentin said, bending to buzz his lips across Jessica's cheek. "I gotta say I'm glad to see your enthusiasm hasn't waned."

"Sorry, sir," Jessica said, though her tone belied the truth of her statement. "I just couldn't believe it when Master Brody said you were coming back but oh, I'm so very glad you did."

"Okay, honey, you can let him go now."

Quentin felt her arms release him but she didn't step back more than an inch. "Um, I-I can't," Jessica said, her eyes widening.

"Why not?" Keith asked.

"I-I seem to be stuck."

Keith chuckled. "The whole room has seen you sticking like glue. Not a very good example for the newbies, Jess. Now, come away."

"I really can't," Jessica said. "My um, nip... um, I'm

really stuck, sir."

Quentin looked down to see her face turning scarlet and grinned. She'd always been a bit uneasy talking about her body and it seemed some things hadn't changed. But she did indeed appear stuck. "Permission to touch your sub?" he asked, the proper protocol easily coming back.

"Seeing as how my wife threw herself at you, I'd say you don't even need to ask. Touch away."

"I'm sorry I couldn't make the wedding," Quentin said.

"You were missed," Keith said, then grinned when his wife gave a soft sigh of exasperation. Lifting an item hanging from his belt, he said, "Your gift has been very much appreciated by me and, well, tolerated by my little miscreant."

"I'm glad you've enjoyed it," Quentin said and then chuckled when Jess gave a little snort. "I seem to remember a good spanking did wonders toward settling this one."

"A memory that shall be tested as soon as you manage to release her." Both men chuckled again as another squeal of protest sounded.

Quentin moved his hand and worked to untangle the small chain from around the button of his vest. Jessica's sharp yelp told of the discomfort she felt when he had to release the clamp attached to her nipple that had been hidden by a spray of purple flowers. "Sorry, little one," he said, helping her to step back. He considered dropping the clamp but felt Keith's eyes on him. Remembering his place, at least for the next few weeks, he said instead, "Deep breath."

Jessica nodded and once she'd obeyed, he placed the jaws of the clamp around her pinched nipple and slowly allowed the teeth to close, once more trapping her tender flesh in its bite.

"Than-thank you, sir," she said.

"You're welcome. Very pretty jewelry, Jessica."

"Isn't it? It was a wedding gift," she said, turning to smile at her husband. "One that I also both adore and hate."

Keith laughed and taking her arm, turned her slightly in order to apply the flat of his hand to her right cheek. "Go over to the spanking bench. I'll be there in a few minutes."

"Yes, Master," Jessica said and then giggled, turned back and lifted herself onto her toes to press her lips against Quentin's cheek. "Welcome home, Master Quentin." She yelped when another swat added a matching red handprint to her left cheek and then, giving a little wave, bounced across the room toward the waiting spanking bench.

"You know, kudzu is said to be eating the south," Quentin said, recognizing the pattern of the body jewelry worn by the precocious sub.

"Yeah, but since she's managed to wrap herself around every part of my soul, I couldn't think of a better design," Keith said, his pride in his wife evident in his tone. He slapped Quentin on the back. "Come over in a few minutes and you can see the pattern repeated across that lovely little arse of hers."

"Ah, now I understand the request," Quentin said. He was known to provide a custom paddle to those few who he'd come to consider more friend than client. When he received his invitation to their wedding, he'd known he wouldn't go but had also known he'd do his best to fill Keith's request for a depiction of the kudzu vine and its flowers on the surface of the leather paddle he'd created as his wedding gift. "I'll be over in a bit." Keith nodded and turned to follow his wife's path, this time with a definite bounce in his step.

Quentin approached the bar and shook hands with Adam, who was on duty. He didn't even have to order as an ice-cold bottle of his preferred beer was set before him. "Thanks."

"I considered leaping over the bar to plaster myself to you but, well, seems someone else had the same idea, and she makes a much better leech. All the same, welcome back."

Quentin just shook his head and both men turned their attention to the spanking bench when a sharp cry immediately followed a rather solid thwack testified that Jessica's spanking had begun. Quentin could remember the day Jessica had come to her first class. She'd been as bouncy then as she was now. Her earlier stumbling words told him that while she'd come a long way, proven by her instant obedience to her Dom's order, she was still coming to terms with her submission. She'd found her perfect match in Keith, who would never hesitate to correct her, but would also never fail to let her know he loved her dearly.

When he'd finished half of his beer, Quentin stepped back and moved to observe the punishment. Several others had gathered to watch, all keeping a respectful distance and maintaining silence out of respect for the couple. The only one making noise was Jessica who was yelping with every stroke of the paddle yet not attempting to rise even though she wasn't restrained. Yes, she'd come quite a long way as each stroke left the imprint of the same design she wore around her neck, at her breasts, around her waist and, from this vantage point, even held deep within her body if the spray of three blossoms nestled between her reddening buttocks was any proof.

Gradually her yelps turned into softer moans as the pain began to morph into pleasure. Quentin saw smiles of approval on both the faces of the subs and their Doms surrounding the area. This was the true meaning of the club's name. *Plaisir*, translated from French, meant pleasure. Though pain was freely given and accepted, it was one way to ultimate pleasure for the women who gave the gift of their submission to their partners within these walls. As the spanking drew to a close, couples began to drift away. At the last stroke, only Quentin and a woman staff member remained.

"As I said, beautiful," Quentin said, looking down at Jessica's now very red ass.

Keith helped his wife up, holding her close as her

legs were a bit wobbly. She lifted her cheek from his chest to give Quentin a smile. "I really do love you, sir, but that paddle..."

Quentin chuckled and bent to kiss her cheek. "Remember, little one, lying will get you paddled again. Now, go and let your Master take care of you." Keith swept her up into his arms and carried her toward one of the more secluded couches. Before Quentin could say a word, the staff member was wiping down the station.

"Thank you," he said, giving her a smile.

"It's Molly, sir," she said with her own smile.

"Thanks, Molly," he repeated and left her to her work. These staff members were almost invisible, and yet they made sure that the clients didn't have to wait for a station to be cleaned and sanitized between uses, or ask for a condom as bowls were placed and kept filled within easy reach of both the seating areas as well as the equipment. They helped secure subs to apparatus and were also available to step in and play if requested. None were attached permanently to any one Dom but while they were all expected to obey any order given, they were women who found their own happiness in serving a variety of men.

Quentin made a circle of the room, greeting those he knew and introducing himself to those few faces he didn't recognize. He returned to the bar to see that Conner had taken a seat.

"So what do you think?"

Quentin had just taken a sip of his beer and was about to answer he thought everything looked as if it were going great when Conner qualified his statement.

"I mean about the club. I know you and Brody don't think I can handle the class."

"Hey, give him a break. He just got back," Adam said.

Not one to react to what he considered basically a pout, Quentin finished his beer before saying, "The club looks great and the clients seem happy. Let's get together tomorrow to catch up and discuss it then. How about noon? I'll put in a request to Hannah for lunch."

"Sure," Conner said. Quentin nodded, thanked Adam for the beer and dropped a ten-dollar tip on the bar. As an owner, his drinks were free but he never failed to tip his staff. They provided more than good service with their bartending skills. They provided complete confidentiality for any one of the rather affluent members of New Orleans' society who valued their privacy outside of those who shared in the lifestyle.

"Night, boss," Adam said, as if to remind Conner exactly who he was talking to.

"Night," Quentin said. As he nodded to Ellen and entered the elevator, he realized how exhausted he was. Though he had to admit once he was in his bedroom stripping off his clothes, it hadn't been as hard or as foreign feeling as he'd imagined it would be. He slid naked between the sheets, and instead of tossing and turning as he'd feared he'd do, he was sound asleep almost before his head hit the pillow.

3

GRACE DIDN'T KNOW what was worse. Having to keep a smile on her face as she mingled with complete strangers or having to do so while wearing the devil's shoes. Her feet were killing her in the four-inch stiletto heels. She had just begun to toe off her left shoe when she gave a startled gasp, her drink sloshing over the rim of her glass as she twisted to see who had just grabbed her arm. The move had her ankle twisting as she toppled forward.

"Easy," the man said, tightening his grip, grinning as she bounced off his chest.

"I'm so sorry," she said, finding it awkward to attempt to shove her toes back into her shoe while pushing against him as he maintained his grip on her arm. "You can let me go."

"Are you sure?" he asked. "It wouldn't be the first time an artist overindulged in cheap liquor waiting to see if they will be the new toast of the art world or... well, simply toast."

Feeling her face flush, Grace no longer cared how it looked as she planted her palm against his chest and pushed up. "I'm not tipsy; you just startled me." At his look of disbelief, she lifted her glass. "It's ginger ale, not champagne."

"Ah, so you can't even blame alcohol for your lack of grace, Grace."

His chuckle had her really having to fight not to remind him that if he hadn't grabbed her, she wouldn't have to hear a phrase she'd heard ad nauseam throughout her life. She also didn't appreciate the fact that he had yet to release her arm even as he lifted his own glass to clink against hers.

"David Brooks at your service."

Of course he was, Grace thought with a silent moan. Who else would it be except for the critic Charles had warned her to be nice to. "It's nice to meet you, Mr. Brooks. Again, I apologize for stumbling into you. I hope I didn't spill anything—"

"Relax, you only spilt on the floor." Looking around he spotted a server and snapped his fingers, pointing to the small amount of liquid pooled at their feet. The girl immediately came over and dropped to mop up the ginger ale. Once she straightened, he plucked the flute from Grace's hand and handed it to her. "There," David said, "problem solved. No more fake champagne for you and no more mess for the help."

Grace hadn't liked his snatching her glass from her without even asking, but she was really affronted by the snapping of his fingers, his comment about those catering the event, or the fact that he hadn't even bothered to thank the young woman. She also didn't like that despite her slight tug, he'd yet to release her arm. It took everything within her not to tell him he was a pompous ass, but managed to refrain as Charles had told her this man could either help make or break her career.

"I must say, I wasn't quite sure what to expect but your work has definitely kept me from being bored."

"I'm glad you are enjoying it," she said, hoping the grimace she couldn't quite conceal as she forced her toes back into her shoe didn't have him question her veracity.

"I'd enjoy it far more if you'd join me after the show for a more in-depth discussion of your work." His eyes raked up and down her small frame. His smirk had her practically able to read his mind before he spoke again. "You could slip into something more comfortable and tell me how you convince your subjects to agree to be forever frozen in such... ah, shall I say titillating poses? While I consider myself a man of the world, I'm afraid I'm in the minority."

Grace just barely managed not to roll her eyes. "I disagree. I believe people can appreciate art even if they don't understand or agree with the subject."

"I hardly think the subject matter is difficult to understand. After all, we're not talking physics."

"If we're discussing the sciences, I'd have to point out that physics is the study of motion, forces, and energy in our physical world." She met his gaze and realized he didn't appreciate her attempt to educate him but she didn't appreciate his thinly veiled insults of her art... her passion. Forcing a smile, she shook her head. "Perhaps it would be better to consider the fundamentals of raw chemistry, the way people interact with another without even truly understanding—"

"Or we could simply tell it like it is. Aren't you afraid your work will be labeled as pornographic?"

Again, tugging did nothing to release his hold, and she was afraid she was about to release a slew of words that would definitely be considered vulgar. Forcing herself to take a deep breath, she looked over his shoulder and saw a familiar face, pleasure rushing to replace her growing anger. Turning her gaze back to David, she said, "Only by those who don't understand the difference between erotica and porn. Now, if you'll excuse me, I see someone I must speak to."

His hand tightened a bit as he spoke. "I'd think you'd be interested in continuing our discussion. After all, I'll have my review written in my head before we part... unless, of course, you are smart enough to take me up on my offer. We can have a much more detailed discussion over a glass of good wine instead of this godawful swill."

"As lovely as that sounds, I'm afraid duty calls. I'm sure you'll agree that an artist who ignores any of her guests is lacking in both manners and the appreciation that they've taken the time to come to her show. Now, please, let go of my arm."

David did so and she immediately began walking

toward the doorway, only to be pulled to a halt yet again, the recapture of her arm causing her to stumble off her heels for the second time. Before she could speak, David practically growled, "How do you know Doucet?"

Grace couldn't believe he'd grabbed her yet again and also had no idea who he was talking about. "Please let go of me."

"Is that what Doucet calls it now—duty?"

"What? Who?"

"Don't pretend you don't know what I'm talking about," David said, shocking her by squeezing her arm tighter. "Doucet... the man with the blonde."

His words and his actions were the last straw. Looking up, she saw that Laurie was practically dragging her escort toward where David had her trapped. Grace was aware of two things. Laurie evidently understood she was in trouble and, if the tick in his jaw was a reliable indication, the man with her wasn't pleased, either. The reason became clear when David spoke again.

"Well, it if isn't Quentin Doucet. What's the matter? Discover that not even the gators wanted you? What brings New Orleans' prodigal son slinking out of the swamp?"

Grace recognized the name Quentin, as Laurie and Brody had often talked about their absent friend. What Laurie had failed to mention was that Quentin Doucet was an artist's dream subject. He wore a black leather jacket that had to have been custom tailored. It fit perfectly across a pair of the broadest shoulders she'd ever seen. His white shirt accentuated the bronze color of his skin where the buttons gaped at his throat. She could see his pulse beating in the vein on his neck and felt an almost irresistible desire to press her lips to it to soothe his tension. She felt her body quicken as her eyes dropped down the flat expanse of his abdomen and locked onto the buckle of his black leather belt. His legs were a mile long, encased in a pair of starched jeans, and the fact that he was wearing a pair of scuffed cowboy boots instead of some fashionable dress shoes had her smiling. The man could have stepped out of the pages of any fashion magazine and yet she knew without a doubt that he'd never truly considered his looks. He exuded the sense of confidence of a man who was comfortable in whatever he wore... or didn't wear. She felt her face heat as she forced her eyes back up to meet his. Again, her breath caught and her fingers itched to be holding a camera. Could she capture the different shades of gray of his eyes? Would any artist be able to translate the expression she saw onto canvas? What would his eyes look like if they softened in pleasure? It took her a moment to realize that his gaze had seemed to harden even more, the reason becoming clear when the tail end of David's words finally registered.

"...like I said, if you know what's good for you, stay away from Doucet. Women have been known to disappear around him."

Grace no longer gave a damn what the man wrote. She'd not only heard Laurie's gasp, she'd seen the flash of pain cross Quentin's eyes before they became the color of molten steel. Jerking her arm free, she didn't even care that her other ankle twisted a bit as she moved toward the couple.

"It's such a pleasure to meet you, Mr. Doucet," Grace said, extending her hand. "I can't thank you enough for escorting Laurie to my show."

"It's my pleasure," Quentin said, taking the offered hand.

Once he released it, Grace hoped the shock she'd felt as his hand engulfed hers wasn't obvious as she threw her arms around Laurie. "Get me out of here," she whispered.

Laurie hugged her back, then linked her arm with Grace's and began to lead her away. "If you'll excuse us, Mr. Brooks? It's my turn to monopolize the artist." Grace was grateful when Quentin joined them but didn't miss the look on the critic's face as he was left standing alone.

"I don't think he's too happy," Laurie said quietly as they walked away. "I hope he doesn't make trouble for you. He did his best to discredit Quentin—"

"Laurie."

Grace wondered at both the single word and the look the two exchanged even as she shook her head. "Despite Charles' warning to play nice, I refuse to do so simply to get a better review."

"Review?"

"Yes. Mr. Brooks reviews restaurants, social events and gallery showings. Why? Oh..." She paused, remembering that Brody had spoken of a reporter who seemed determined to convict Quentin for the death of his girlfriend even after he had been excluded from the list of suspects. From the tension surrounding them, she understood that the reporter had been Brooks. "I'm sorry—"

"Nothing to be sorry for. If you'd prefer, I'll wait outside," Quentin said.

"Absolutely not." Grace reached without thought to link her free arm through his. "The man's a total jackass."

"That may be but there's no reason for my presence to taint your show."

"Honestly I don't care; let him write what he wants. I create for my soul and not for the approval of people who form their opinion based on some biased reviewer who is either pissed that I won't sleep with him or holds some sort of grudge." She felt her heart skip a beat at the surprised look that did indeed soften the gray color of his eyes for a brief moment before they once again became unreadable. When he gently disengaged his arm from hers, she was disappointed, but understood she'd invaded his personal space just as David had hers. Still, she didn't apologize as she'd enjoyed the feel of his arm beneath her fingers. Before her mind began to take her to places she didn't belong, she turned to Laurie.

"So, what do you think?"

"I think you are one of the most talented artists I've ever known. My God, Grace, seeing what you've created from a photograph has me almost speechless." Laurie pulled her toward a large canvas that was centered on a wall in a circle of light. Grace stood silently, her eyes not on Laurie but on Quentin as he moved to stand directly in front of her featured piece. She didn't truly care what David thought but found she really did wonder how this man perceived her work. Every other person in the gallery disappeared as the artist stood with bated breath, waiting for the only review that mattered to her.

QUENTIN FELT ALMOST TRANSPORTED as he stood before the painting. It was not simply oil on canvas. Instead of brush strokes, he saw living tissue. He could practically feel the raw sexuality pouring from the frame. His eyes roved over every inch and yet found not a single flaw. It was as if the artist never once hesitated in her work; as if her hand had simply been the tool but her soul had been the true creator.

"It's stunning," he said softly. Looking at the small plaque mounted to the left, he smiled. "*Entwined*. I can't imagine a more perfect title."

"Thank you," Grace said, her heart beginning to beat again.

"You made the jewelry as well? I saw it last night."

"How? We only hung it this morning."

"No, I mean, I saw the actual jewelry last night. How you made gold seem to flow like water around a body is truly incredible."

"Oh," Grace murmured and he turned his eyes from the painting to her. He wondered if the flush on her cheeks was due to his praise or the fact that she must be wondering how he'd know how the jewelry would fit its owner.

"Is gold the only metal you work with?" he asked, not particularly caring to share the events of last evening with someone outside the club.

"No, I work with all sorts of materials. Silver is actually the most requested due to its lower cost, but I admit, gold is my favorite. There is just something about looking down into a golden molten pool and picturing what will emerge... what I can bring to life from its depths."

Giving another long look at the painting, Quentin couldn't stop a grin. Perhaps times had changed more than he'd thought. After all, whereas he was adamant about keeping the names of their clientele strictly confidential, he was looking at the same couple he'd seen playing at *Plaisir* the night before. Though her face was shadowed by the fall of her hair from where she'd tucked her cheek under her lover's neck, and the man's face was turned away, his cheek pressed to the top of her head, he knew without a doubt that the painting was of Jessica standing in front of Keith. His left hand was at her throat, a finger slid beneath the collar of golden leaves that encircled her neck. His right hand was splayed against her abdomen, the darker color of his skin contrasting with the paleness of hers. The jewelry that began at her neck continued down her body. A thin chain led from the center of her collar to a small ring that hung between her breasts. Golden kudzu leaves covered the slopes of her breasts. Amethysts had been used to define the small purple flowers that had topped the clamps he'd held the night before which had concealed Jessica's nipples. Another thin chain ran down her stomach, disappearing briefly under Keith's palm and reappearing at the apex of her thighs. Though his leg was crossing hers, drawing her legs apart, her sex was hidden by another cluster of leaves.

Quentin knew for a fact that what the painting didn't show was that the chain continued to run between her legs, ending in a final cluster of flowers adorning the end of a butt plug that was buried deep within Jessica's body. Every line, every curve of each leaf, each petal of the flowers looked as if they could be plucked from the canvas but he knew that there was not another soul on earth who could state that the jewelry truly belonged to them... they only came alive on the body for which it had been created.

"Every piece is custom, isn't it?" he asked, finally dragging his eyes from the canvas.

"Yes," Grace said, a smile on her face that showed her appreciation of his pleasure. "I know some people think it's silly and poor business but I don't care. I've lost customers because I won't replicate a piece, but I want those who do me the honor of choosing my art to know they are unique."

Quentin nodded and allowed Laurie to pull him to stand before the next painting. It was titled, *Expectations* and depicted a woman, obviously well along in her pregnancy, with her hands splayed across her distended belly. He remembered how people said women glowed when expecting and he could easily believe it as he looked at the painting. Her expression seemed to reflect a myriad of emotions: love, hope, fear, joy and... yes, expectations of what the future might hold for the life she was carrying. It took him a moment to realize the woman also wore pieces of Grace's unique collection. Small silver bracelets adorned each of her wrists and ankles and she wore a collar around her throat. This woman had given the ultimate gift of herself to someone in more ways than one. She'd given her heart and soul and would soon be giving the living gift of a child.

"It was a little boy," Grace said. "They had tried for years to become parents but she couldn't seem to carry one to term. She was terrified she'd lose this baby as well. I remember praying daily that their miracle would happen, and cried when he called me and said she'd given him a son." She paused and Quentin realized she was wiping her eyes.

"I'm glad," Quentin said and truly meant it. Suddenly, he stepped closer and studied the collar. What had looked like a solid band from a distance, wasn't. Instead, tiny links, actually, tiny heart-shaped links, interrupted the band. Two small hearts bracketed a larger one that was nestled in the hollow of her throat, breaking the solid ring of silver. Quentin stood for several minutes, his head slightly cocked as if the painting were speaking to his soul. Turning, he looked at Grace. "They lost two babies?"

"Yes."

"Oh, God, that's... so sad," Laurie said.

"It is," Grace agreed, her eyes on the painting. "Most people believe the three hearts represent the baby and his parents." She looked at Quentin. "Very few understand the true meaning, the great loss." She paused and lifted her eyes to the painting again. "And yet, they found a way to keep each lost angel in their hearts and not allow the sadness to stop them from finding the greatest joy in becoming parents. I have no doubt that there will never be a single moment in their son's life where he doesn't know how much he is loved."

When an older gentleman approached, Grace smiled and introduced Quentin to the gallery owner, Charles Westing. Quentin wasn't surprised to see the obvious pleasure the man felt toward his featured artist, but was very surprised to feel disappointed when she allowed Charles to pull her away. Once she was out of sight, Laurie slipped her hand through his arm. They continued to look around and spent another hour studying several pieces of jewelry artfully arranged in glass display cases. He smiled, noticing that this jewelry could be worn by any woman, as the offerings consisted of rings, bracelets and necklaces that were not intended to be worn specifically as a submissive's collar. Several had red stickers placed next to them.

"I knew her show would be a success. I'm so happy for her."

"She has an amazing talent," Quentin agreed

The crowd had thinned out considerably as the night grew later. Quentin had managed to avoid the art critic until the end, when he saw Grace shaking her head as David spoke to her. The man turned and gave Quentin a sneer before he stomped out the door.

"Shit. I have a feeling that Brooks is going to trash her just because I'm here."

Laurie shook her head. "I really don't think Grace would care. She meant what she said about creating from her soul."

"That's obvious in her work, but still, the man is a little shit."

"I couldn't agree more but Grace isn't a pushover. Hold on, I'll be right back," Laurie said as she moved toward Grace. He watched as the two spoke and his suspicion grew as he saw Laurie's grin when the two begin to walk toward him.

"You can do us both a huge favor," Laurie said, her batting lashes putting Quentin on full alert. "It's a shame that poor Brody is stuck in that bed and couldn't enjoy the show. I want to go pop in at the hospital, which would leave room for you to take Grace home." When he didn't immediately respond, Grace spoke.

"It's okay, I can take a cab."

"Nonsense," Laurie said. "I'll grab a cab. I can't wait to tell Brody about the success of your show, and besides, it would be a waste of a good dress if he didn't have the pleasure of seeing me in it. Don't you agree, Quentin?"

Quentin definitely felt manipulated but when Grace gave a soft groan as she wobbled on her heels again, he capitulated. "I'm sure Brody would appreciate a visit, and I'd be glad to see Grace home."

"You're the best!" Laurie said and after giving him a hug, she added, "Oh, there's a cab. See you later, Grace. Great show!"

Quentin watched her dash out the door and flag down the cab. It didn't escape him that she managed to run without a single misstep, wearing heels higher than those currently torturing the woman standing next to him.

"I really don't mind taking a cab," she said.

"No, it's fine."

"If you're sure, I'll change and be right back, okay?"

At his nod, she turned, walked toward the back of the gallery and disappeared. Charles was walking around, a tablet in his hand, entering what Quentin thought was probably the commission he expected on Grace's sales. From the look on the man's face, he too was pleased at the outcome. When Grace reappeared, Quentin watched the impeccably dressed man's face morph into one of dismay at the change in his featured artist. Gone was the little black dress and the designer stilettos. Instead, she wore a pair of black leggings that fit her like a second skin and a white, loose cotton sweater. He could see the heels stuck in her oversized tote bag, their red soles attesting to the fact that while she might appreciate the design of another artist, she'd had enough of Louboutin for the evening, changing into ballet flats instead. As she joined him, he realized she'd lost a good four inches in height, the top of her head barely reaching the middle of his chest.

"Ready?" he asked.

"Yes, thank you. I just couldn't stand another moment in those heels. Um, I hate to push my luck, but I'd be eternally grateful if we could stop for coffee? I didn't have time to eat all day." Flashing him a grin, she added, "How do you feel about beignets?"

"Fried dough is not a healthy choice," Quentin said.

"You only live once," she countered. "Besides, I'm considering it my reward for not breaking my neck and keeping my temper. Come on, my treat?"

"All right," Quentin agreed, holding the door open for her to precede him outside. "This way." He led her to his bike and watched her mouth drop open. "If you'd prefer, we can walk—"

"Are you kidding? No way! I've always wanted to ride on one of these. God, this is a beautiful machine. It's an Indian, right?"

He was surprised by both her knowledge and her enthusiasm. Her giggle grabbed his attention.

"How did you get Laurie to ride on this? She was wearing a dress!"

"Let's just say she didn't choose to walk," Quentin said, not adding that Laurie had no problem hiking her dress up and straddling the bike, wrapping her arms rather tightly around his waist. Nor did he mention the fact that she'd teased and pleaded he keep riding about the city until the vibrations of the bike did a proper job of rewarding her for her tolerance of this means of transportation.

He took the bag from Grace and put in in the saddlebag as he lifted a helmet out. He watched as she eagerly plopped it on her head and then struggled to adjust it. "Here, let me," he said, moving her fingers away from the strap in order to secure it properly. He felt a jolt of pleasure as she tilted her head back, exposing her throat. He ignored the look of puzzlement on her face as he rather brusquely told her to get on the bike and pointed to where she should place her feet. As he mounted in front of her, he felt a twinge of guilt when she asked if she should put her arms around him or just hold on to the seat.

"It depends, how fast do you want to go?" he asked, turning back to look at her.

"How fast does the wind blow?"

He couldn't help but grin as her question sounded more like a challenge. "Hurricane gale force it is. Hold on to me," he said, starting the motor. Once he felt her arms wrap around his waist, he allowed the machine to leap away from the curb, hearing her startled gasp and then her laughter as the wind blew by them. It took less than ten minutes to arrive at the famous outdoor café, Café du Monde, where chicory coffee and fried dough liberally dusted with powdered sugar were served twenty-four hours a day. Helping her from the seat, he was a bit disappointed when she removed her own helmet and handed it to him.

"Thanks, that was incredible." He watched as she

tilted her head back and listened to her inhale deeply. "Do you smell that? It's the aroma of the nectar of the Gods. Come on!"

He chuckled, thinking she was acting as if the coffee supply would disappear before she got her fair share. "You pick a table and I'll get the coffee."

"No, I said I'd treat," she said, attempting to step in front of him.

"No, you'll sit." When her mouth opened he added, "Unless you'd like your coffee without benefit of beignets?"

Her mouth snapped closed and she smiled. "In that case, how about I pick a table and you bring us a large serving?" When he nodded, she turned back. "Oh, and don't forget ask for lots and lots of powdered sugar, please."

Quentin pointed to a silver shaker on a nearby table. "Isn't that sugar?"

"Well, yes, but..." Looking from the table to him, she smiled and picked up the shaker, upending it to allow the sweetener to fall on to her palm then pursed her lips and blew across the white surface, sending a brief snowfall into the air. Green eyes sparkled as she laughed. "The powder sticks a lot better when the dough is piping hot directly out of the fryer. This is just extra."

He shook his head as she ran her tongue across her skin, licking up what hadn't blown away. "You must have quite the sweet tooth, sugar."

"Life is too short not to enjoy its pleasures," she

returned, brushing a dusting of sugar from his jacket before turning away to find a table.

Quentin was watching slim hips sway as she walked away when he was jostled as another customer passed him, snapping his attention back to his task. The place was hugely popular and Saturday nights were especially crowded. Still, by the time he had a tray containing two steaming mugs of coffee and a plate piled high with almost molten golden fried dough, she'd secured a table that faced out onto Jackson Square across the street.

"Oh, thank you," she said, reaching for a beignet the moment he set the plate down. Her first bite had powdered sugar rising in a cloud and falling on to her sweater. She giggled and shrugged. "At least I wore white," she managed to say around a mouthful of dough.

"Good thing," he agreed, and felt another stab of arousal as his fingers twitched, wanting to reach across the small table and brush the powder off the small mounds of her breasts. He sat back, raising his own cup to his lips and pretending that the big swallow of the piping hot brew was the cause of his discomfort. This little woman was causing him to think of things best left alone. The sooner she ate her sweet reward, the sooner he could get her home.

"How long have you lived in New Orleans?" he asked.

"Oh, I don't live here," she said and his cock jerked as she ran the tip of her tongue along her fingertips as if to capture every bit of sugar clinging to them.

"Well, then, where are you staying?"

"I'm staying with Laurie," she said, taking a sip of her coffee, her soft moan of pleasure lengthening his cock further before his brain processed her answer.

"Laurie?"

"Yes, Brody thought it would be a good idea. I save time traveling back and forth and money for a hotel, but the best part is Laurie isn't left alone." She bit into another beignet and he watched her eyes widen. When she'd swallowed, she said, "Oh, I guess she's not alone now, is she? I mean, don't you live there, too?"

"In the same house, yes," Quentin said, "not in the same suite of rooms... apartment really, as we converted the second floor into just the two apartments."

"Oh, that's good... shit!"

"Watch the language," he said without thinking.

"Sorry, it's just that I realized Laurie didn't give me the key."

"No problem, as you said, I live there as well."

"Um..."

"Relax, I mean I've got spare keys to their place."

"I-um, okay," she said, her face flushing a bit. "That will keep me from having to go to the hospital and bother them to get the extra Laurie was to have made for me." Instead of meeting his eyes, she concentrated on finishing her third beignet and then sat back with a small moan. "God, I can't believe you let me eat every one of those!"

Quentin couldn't believe she'd managed to do so.

Picking up a napkin, he dunked a corner of it into his glass of ice water and leaned forward. Cupping her chin with his thumb and forefinger, he proceeded to wash her face, ignoring the desire to simply bend and lick off the last bit of powdered sugar from the corner of her mouth. Meeting her eyes, he found himself wondering if she might not have been averse to his more intimate grooming. Forcing himself to sit back, he said, "How well do you know Laurie?"

He watched her cheeks pinken and saw her shift a bit on the seat of the wrought iron chair. "Well enough to know that if I did have to go get the keys, Laurie would most likely be sleeping on her tummy tonight. It seems Brody isn't all that happy when she forgets things, and doesn't hesitate to let her know it." She smiled and looked out toward the street where they'd left the motorcycle. "She might be a little less willing to straddle your bike if her ass is as red as that sexy dress she ran off to show him."

Her casual comment had him wondering exactly how she'd feel over his knees, learning how to be a tad more tactful. Tossing the soggy napkin down, he stood and held out his hand. "Ready?"

4

GRACE HADN'T MISSED the darkening of his eyes. It was almost as if shutters had slammed down, the light she'd seen as he leaned forward to wash her face gone. She stood and hadn't intended to take his hand, yet it seemed to slip into his of its own accord. "Yes." Her heart was pounding as he nodded and led her in a zigzag path through the cluster of tables until they reached the street. God, what was he thinking? She'd just basically stated that she knew Laurie was spanked by her fiancé. In fact, she'd blurted it out in the middle of a crowded restaurant and hadn't even bothered to lower her voice. She knew that while she and Laurie were close, Brody and Quentin had grown up together and Quentin had most likely taken offense at her comments. Surely he had to think she was the rudest person he'd ever met.

She tried to take the helmet from him but he brushed her hands aside and once again made sure it was properly secured. For a moment, she seriously considered stating she'd take a cab but before she could, he'd lifted her off her feet and she had no choice but to spread her legs to straddle the motorcycle. He mounted and looked over his shoulder. "Hang on."

Obeying, she wrapped her arms around his middle and prayed he couldn't feel her trembling. She was grateful conversation was impossible as he wove around the cars and took back streets through the city. She caught glimpses of people strolling along Bourbon Street as it passed by in a blur, and wished she'd chosen a Hurricane from Pat O'Brien's instead of the sweet pastry that was threatening to turn into a sodden wad of dough in her stomach. When he hopped off the bike, she scrambled off as quickly as she could. His look showed his disapproval as he unlocked the gate and mounted the bike again. She walked through the gate after him and closed it when he looked back and nodded before driving off toward the garage. Only the fact that she needed to return his helmet had her following him.

"Thanks for the ride," she said, shoving the helmet toward him. Turning, she managed only a few steps before his voice stopped her.

"You forgot, I've got the keys."

Crap, she had forgotten. Now she couldn't run and hide until he unlocked Laurie's door. When he joined her, he led her not outside the gate but to a door she'd not seen before. She watched as he pressed his ring and his thumb against sensors, and gave a little yelp when she heard locks being disengaged.

"Oh, this is like some sort of secret society," she said. "What's the password? Open Sesame?" At his look, she wished she'd kept her mouth shut, her attempt at levity falling flat. "Sorry."

He just took her arm and led her to an elevator. Once again using his ring and thumbprint, he had the door opened and pressed the button for the second floor. Exiting, she looked down the hall to where his apartment must be before turning toward Laurie's. After he did his magic trick to unlock the door, she reached out and put a hand on his arm before he could open it.

"Look, I'm sorry. I know that I was incredibly rude." She took a deep breath and continued. "I know that Brody is a good man and that Laurie loves him with her entire heart and soul." She took it as a sign he was listening when he didn't open the door and shove her inside. "I know that even though he spanks her... it isn't any sort of abuse. I'm sorry if I gave that impression. I-I know they are in a D/s relationship and that Laurie accepts both his punishment and his forgiveness when they make love afterwards. Surely you understand that I didn't mean to be flippant or make light of their commitment..."

"What you need to understand is that while you've got Brody pegged, there is a big difference between us."

"I wasn't talking about you or... or what you might do in a... well, whenever—"

"Instead of you and Laurie concocting some sort of scheme to throw us together, what Laurie should have shared is that I don't *make love*. I *fuck*. I'm not interested in a relationship. So, Grace, if you have an itch, we can go upstairs and I'm sure someone would be happy to scratch it for you."

Jerking her hand free, she wasn't sure who was more shocked, her or Quentin when she slapped him.

"I'll take that to mean you're not interested," he said, pushing the door open.

She knew she should apologize but just couldn't. Instead, she ducked under his arm, entered the apartment and then turned and slammed the door, slightly disappointed when it didn't close in his face as he'd already turned away. Leaning against it, she wondered how the night could have gone so very wrong. It had been a stressful day and yet, the moment he'd appeared with Laurie, she'd felt a sense of calm that actually allowed her to enjoy a few brief moments of her show.

Pushing away from the door, she entered the guestroom. She didn't bother turning on the lights or brushing her teeth. She peeled out of her clothes and climbed into bed. How in the world was she going to tell Laurie that she'd managed to so anger Brody's friend? Turning onto her stomach, she admitted that if anyone needed a good hard spanking to remind them what happened when unable to first engage their brain before opening their mouth, it was she.

Just before exhaustion finally pulled her under,

she heard the faint pinging of the elevator and wondered where Quentin was going.

—

QUENTIN GAVE Ellen a nod but didn't speak as he entered the club. Though it was late, the place was even more crowded than it had been the night before. He gave a nod to Adam, who again had his beer ready by the time he reached the bar.

"How's it going?" Adam asked.

"Just keep them coming," Quentin answered, not caring that Adam's eyebrow rose but noticing that he did nod, indicating he understood. It took him halfway through the second beer before he began to feel some of his anger slipping away. "Sorry," he said when Adam approached after serving a couple at the other end of the bar.

"Nothing to be sorry about, boss."

"Anything happening I should know about?"

"Just a regular Saturday night. Though you and Brody might consider interviewing a few more floaters. Seems the male to female ratio is only growing further apart."

At his words, Quentin turned to give the crowd a closer look. He could see that Adam was correct. There were several men who didn't appear to be involved in any scene other than as observers. The three women who worked to keep the equipment clean and the bowls filled were all involved with someone. He noticed that Molly was draped across the horse and that her bottom was well striped from the flogger a Dominant was wielding. Quentin was glad to see that the man obviously knew what he was doing, the falls of the leather implement landing with precision across the fleshy mounds of Molly's ass, her shoulders, and upper back. Debbie was presently on her knees, her head bobbing up and down on another Dominant's cock, the halter top of her dress unfastened and hanging at her waist, ample breasts bouncing as she pleasured the man. Though it took a bit longer, he finally spotted the third floater to see that Sarah was being released from the St. Andrew's Cross that took up a far corner of the room. He frowned when the Dominant simply tossed aside the paddle he'd been using and walked away, leaving the woman swaying on wobbly legs.

Pushing off his stool, Quentin strode toward her, and she gave him a smile when he reached out and took her arms. "Take your time," he said, allowing her to regain her balance as the endorphins caused by the scene flooded through her system. "He should know better."

"He's new," Sarah said. "Maybe he didn't like my performance..."

"I'm sure that's not it," Quentin said, looking down to see that her nipples were tight buds and that her skin had broken out in goose bumps. The glaze of her eyes told of her arousal, as did the distinct glistening he could see on her inner thighs. He led her to a sofa and sat, pulling her between his legs. She instantly crossed her arms behind her back, shifted her feet apart, and lowered her eyes. Yes, she was definitely aroused, and he knew he ought to find the Dominant and reprimand him for leaving her unfulfilled.

"May I offer myself, sir?" she asked, her eyes briefly lifting to his, hers bright with anticipation.

Quentin hesitated for a moment and then pulled her down. He was a bit shocked when he realized he wasn't guiding her to her knees but onto his lap. His erection was evident against the front of his jeans and yet he didn't move to release it. Instead, he pushed her head to his chest and stroked her arm as she relaxed against him. Moving to cup her breast, he enjoyed her soft gasp as his thumb flicked over her nipple, and she arched to offer him more.

"Relax, let me pleasure you," he said softly, his fingers playing with her nipples until she was squirming. Sliding his hand down, he felt her opening her thighs to allow him better access and then heard her soft moan as he cupped her sex. She was dripping wet, her arousal easily allowing him to slip two fingers deep inside.

"Oh, please," she whispered, "harder..."

He increased the speed of his thrusts, knowing he'd hit her g-spot when she arched again and groaned. He was aware that they'd drawn some onlookers but ignored them as he concentrated on rewarding Sarah for a job well done. Continuing his thrusts, he moved to slide his thumb and index finger over her clit, enjoying her small yelp as he gave it a pinch.

"That's it, come for me." He continued to finger

fuck her and rub and pinch at her clitoris until he could feel her pussy walls tighten around his fingers. "Good girl, come... come now." With his order, he pinched the small sensitive bundle of nerves hard and she came apart, her body jerking on his lap, her juices streaming down to wet his trousers. He continued to hold her and stroke her until he was sure she was sated. Once she sighed, he slowly removed his hand from her sex and bent to kiss the top of her head. "Good girl."

"Thank you, Master Quentin," she said.

"If a Dominant isn't man enough to make sure you are satisfied after your play, then don't play with him again." Quentin looked up, pleased to see that the Dominant who'd paddled her had the grace to flush.

"I was only getting her a drink..."

"She didn't need a drink, she needed you to make sure she was okay."

"I realize that now and I apologize. Sarah, I'm really sorry."

"That's all right," she said, accepting his hand as he helped her rise off Quentin's lap. "If you still want, I'd like a drink now."

"Certainly."

Quentin watched with approval as the man took the time to help her back into the black dress the floaters wore as their uniform, carefully pulling it up over her bottom and then gently moving her hair to lie over her shoulder so that he could tie the ends of her halter top at the nape of her neck before leading her toward the bar. He smiled as she thanked him, her reddened cheeks peeking out beneath the very short hem of the dress. Standing, Quentin made use of the bottle of hand sanitizer and dropped the thick paper napkin into the trash before returning to the bar to finish his beer.

"You're right," he said, lifting the bottle. "We need more floaters."

"Better watch it, boss," Adam said with a grin. "If word gets out that you are willing to personally step in without asking for service, you might find a bunch of their friends applying for the job."

Quentin knew it was a joke but also knew it was highly unusual for a Master to forego his own needs. Still, the moment he had considered having Sarah open her mouth to take his cock inside, all he'd seen was the heart-shaped face of another woman, her eyes showing her shock at his words. He didn't deny he'd earned the slap Grace had given him but was also unable to deny that she had needed to hear what he had to say. Laurie was a great girl but he'd forgotten she tended to play matchmaker.

Slipping a tip under his napkin, he said goodnight and returned to his apartment. Stripping out of his clothes, he tossed them into the hamper, and looking toward his bed, knew his own words had just come back to haunt him. Sure, he didn't make love, and it seemed he didn't fuck, either. He stepped under the hot spray of the shower and took his erection into his fist. No, instead, he jacked off like some horny teenager. Squeezing and releasing as he moved his hand up and down his shaft, he closed his eyes, groaning as the woman only feet down the hall once again appeared in his mind. In the privacy of his rooms, he allowed his fantasy to imagine the little artist falling to her knees, her tongue and lips replacing his fist. Picturing her curly auburn hair becoming a darker red from the falling water and her green eyes lifted to his as she pleasured him, he groaned as the first jet of his seed splashed against the tile.

He pushed the erotic picture from his mind and finished his shower, trying not to notice that his cock was already semi-hard again. Damn it, he was not interested! Pulling on a pair of sweat pants and a t-shirt, he grabbed a beer from his fridge and the stack of reports that he and Conner had started going over that afternoon. It would be far better for him to immerse himself in his work instead of a fantasy that he had absolutely no intention of pursuing. He'd shirked his responsibilities long enough. The very least he could do was make sure that by the time Brody returned to the club, it would have the proper amount of staff, and a newly graduated class of submissives just waiting to find their perfect dominant partner, ensuring the club continued to be both a safe place for those who enjoyed kinkier play, and a profitable business for the man whom he'd called a friend for as long as he could remember. He made a mental note to again remind Conner that he wanted to see the individual applications of the women who had signed up for class, wondering how many would actually remain to the very end.

He didn't stop working until he heard the ping of the elevator and knew that Laurie had returned home safely. He'd speak to her tomorrow about her little scheme. Then again, he'd be willing to bet that while Brody might have enjoyed her late night visit, he would wonder exactly what had her thinking he'd approve of her ditching the escort he'd provided in order to do so. With a grin, he wondered if the little nurse did indeed have a red ass or if she had simply been instructed to add the transgression in her journal to be atoned for at a later date. Quentin flipped the file folder closed and stood to go to bed. Before he could, he heard a soft knock on his door.

Looking through the peephole, he realized he'd be getting his answer sooner than expected. He grinned seeing Laurie give a small shrug as she turned away, obviously intending to be able to truthfully state that she'd knocked but he hadn't answered. He waited until she was halfway down the hall before he pulled the door open, causing her to give a short shriek.

"Going somewhere?" he asked.

"Um, I thought you might be asleep. I didn't want to bother you."

"No bother at all. You know I'm always available to you. What can I help you with?" He paused a moment and then said, "Oh wait, don't tell me. You've got another friend who just happens to be without transportation? Or perhaps you've got someone else who needs a place to crash?"

She gave him a look that told of her guilt. "I'm so sorry, Quentin. It's just that well, you seemed to like her, and I love her, and I thought—"

"Do you have any idea how your little game played out?" he asked, sternly.

"From the way your arms are crossed and your tone, I'm guessing not so well?"

"That's an understatement. I not only felt manipulated, I was mad, and rude to a woman who didn't do anything to earn it."

"Oh, God, I'm so sorry, Quentin. Really, Grace had no idea. I just thought that if I was out of the picture, you two might..." She stopped speaking and walked toward him. "I know it was a shitty thing to do. It seems Brody agrees and, well, he sent me to ask that you take care of it for him."

For a brief moment he wondered if perhaps this was Brody's attempt to draw him back into the world he'd walked away from. But when she pulled an object from her tote bag, her trembling hand showing her reluctant obedience to her Dom, his suspicion evaporated. Without a word, he reached out and accepted the hairbrush before stepping aside to let her pass him. Closing the door, he entered the living area and sat down on the middle of the couch. This time he wasn't sitting to reward a woman, he was sitting to punish one.

"Dress up," he said brusquely.

Laurie instantly obeyed, tugging the dress up to

her waist. Quentin patted his knee and she draped herself across it, her torso resting on the couch, her toes scraping the floor. He appreciated her soft groan when he draped his free leg over hers. She would now understand that this was not going to be a few light swats. No, she was most likely remembering that Quentin was very capable of making her ass burn just as hotly as Brody did when delivering what the men considered a *lesson*.

Hooking his fingers into the waistband of her underwear, Quentin slowly pulled them down until they rested at the top of her thighs. "It's been a while since I've paddled a naughty girl. Your choice of red panties gives me the exact shade of crimson I should strive to achieve." When she gave a murmured sound of protest, he lifted his hand and began.

From the first bounce of his palm against her flesh, Quentin realized it was just like riding a bike. Once mastered, one never truly lost the skill. He also had to admit that once tasted, it was hard to walk away from the delicious satisfaction in delivering a well-deserved spanking. He didn't begin to lecture until he'd turned every inch of her backside from white to pink. Only then did he reach for the wooden hairbrush she'd so thoughtfully provided.

"I love you, Laurie," he said, rubbing the smooth back of the brush over her pinkened skin. "But, young lady, you've been warned repeatedly about trying to set people up, haven't you?" When she didn't answer, he lifted the implement and brought it down with a solid thwack onto her right buttock.

"Ow, yes, I mean yes, sir," she said, her bottom wagging to one side as if he'd be unable to follow its path with the brush.

He had no hesitation in proving his aim was flawless as he gifted her left cheek with a stroke of its own.

"How many times have you been across either mine or Brody's lap getting your ass heated for playing matchmaker?"

"I don't know..."

A stroke across the center of her ass refreshed her memory.

"I mean, too many. Ow, please, Quentin, not so hard!"

The brush flew to kiss her bare skin—right, left, center—in rapid strokes.

"Excuse me?"

"Sir, I meant, sir."

Reversing the pattern just as rapidly, he gave her three more strokes, her flesh depressing beneath each one before springing back as if waiting for the next.

"That's better. Stop trying to swim off my lap. You know it won't do any good and will only ensure your spanking continues."

"Yes, sir!" she wailed, her back arching as he gave each cheek a harder swat. Two more followed and then he saw her wilt, her body relaxing as she submitted to her punishment.

"I'm really sorry, sir. I didn't mean to hurt you... or Grace."

"That might not have been your intention, but that's what happened. Let this paddling teach you what you can expect every time you attempt to meddle where you don't belong." He peppered her bottom with another dozen swats before he rested the wood on the red mottled surface. He couldn't help but notice the color almost perfectly matched that of her panties. He set the implement aside and pulled the red silk back into place before lifting her to sit on his lap.

"Shh, it's over. You're all right now," he said, holding her as she cried against his t-shirt. He continued to hold her until she quieted. When she pushed up, he bent forward and plucked a tissue from the box on the coffee table. Handing it to her, he grinned. "I don't remember putting that there," he said. "Perhaps you knew that you'd be needing a tissue sooner or later."

Shrugging, she smiled and then blew her nose. "Let's just say I remembered both you and Brody were boy scouts. Always prepared?"

He chuckled and gave her a hug as he helped her to stand, smoothing her dress down her hips.

"I'm sorry. It's just that I love you so much and want you to be happy."

"I know," Quentin said, standing and then bending to kiss her cheek before leading her to the door.

She reached up to lay a palm against his cheek. "Welcome home, Quentin. I've really missed you."

He felt his heart tighten a moment and knew she

meant every word. "I've missed you too, honey. Now, go get some sleep."

He waited until the door to the apartment that now belonged to her and Brody closed behind her before he shut his own door. Flipping off the light, he stripped out of his clothes and climbed into bed. He couldn't help but remember Grace's prophecy that Laurie might well be sleeping on her tummy that night. He wondered if the woman had even once thought that it might be the man across the hall who would be the one delivering the lesson. Sighing, he knew that he needed to do some apologizing himself. He'd been nothing short of an ass.

5

QUENTIN DIDN'T GET a chance to apologize the next day. When he'd knocked on Laurie's door, she'd answered, looking quite adorable in a wrinkled, oversized t-shirt that belonged to Brody, her hair in desperate need of a brush and her yawn indicating she would much prefer to still be sleeping.

"Sorry to wake you, but I wanted to talk to Grace."

"You just missed her," Laurie said. "I woke up when she was attempting to be quiet." She shook her head. "She must have tripped over something because she was cursing and it sounded like she was hopping around. By the time I got out of bed, she'd gone, but there's a note." Plucking a piece of paper off the back of the door, she handed it to him, tape and all. "Now, go away. I've got to get some sleep. I swear I had barely closed my eyes before Grace woke me up." She gave him a scowl. " I hate sleeping on my stomach, you know."

Quentin chuckled. "Another reason to remember

to behave. Go on, back to bed. No one likes a grumpy nurse." Pretending he hadn't seen her sticking her tongue out as she closed the door, he looked down at the note. Grace wrote that she was sorry she had to cancel their plans for the day, but that she needed to return to the gallery to help pack up her things and discuss the showing with Charles. She said not to worry about her, she'd grab dinner somewhere and be back that evening. He was a bit disappointed when she said that she'd found the key Laurie had left her so no worries. Quentin felt a bit disquieted. Not because Laurie had given the woman a key, because he knew that it would only allow Grace into that one apartment. No, he'd been entirely prepared to apologize and now, being unable to do so, left him feeling unsettled.

After returning to his apartment to change into leathers, he left and took the stairs down to the first floor. What he needed was to ride. An hour or two on his bike would clear his head. The moment he started the motor, he felt himself relax. It wasn't long before he was taking an exit ramp off the highway and turning onto barely discernible tracks that he knew like the back of his hand. The only thing better than feeling the wind rush by that the speed of highway riding gave him was the silence that descended on him the moment he became enveloped by the trees, vines and bushes that made up the swamp. He knew exactly what paths to take to avoid the marshes that were capable of swallowing a man whole. Pulling to a stop, he realized where his subconscious had brought him. He dismounted and, for the first time, sank to his knees and allowed himself to give voice to the grief that had consumed him for two years. His sobs over Beth's death were accepted and muffled by the green living plants that surrounded him. When he had no tears left, he felt his mind shift as a breeze caressed his face, drying his cheeks.

While he'd never feel completely free of guilt, he could finally accept what Brody and Sammy had been telling him—her death wasn't his fault. Shaking his head, he also accepted the fact that he'd never rest until the person who had robbed an innocent woman of her life and defiled a place that he considered sacred was brought to justice. It was another half-hour before he got back on the motorcycle. He might not be able to talk to Grace, but there was another person he needed to see. Once he had a signal on his phone, he made a call. With an assurance that he'd be welcome, he turned the bike back toward the city.

It was dark by the time he entered Brody's room. He hadn't bothered to change out of his leathers though he'd unzipped the jacket, leaving it to hang open.

"Hey," Brody said.

"Hey," Quentin replied, moving to the bed and pulling the tray table into position before placing a foil wrapped plate down. "Thought you might enjoy this." Peeling back the foil, he revealed a mound of crawfish with ears of corn and new potatoes that were still warm.

"You thought right," Brody said, pushing himself up a bit more. "Though the least you could have done was peel them for me."

"Your leg's broken, not your hands," Quentin said, reaching for a bright red mudbug. "Want me to eat them for you as well?

"Hell no!" Brody said, slapping at his hand. "All I've had to eat today was a shrimp po'boy that Laurie brought. She didn't tell me that Sammy was putting on a crawfish boil."

"This isn't from Sammy," Quentin said, pulling a bottle of Coke from his jacket pocket. "It's courtesy of Jason."

Brody's hand stopped in mid-reach as his eyes lifted. "Jason as in Detective Stewart?"

"Yes."

"Tell me," Brody said, cracking the first crawfish as Quentin dropped into the chair and told how he'd spent his day.

"At first I planned to ride along the highway but something pulled at me and I wound up in the swamp. I know I live in one but I didn't go home. I went back to where Beth was found."

Brody didn't speak, just nodded and continue to shell and eat the crawfish, allowing his friend to tell the story in his own way... at his own speed.

"I finally broke down," Quentin admitted. "Cried like a baby at the fucking unfairness of it all. She didn't deserve to die like that. Hell, no one deserves that." He paused again and this time when he reached for a crawfish, Brody didn't slap at his hand.

"Anyway, I called Jason and he invited me over. He's a good man. Didn't even bat an eye that I appeared out of nowhere during a family get together. He introduced me to his family, made us both plates, and then took me down to the creek. I read him the riot act about how no one cared about finding the asshole who killed Beth but me, and he just listened. When I finally stopped shouting, he didn't tell me to quit being an arrogant prick, but told me that a day didn't go by when he didn't think about Beth. He said that he'd never stop investigating until the day he put her murderer behind bars."

"Does he have anything new to go on?" Brody asked quietly.

"Nothing new really, but he says he is still certain that she wasn't killed by a stranger."

"What do you think?"

"I don't know. Part of me can't believe that anyone she knew, hell, that we might know, would do something so horrid. It would be better to think that Beth hadn't known her killer rather than discover someone she trusted turned out to be evil. But, God, man, it makes sense. What I don't understand is how no one remembers seeing her that night. Her ring registered as being used to enter the club. Last night I realized that with how busy and crowded the club is on a Saturday night, it might be possible, but she disappeared on a Friday night. There weren't half as many people on Friday as there were last night."

"But that night was unusual," Brody countered. "Remember, it was an open night for prospective members to visit the club."

"Shit, that's right. So with a lot of new faces, Beth might have just been overlooked by other members used to seeing her there."

"Could be," Brody agreed. "But you said Jason believes she met up with someone while at the club?"

"Yes. Shit, if we'd known she was taken, they might have found clues left behind. By the time I reported her missing, the club had been thoroughly cleaned by the staff."

"Not your fault. Okay, even if that's the case, how can we be sure she didn't visit the club and then leave to go somewhere else to party? I mean, she was angry at you and was obviously determined to show you that if you weren't interested, she could find someone who was."

Quentin took a while to answer, knowing that Brody was stating facts and not attempting to judge his behavior.

"She didn't take her purse or her phone. They found both in my apartment, remember?"

"That's right," Brody said, uncapping the Coke and taking a long drink. "We went over the list of members at the time, despite some of them making noises about suing when we cooperated with the investigation."

"I know, but maybe we didn't go over it well enough, especially with guests attending. Jason asked me about the list and then, well, he asked me how well I knew the staff."

That got Brody's attention. "Hell, you're not thinking one of our own could have done this?"

"I don't know what to think," Quentin admitted. "Even with non-members being there, would they know about protocol? All I know is that whoever did it knew about the club, knew he'd have to use a ring to gain admittance, and managed to do so without raising suspicion. What else makes sense?"

The men were both quiet for several minutes. Finally, Brody sighed and pushed away the remaining food. "All right. We'll go through the list again, this time with a fine tooth comb. I know we vet our employees but hell, we'll vet them again. The records are on flash drives. Do you remember the combination to the safe?"

"Yes."

"Good, don't ask for anyone to help. In fact, don't even mention visiting Detective Stewart. The less said, the better. Bring me my laptop and the videotapes from that weekend and I'll start compiling a list."

"I can do it—"

"I know, but two heads are better than one. Besides, it'll give me something to do. We've got the funds to hire our own investigators. If someone we know is responsible for Beth's death, you better believe we'll find him."

"Thanks, Brody," Quentin said, lifting his eyes to his friend's. "I know it's been a long time, but—"

"It won't be over till it's finished," Brody said, reaching out to clasp Quentin's arm. "We are in this together until the end."

Quentin nodded and then stood to step into the bathroom. When he returned, Brody seemed to know that he'd discussed it as much as he could in one day. Instead, he popped a boiled potato in his mouth and, after swallowing, said, "Now, tell me, how did my girl behave while your paddled her ass?"

"Like she does every time," Quentin said with a grin. "Kicking and squirming and making continual promises that she'll never be naughty again."

Brody chuckled. "That seems to be a mantra of all submissive women. Making promises they can't possibly keep and then repeating the same thing that got them across a lap in the first place." He took a drink and then said, "Seriously though, thanks for giving her what she needed. I honestly don't know what she was thinking. She breezed in here with a big smile on her face and told me all about how you thought Grace was great. I knew the moment she took a breath that you were most likely seething."

"No, not really," Quentin said, dropping back down into the chair. "I admit, I was pissed but, well, it wasn't until I managed to make a total ass out of myself that I realized that she was at least partially right. I mean, yes, I do think Grace is great. She's an incredible artist, and I mean that she has serious talent. You've got to ask to see her work sometime. It blew me away."

"So I heard from Laurie. But that doesn't explain how you made an ass out of yourself."

Quentin ran his hand over his face, feeling the stubble of his five o'clock shadow. "Well, it came as a shock when I realized that I wasn't just thinking of her as an artist. Hell, she's a beautiful woman. For being so tiny, she can stand toe to toe with the big guys. She practically dared David Brooks to trash her in his column simply because she overhead him trashing me... hell, a guy she doesn't even know. Do you know she has a sweet tooth?"

"Can't say that I do."

"Well, she does. She managed to down an entire plate of beignets in record time. She was practically wearing a pound of powdered sugar by the time we left."

"You know, that's a sweet tale, but can we get to the part where you tell me what you did? The asshole part?" Brody asked, his tone having Quentin appreciating that he was attempting to keep his grin to himself.

"I'm getting there," Quentin said, pushing to his feet and walking to look out the window. He could see Brody's reflection in the glass. "I know she didn't mean it to sound like anything other than an honest answer to my question. I asked her how well she knew Laurie, and she explained that she knew her well enough to wonder how you'd feel about her ditching me and forcing me to take her home." He sighed and turned around. "Instead, I let her believe I was offended she'd suggest you would appreciate her honesty in sharing the fact that you spanked her friend. I practically threw her on the bike and didn't bother to speak until I had her at your door."

He walked back toward the bed and braced his hands against the back of the chair. "And this is where the real asshole comes in. Instead of apologizing, I listened to her stumbling as she apologized to me and then, when she assured me that she knew Laurie and you loved each other, I told her in no uncertain terms that I'm not interested unless she just wants a quick fuck. To top it off, I offered to escort her upstairs, assuring her that someone was bound to be willing to scratch any itch she might have."

"Whoa, you're right," Brody said, once more pushing the table tray away. "You were a total ass. Question is, what are you going to do about it?"

"I was going to apologize but she wasn't home."

"That might be, but I guarantee she'll be home again. She's staying with us, and if I find out she plans on leaving because of you, you can guarantee I'll be doing a bit of ass kicking myself."

"I get it," Quentin said, straightening and running his hand through his hair. "I'll make sure she knows I'm sorry."

"That'll do for a start," Brody said. Quentin couldn't help but notice that he hadn't bothered to suggest what might come next. The door opened and a different nurse came in. Seeing the plate of crawfish shells, she shook her head.

"You are one very incorrigible patient," she said,

moving to wrap a cuff around his arm.

"Yeah, but you love me anyway," Brody said with a grin that never failed to make a woman smile back.

"We love Laurie," the nurse corrected, pumping the ball to inflate the blood pressure cuff. "And because she loves you... well, we look the other way." After making note of his vital signs, she took the plate off the table.

"I promise I was planning on getting rid of that," Quentin said.

"I have no doubt that you are his partner in crime," the nurse said, opening the door. "How about the next time you bring a feast, you bring some to share? I've heard about Sammy's wife's pies. I think a couple of pies would go a long way toward us keeping our heads turned when our patient has visitors with unapproved bounty."

"You can count on it." Quentin chuckled as she gave him a finger wave. He made sure Brody's water mug was filled and within reach before walking to the door. "I'll bring you the laptop and tapes tomorrow."

"Good. Hey, you haven't forgotten you've got a class starting tomorrow?" Brody reminded him.

"No, but that reminds me, I still haven't gone over the applicant files. Conner seems to be having a pity party, and I'm wondering how much help he'll really be."

"He damn well better do his job," Brody said, his voice turning harsh. "You are in control for a reason, and if you need me to intervene..."

"No, I'll handle it. Now, get some rest." He opened the door and turned back. "Thanks for everything."

Brody gave a nod and was reaching for the remote as the door closed. Quentin rode the bike at a far more sedate pace and took the time to actually look around instead of letting things pass by in a blur. After parking the bike, he pulled two boxes from the bed of his truck and carried them to his apartment. He took a shower and then pulled out his phone and called Conner. When he didn't answer, Quentin left a request that he bring the applications to him early the next morning. Ending the call, he hoped that he wasn't going to get into some pissing contest with the man. While he understood that Conner most likely felt slighted that he'd not been told he would head the class, his position usurped by a man who'd just breezed back into town, he'd have to get over it. Until Quentin convinced Brody to take over his share of the business, he intended to step up to the plate and keep his part of the bargain.

Quentin spent the next couple of hours working with the medium that had the power to soothe him. As he worked the strands of leather he'd carefully cut, he made sure each one was supple and layered perfectly so that when attached to the braided leather handle he would make next, each individual piece would become part of the whole. It would be the perfect wedding gift for Brody and Laurie. She was a huge fan of the flogger, and he'd often watched her drift into subspace when her Dominant wielded one all over her body.

6

"HEARD YOU'VE GOT a slew of ladies coming in today," Sammy said, setting the tray he'd carried from the kitchen down on a table in the back dining room.

"What?" Quentin said, looking up from the pad of paper he'd been writing on.

Sammy chuckled. "That list must be promising if it has you so engrossed that you've forgotten our lunch date," he said, nodding toward the pad.

Quentin flipped the pad facedown and didn't answer. Instead, he said, "That smells divine."

"Of course it does," Sammy said, placing a steaming bowl before him. "Can't go wrong with Pop's gumbo recipe." He finished unloading the tray, adding a basket of jalapeno cornbread muffins and a basket of fried clams within easy reach. Taking his seat, he added a very generous amount of his own brand of hot-sauce to his bowl.

Quentin rolled his eyes and waved his hand as if

to dissipate the spicy fumes coming from the bottle. "Your stomach has got to be made of cast iron."

Sammy just dipped a large spoon into his bowl and took his first huge bite before saying, "How do you doing, son?"

Breaking his muffin in half, Quentin crumbled it into his gumbo to soak up the broth. He wiped his fingers on his napkin and then lifted his spoon. "I've got to hand it to Brody. He's done an outstanding job..."

"I didn't ask about Brody. I asked how you were doing," Sammy said, dunking his own bread.

"Fine."

Sammy shook his head and reached across the table to pull Quentin's bowl away, causing the spoon that he'd just dipped into the bowl to splash gumbo onto the table's surface.

"What the hell!"

"You don't deserve the best dish on the menu if you don't respect that hands that made it," Sammy said, not releasing his hold despite the fact that steam still rising from its contents testified that the ceramic bowl's surface had to be burning hot.

"What the fuck are you talking about? You know I respect you—"

"Son, when are you gonna learn you aren't going through life alone? You can lie to yourself all you want, but don't lie to ol' Sammy. Now, you've got a choice to make. You can really piss me off by making me throw this in the garbage, or you can remember I'm not only your cook, I'm your goddamned friend!"

Quentin had instantly tensed at the older man's actions, his hands gripping the table's edge. Sammy's first words had immediately put him on the defensive. Who was he to judge him? He'd come back, hadn't he? But, with Sammy's last statement, Quentin once again felt a shift in his mind. God, he was tired... tired of pretending he didn't need anyone, tired of pushing his friends away, tired of living in what amounted to limbo. It was time to stop trying to be some sort of macho man and accept what had been right before him. Instead of staying and acknowledging that Beth had been friends with them all, instead of being there for those friends in their grief, he'd let it all be about his loss—like he was more important than the others. No, he hadn't been a man, much less a friend. He'd taken the easy way out by walking away to lick his wounds like some fucking animal. Reaching out, he pulled the bowl back.

"I'm trying, and will keep trying every day. Brody deserves that and, yes, so do you and Hannah. I promised to give it my all and I will, but, hell, it's not the same—"

"And will never be," Sammy said. "It will be different but it can be better. Life throws shit at people that disrupts their well-laid plans all the time. The smart ones know there is more than one road to travel." He paused to finish his gumbo and then reached for a handful of fried clams, again dousing them in hot-sauce. "I heard you tear out of here on your bike yesterday morning—"

"Afraid I wasn't coming back?" Quentin

interrupted, not with anger but with resignation, knowing that he'd run away before.

"Never crossed my mind. You might be a pain in the ass, son, but you've never broken your word. Did you find the answers you were seeking in the swamp?"

Quentin didn't ask how the man knew where he'd gone. Sammy was not only a surrogate father to him, he was a man born of generations who'd come from the darkest shadows of the swamp. He seemed to know things without being told, and experience had told Quentin not to make light of what was considered as having the 'sight'. Making a decision, he pushed his empty bowl away and reached, not for the clams, but for the pad. "Not all of them," he said, meeting the man's eyes. "But I did discover that while the past will always be a part of my life, I think I'm ready to see what's in my future." Sammy just nodded, as if knowing Quentin wasn't finished. "I can't give my all to that future until I can say goodbye. I'll never be at peace with what happened, but I owe it to Beth to let her rest in peace." Turning the pad so that Sammy could read it, he tapped a finger on the top sheet.

"I went to see Detective Stewart." Quentin repeated the story, grinning when he admitted he'd eaten his fill of crawfish. Sammy snorted as if to state the crustaceans served had to have been below par, and Quentin didn't dispel him of the thought.

"We're going to look at everything and everyone again."

Sammy took a few minutes, flipping through the top few pages of the tablet. His brow furrowed and he returned to the list of names Quentin had written down on the top page.

"What's wrong?" Quentin asked, setting down his glass of ice tea.

"I don't see Farraday's name on here, and wasn't there some other woman who was assisting with hostess duties at the time?"

Quentin leaned forward. "Shit, you're right. We had two girls at the desk that night because we knew there would be more people. I don't remember her name, but Brody probably does. As for Farraday, I just forgot. Mike quit..." Pausing, he lifted his eyes to Sammy's. "Hell, he quit right after Beth disappeared. Okay, I've got to give this list another go. Going back is gonna be useless if we leave someone out, but I believe it's the only way forward."

"Stirring the pot is the only way to bring things up from the bottom," Sammy said, beginning to pile the empty dishes onto the tray. Reaching across the table again, he laid his hand over Quentin's. "Be careful, son. Whoever killed Beth thinks they got away with it, but once a person gets a taste for killing, it makes it a whole lot easier to kill again."

Quentin nodded and, when the older man stood, he did as well and moved to wrap his arms around him. They stood like that for a few moments and then released each other, secure in the knowledge they were more than friends—they were family.

QUENTIN WENT UPSTAIRS after stopping in the kitchen to ask Hannah if she would be willing to help keep her favorite person out of trouble. She'd beamed with his request for two of her pies and promised to have them ready in a few hours. She'd also pulled him into a hug and though she didn't speak, he knew it was her own way of making sure he was all right.

Grabbing a box he'd emptied the night before, he tossed in the tablet after adding Mike's name and noting they needed the missing name of the temporary hostess, and then took the box down the hall. When his knock wasn't answered, he opened the door, figuring that Laurie was at the hospital. He looked around and smiled. Though he'd been at the door, he'd yet to step inside since his return. The apartment he remembered had definitely been far less colorful. Touches of Laurie were everywhere. Brightly colored pillows now decorated the black leather sofa. Not one but two pairs of high heels had been abandoned in the middle of the floor, a pink sweater had been tossed over the back of a chair, and several magazines were scattered across the surface of the glass coffee table. Shaking his head, he went to the set of built-in bookshelves and was reaching to remove a set of books when he paused.

He'd noticed several framed photos on the shelves and yet this one had him momentarily forgetting his mission. Picking it up, he gazed down at a photo of Brody, Laurie, himself and Beth. All four were smiling, the wind tossing the girls' hair about as they'd stood in the bow of the boat. He remembered that night. They'd taken their dates out for a dinner cruise onboard the *Creole Queen*, an old paddlewheel boat that ran down the Mississippi River. It had been only a couple of weeks before Beth disappeared. The four had eaten and danced the night away before going up to the top deck to cool off. A photographer who worked for the cruise line had taken their picture, and evidently, Brody or Laurie had purchased a copy from the website. Quentin smiled, relieved that the memories of that evening were good ones, and that looking at the photograph wasn't tearing him apart. Replacing the frame, he removed the set of books, revealing a hidden panel. Pressing his ring into the impression, the door clicked open. Turning the dial of the safe, he opened it and reached in for the box of flash drives. Shit, there were so many. He realized that there was a date written on the top of the box. These weren't the ones he needed. Putting it back on top of the stack, he chose another and then another until he finally found the box marked with the proper year. He added the small box to the one he'd brought with him, knowing he didn't have time to go through the individual flash drives. Closing the safe and twirling the dial, he shut the panel and replaced the books.

Glancing around, he spied the laptop on the small kitchen table. Approaching it, he saw a mug of coffee sitting on the table as well. Moving it aside, he felt its warmth and wondered why Laurie hadn't poured it into a travel mug to take with her to the hospital. Shrugging, he turned his attention to the computer, noticing that there was no power cord attached and he didn't see one lying around. Lifting the lid to check the remaining battery power, he stopped considering cords as the photos on the screen grabbed his attention. He bent forward, his finger moving across the touchpad to enlarge the array.

"What the hell do you think you are you doing?"

It took a moment for Quentin to even understand that he'd been asked a question. Grace stood a few feet away wearing only a towel. A very small towel. Beautiful, trim legs, still damp from her shower, ended in bare feet with the cutest little toes, the nails painted a bright pink. His eyes traveled up to see her tugging the towel a bit tighter, but all that did was have him imagining what lay beneath the terry cloth. Her auburn hair was wet, darker red-tinged tendrils clinging to her face, and he could see the swell of her breasts peeking out the top of the towel. His cock instantly responded as he remembered his fantasy of seeing this woman on her knees, her hair wet, her green eyes on his as they shared a shower. When he saw her skin begin to flush, he remembered she'd asked him a question.

"I knocked," Quentin said.

"Well, obviously I didn't hear you. You might have a key, but that isn't an excuse to invade my privacy."

"Look, I didn't know anyone was here. I just came in to get some stuff for Brody."

"That's not his laptop," Grace said. "Why would his be out when he's in the hospital?"

"I didn't even consider that," Quentin admitted. "Forgive me, I really didn't mean to invade your privacy." He looked down at the screen and said, "Does it help if I say that you are as good a photographer as you are a painter?"

"Not particularly," Grace said bluntly, pointing to a small desk built into the wall. "What would help would be if you get what you need and leave. Brody's computer is in the drawer."

Quentin shut the lid of the computer and saw she had turned away. God, the towel clung to the globes of her ass, the contours promising a plump bottom that his hand itched to both fondle and spank. Forcing himself to look away, he moved to the desk and added the laptop that did have a power cord, though it was not plugged into anything. Placing it in the box, he moved out of the kitchen to find Grace standing by the door.

"I tried to find you yesterday," he said. "I wanted to apologize. Hell, now I owe you two." When she didn't say anything, he continued. "I was an ass, and shouldn't have given you the silent treatment, and was an even bigger ass when I did speak by saying what I did. You didn't deserve either." He was pleased to see her posture relaxing slightly, her green eyes no longer flashing in anger, but she hadn't smiled either. "And I apologize for barging in. I didn't even consider you'd be here."

"Why? Did you think I'd run away after

discovering that the next-door neighbor was... how did you describe him? Ah yes, an ass."

Quentin squashed his first instinct, which was to drop the box, pull the towel off her little frame and bend her over his thigh for a spanking. Instead, he took a deep breath and nodded. "Fine, I deserved that. However, when a person apologizes, it is expected that it be accepted with grace."

"Like the grace you showed me when I apologized last night?"

"No, as I said, that wasn't grace... it was me being an idiot." He took a step forward. "I won't barge in again."

She reached for the doorknob and then sighed. "I'm sorry. I don't know why I said that. It was rude." Removing her hand, she held it out. "Truce?"

Adjusting his hold on the box, he took her hand in his, praying the box's position would disguise the fact that his cock jerked as his fingers enveloped hers. "Truce." He was disappointed when she pulled her hand free and opened the door to allow him to leave. He stepped out and turned back. "Just in case you'd like, I'll stand right here and let you slam it in my face."

She seemed to consider it for a moment and then finally gave him a small grin. "No, I'm good." He was about to state that she definitely was when she did close the door, but quietly. It took the box slipping a bit for him to remember his mission. He had just enough time to drop it off at the hospital before he needed to be back to greet the women coming for the first class. After securing it on the back of his bike and setting off, he arrived at the hospital to find Brody sound asleep, a line on his forehead reminding Quentin that despite Brody's cheerful attitude, his friend was indeed dealing with an injury that was quite painful. Setting the box onto the cushion of the built-in bench seat beneath the window, he left just as quietly. He'd be back later, and they could begin.

7

"I EXPECTED THESE THIS MORNING," Quentin said as he stepped off the elevator to find Conner waiting, a pile of manila folders in his hand.

"Sorry, I was busy," Conner said with a shrug. "I've already gone through them and they look fine."

Quentin held his temper in check, taking the folders. It was too late to go through them now. The women were already gathering in the back dining room. He'd have to get his first impression from the actual students instead of whatever they'd written on their applications as their reasons for seeking a place in the class.

"So, I think we ought to just split them up," Conner said as the two began to walk down the hall. "Between us and Trent and Sloan, we can each take three."

"What do you mean? I thought there were only ten scheduled."

"Well, yeah, but we had a couple more come in. Before you ask, I've checked them out. Besides, if there's more than six total left by the end of the day, I'd be surprised. And when they begin to drop like flies, you can let the three of us handle them."

While that was quite possibly true, as several students quickly discovered that their fantasies were a lot less demanding than the reality of submission could be, Quentin was still pissed. Before they entered the room, he turned to Conner. "Let me make this perfectly clear. You do not lead, you follow. The next time I ask for something, I don't give a shit how *busy* you are; I expect you to do as asked." When the man's lips thinned, Quentin truly didn't care. "If you don't like the way I do things, you are free to leave."

"Don't get your panties in a wad, man, and I don't think Brody would like you threatening me," Conner said. "This place is already short-handed, and if I quit—"

"Another comment like that and you won't have to quit; I'll fire your ass. Either leave now, or stop trying to be cock of the walk and take the opportunity to learn something. Your choice." Without a glance back, Quentin opened the door and entered the room.

"Oh my God," he heard a woman mock-whispering. "Talk about a walking mountain of testosterone." Her statement had a few others giggling and Quentin lifting his eyes from the folders. The moment he'd crossed the threshold, he was in his full dominant role, and his expression didn't change when he found the cause of the wave of tittering that was running around the room. Looking down, he matched the woman to a photo on one of the files and then looked up again. His hold on the folders tightened when he realized who was seated next to the blonde. What the fuck?

OH, shit, Grace thought to herself, attempting to sink a bit lower in her chair as Quentin looked up. She had to admit Gretchen was right. While she'd thought the two men who had greeted them, checking IDs against a list, were handsome and sexy, both paled next to Quentin. His black leather pants fit him like a glove, not a single line disturbed the perfectly molded expanse to indicate he was wearing either boxers or briefs. The fact that he was going commando, and the bulge behind the zipper telling her he was very well endowed, had her breath catching and her nipples tightening. She wondered how the long-sleeved black t-shirt didn't burst at the seams as it stretched across his chest. Her heart skipped a beat at the tiniest glimpse of a tattoo peeking beneath the hem of one cuff, her imagination running wild as she wondered what ink was worthy of adorning such a perfect body. There was only one thing marring the raw sexuality of his pose. His left eyebrow was cocked over eyes that she was positive had turned the hard gray of cold steel as they seemed to be pinning her to her chair.

She swallowed hard and then pushed herself to sit up straight. She had as much of a right to be here as any of the other women. Mentally kicking herself for dropping her eyes, she pushed her shoulders back, watching as yet another man walked to the front, pausing for a moment before moving to join the two men standing slightly behind Quentin. Of course Quentin was the leader. Grace seriously could not picture him in any other role. She slid her glance to him again, noticing that he was flipping through what appeared to be a set of folders.

"Sorry, I think he believes it was you who started the giggle fest," Gretchen truly whispered this time. Grace wished she'd chosen any other chair in the room when Quentin's voice had every giggle ending and every single woman freezing in their seats.

"Is there something you'd like to share, Miss Kennedy?"

"Um, what?"

"I believe you heard me," Quentin said, his eyes now on the blonde, obviously understanding exactly who had made the comment.

"I'm sorry, I was... um... well, it *was* a compliment."

"It was a compliment, what?"

"Huh?"

Quentin sighed and addressed the entire class. "Ladies, let's get a few things straight. If you've signed up for this class because you're bored and are looking for something to fill your time, you've made a mistake. This class is not intended to teach you a hobby—it is to teach you a lifestyle. There are rules and protocol that will be followed at all times. Infractions of those rules will result in consequences."

Grace noticed that not a single person around her seemed to be breathing until he paused and then, almost as one being, everyone took a breath, herself included. God, his voice was smooth as warm chocolate, and yet the authority with which he spoke had the skin on her bottom crawling, wondering exactly what sort of consequences he was discussing. She didn't have to wonder long.

"To be perfectly clear, in this class and with the hands-on training you'll receive, any one of the trainers won't hesitate to deliver those consequences in the form of their implement of choice being applied to your ass... your bare ass."

At least I'm not the only one squirming, Grace thought, forcing herself to remain still by gripping the edges of her chair, only to blush when she realized Quentin's gaze had once again landed on her. She saw the corner of his mouth quirk and she knew that if he wanted, he could easily lift her off the chair, no matter the strength of her grip. She forced herself to let go and folded her hands in her lap.

"There will be no negotiations. Your opinion as to the fairness of the decision does not matter within these walls." Once again he looked down at the folders, moving one to the top. "Could you tell me why that is, Miss Baxter?"

Grace heard a soft gasp from a few chairs away.

"Um, because we are the sub-submissives and you —I mean all of you guys—are the bosses?"

Quentin's small grin had everyone relaxing the tiniest bit. "Very good, but the proper term would be Dominant. And, ladies, when addressed by a Dominant, you are to respond with respect..."

"Oh, oh!"

Grace saw Gretchen waving her hand furiously, like some first grader in desperate need of the bathroom. She almost winced when Quentin's head swiveled toward the woman.

"Yes, Miss Kennedy?"

"I got it now. I should have ended my answer with 'Master', right?" Gretchen said, and Grace had to bite the inside of her cheek at the woman's obvious pleasure in understanding where she'd messed up earlier.

"No," Quentin said, instantly deflating the woman. "While you will use the word *Master* in front of a trainer's name, when asked a question, the use of the word *sir* given with your answer will denote proper respect." When Gretchen begin to wave again, he shook his head. "Let me continue and then, if you have any questions I haven't answered, we can address them."

"Oh, of course, sir. I mean sorry, sir. Um, yes, sir!" Gretchen said, nodding just as vigorously as she'd been waving. Grace had to hand it to Quentin when he didn't roll his eyes or make any other expression signifying his humor at Gretchen's repetition of the title he'd just instructed they use.

"Thank you. Now, as I was saying, the decision to apply discipline is left to your trainers. If you graduate and enter into a relationship with a single Dominant, it will be his responsibility to determine if another Dominant has the right to punish you." He looked around the room before he continued. "I realize this is the first night of your class but believe me, the sooner you decide to commit or not, the more it will benefit everyone. That said, who has been spanked before?"

Grace's hand went up, along with the majority of the other women's.

"Let me clarify that," Quentin said. "Who has been spanked as an adult—not as a child by a parent?" A few hands went down but still more than half of the women kept their hands in the air.

"Clarifying further, I don't mean a few swats during sex to spice it up a little. I'm talking about being spanked for punishment until your ass felt like it was on fire and you found it hard to catch your breath and difficult to sit for a while?"

Grace lowered her hand and noticed that only two remained in the air. Quentin looked at the women and then at the folders, obviously searching for a match, but not speaking to them specifically. Instead, he nodded to the two before addressing the entire class. "Ladies, this is the time to decide if you wish to stay or leave. I realize we have yet to go into a great deal of specifics of what this lifestyle requires of a submissive, but I promise if the knowledge you'll often go home with a sore butt is not appealing, then you definitely won't like your first hands-on experience. No one will think less of you if you've decided that this lifestyle is not for you. I'll give you a few minutes to make your decision."

"What about the fee I paid?" a woman asked, already reaching for the purse she'd slung over her chair.

"You'll be given a full refund," Quentin assured her. She nodded and stood, and one of the men who'd checked the women in went to the door to escort her out. As he returned to the front, Quentin appeared to be handing out the folders, and Grace understood he was probably going to split the class into smaller groups. Seeing the paddle secured by a loop at his waist, and what appeared to be identical ones hanging from the other men's belts, she also understood that a spanking was most likely in the immediate future of those women who didn't leave.

"You staying?" Gretchen whispered and Grace nodded. "Oh good, me too. I'm praying I get the leader. God, he's so freaking hot."

It took a few minutes and a bit of whispering, but another woman finally shook her head at the friend she'd entered with and stood. At her action, Quentin looked up and gave her a smile, then nodded to one of his men, who again moved to escort her out. Wow, they'd been in class less than a half-hour and their numbers were already dwindling. How many more would leave either the moment before they got spanked, or immediately after? Squirming again, Grace also wondered if anyone else's panties were a bit damp. Then her face turned hot as she realized that no matter who spanked her, they'd know just the thought of being turned over a lap by a dominant man had her wet.

"All right, anyone else?"

Quentin's voice and question snapped her attention back to the front. When no one else stood, he nodded. "Good. Let me state that you are free to leave at any time. Just let your trainer know. You will address me as Master Quentin. These men will also be responsible for your training." He introduced each man by his name as they all gave a nod. Grace noticed that while two also gave the ladies a grin, the blond man who'd entered last just glanced over the group. None of them spoke. Perhaps there was some Dom-code that required them to be the strong, silent type? Her thoughts were interrupted when Quentin... make that *Master Quentin*, spoke again.

"If you'd all come line up before me, please."

Grace pushed herself up, grateful that her legs were stable enough to hold her upright. She joined the group, noticing that no one even looked like they were thinking of giggling.

"Stand up straight, arms folded behind you, legs slightly apart," Quentin ordered, and the line shuffled to allow each other enough space to obey. Once they were in position, Quentin continued. "This is the position of attention, and one you'll assume when any trainer enters the room.

"There are specific commands for kneeling and you'll learn the differences as we go along. Most kneeling positions begin with a slight change in how you'll position your hands and legs. You'll discover that most clubs use variants of the poses used in the Gorean subculture. We'll start with the basic command, which is given with the simple instruction to kneel. As a submissive, you will always need to remain aware of what your Dominant is expecting. The command to kneel can also be given silently by your Dominant using one of a few hand signals You'll need to become familiar with the slightest change of position of his fingers to indicate variations." Every eye was on him as he curled his thumb and two fingers into his palm, leaving his middle and index fingers pressed together as they pointed to the floor.

"Please kneel now with as much grace as possible."

Grace had a fleeting thought that once again she wasn't living up to her name as she tried to sink to her knees with her hands behind her back. Seeing Gretchen stumble a bit, she was glad she wasn't the only one who had to use a hand to brace herself before returning her hands to the required position.

"In this standard kneeling position, you are indicating you are not just a submissive but that you are willing to serve, and by that, I don't necessarily mean sexually." A few nervous titters were overlooked as he continued. "In this pose, you are basically waiting to see what is required of you. You will be comfortable and could maintain this position for a long time. You will learn to rise gracefully to perhaps bring your Dominant a drink or even an implement that he has requested. You'll sit back on your legs, the tips of your toes touching the floor. Legs together, hands on your lap, wrists crossed. This also allows the Dom to easily bind your wrists if he chooses. Back straight, chest out, stomach in, and head up but eyes downcast." He paused and shook his head. "That was an instruction, ladies." Bodies shifted again until each one was in the required pose. Grace watched from beneath lowered eyes and saw four sets of legs move and heard soft voices giving instructions to sit straighter, tummy in, toes pointed against the floor. By the time she felt a presence behind her, she barely dared breathe until she heard, "Very nice, Miss Hensley, but don't clasp your hands together. Just loosely cross them over one another." At her nod, the man added, "I can't hear a nod, sweetheart."

"Oh, okay... I mean, yes, sir."

"Very good."

The next voice was Quentin's again. "Practice going from standing to kneeling until you can do so without having to think about keeping your balance or where to put your hands. It will seem awkward at first but the more you practice, the more comfortable you'll become. There are not only variations of this pose but also additional positions, which you'll learn later. Please rise again, as gracefully as possible."

When they all stood, remembering to return to the proper standing position, he nodded.

"Good, but remember, you'll need to learn to move flawlessly without the use of your hands. Again, it will require practice. Eyes on me, please." Looking at each one, he added, "From now on, I expect to see you wearing either a dress or a skirt, one loose enough to allow your legs to spread widely, and the easier to remove, the better. Eventually, you'll be moving from one position to another in the nude." Grace heard a few gasps but felt her sex clench at the image that popped into her mind, and had to admit it would be a sign of obvious submission if required to drop and spread her legs and thrust out her breasts without benefit of any covering. Again she was pulled from her thoughts when he continued.

"Until then and despite what you might believe, underwear is required. I won't deny that every man with a cock, well, those who prefer their partners be women, love the naked female form, but lingerie is also quite the aphrodisiac." He paused as if to allow the women to give that some thought. Grace was already making a note to immediately do some shopping at the nearest Victoria's Secret. When he continued, she felt her tummy flip. "Having to lower your own panties or having a Dom do it for you is also a part of the experience. And don't be under the impression that wearing a thong will keep your panties up when receiving discipline. Any questions?" When a bunch of heads began to shake, he shook his, as well. "Your Dominant can't read your mind. When you are asked a question, you are to verbally answer. Try again, any questions?"

"No, sir," the line of women said in unison, more than a few voices sounding a little shaky. Before he could continue, a lone voice spoke.

"Sir?"

"Yes, Miss..."

"Alton, Jean," Master Trent provided, obviously having received her folder.

"Thank you. Go ahead, Miss Alton."

"Sir, um, are you... I mean, are we going to actually be... um... well, you know..."

"Spanked?" Quentin offered.

"Um, yes, sir."

"Yes, you are. Do you wish to leave before we begin?"

"Oh no, I mean, I-I just wondered..." Jean took a long, audible breath. "I just wondered about safewords... that's the proper term, isn't it?"

Grace thought the question was an excellent one. From the slight nods she saw from a few of her classmates, they seemed to think so as well.

"The term is proper," Quentin acknowledged. "And we'll be discussing the choice of safewords in a later class. What's important for now is that safewords are not considered during a punishment."

"Really? I mean, what if it... you know, hurts too much?" Gretchen asked.

Quentin turned his eyes to her. "Because, Miss Kennedy, the very purpose for a punishment is that it *does* hurt in order to remind a submissive that the behavior will not be tolerated. It would be rather pointless if it didn't, don't you agree?"

"I-I guess."

"Guess what?"

"Oh, I guess it would. Be pointless, I mean... um, sir."

"Let me reassure you, ladies. It is not our intention to frighten you tonight. It is our desire to help you begin the journey you've all decided to take. We are not monsters with palms itching to light into your behinds. Every lesson and every hands-on demonstration is simply another step along the path. Again, I'll repeat. If at any time you decide this isn't a journey you wish to take, tell any one of the Masters. However, I do ask that you don't do so when in the middle of your first spanking." He paused and ran his eyes up and down the line. "I'll also reassure you that you will survive." A few women giggled and he smiled before continuing. "Any additional questions before we begin?"

This time there was a single chorus of, "No, sir."

Quentin nodded. "When I call your name, please step forward." Looking over to the left, he nodded and one of the men stepped forward. "Miss Alton and Miss Landers, please go with Master Trent but, as I've stated, you'll address him as sir on most occasions, as your conversation will be limited to answering questions." The women stepped forward and followed Trent as he led them to one corner of the room.

Master Sloan stepped forward and was joined by

Miss Rodgers and Miss Torrance. Grace tried not to fidget as he read off the next name, Miss Garrison. She was one of the women who'd kept her hand up as to having spanking experience, and went to stand before Master Conner.

"Miss Wilson, you'll come with me," Quentin said, taking the other experienced woman. From the woman's instant smile, Grace knew she was extremely pleased. When he called two more names, splitting them between himself and Conner, Grace felt her heart begin to pound.

"Miss Kennedy, please go with Master Conner, and Miss Hensley, you'll be—"

"No!" Gretchen interrupted.

"Excuse me?"

"I just meant that I wanted to go with you, sir. It's not that I don't think he—"

"You've been given your assignment, Miss Kennedy—" Conner interrupted only to find himself interrupted instantly.

"But—"

"I'll switch," Grace said. As Quentin's eyes swiveled to her, she flushed but continued. "I mean, if she wants."

Quentin shook his head. "This class is not about what a submissive *wants*, Miss Hensley. It is about learning to take orders and obeying without regard to what your personal choice might be. If either of you can't obey the first order you've been given without argument, then perhaps this isn't the class for you."

Gretchen instantly moved forward to join the

group with Master Conner. Grace took a deep breath. "I'm sorry, sir," she said, stepping forward to place herself in Quentin's hands, trying to ignore the little smirk she saw on Miss Wilson's lips. So much for team unity and support. As Quentin nodded toward Master Conner, she also prayed that he was remembering they'd called a truce.

8

ONCE MASTER CONNER had practically snatched the file folders that Quentin held out and taken his group to the other corner of the room, Quentin turned his entire attention to the three women in front of him. "Miss Hensley, if you'll look at your classmates and tell me what you see?"

Grace looked at the two women and flushed. Of course she'd already screwed up. "Sorry, sir," she said, quickly assuming the standing position she'd abandoned when joining the group.

"I asked you to tell me what you see, Miss Hensley."

Grace took another look, her eyes roving up and down the two other women, understanding that he hadn't just meant that they were in the proper pose. When she reached their feet, she looked back at Quentin, and almost moaned. "They are both wearing really high heels, sir."

"That's correct. What size shoe do you wear, Miss Hensley?"

"What? Oh, um, a six."

When he didn't speak or acknowledge her answer, she felt her face heat. "A size six, sir."

He nodded and she watched him walk to what first appeared to be a piece of furniture where a delicious buffet could easily be set out. He squatted and opened one of the doors. Returning, he held out a pair of heels. "Don't worry, I assure you they've been sanitized." He also held out a pair of nylons, the disposable type used to try on shoes in a store if you'd forgotten your socks.

Unable to even fathom how ridiculous stilettoes and footies would look, she was grateful to be able to say, "Um, I don't need those, sir; I'm wearing hose." He tucked the hosiery into his pocket and she released her position to take the shoes, toeing off her ballet flats. She was sure he wanted to say something about her continued lack of grace as she balanced on first one foot and then the other in order to put the heels on. Instead, he just reached out and steadied her as she tipped to the side to put on the second shoe. "Thank you, sir."

He nodded, released her arm and stepped back. "Please remain in line but kneel." Grace sank to her knees, again flushing when she lost her balance and had to brace herself with a hand. She fought the urge to lift her eyes when Quentin's legs disappeared after bending to pick up her flats. The shiny pair of boots soon returned as he placed a chair down and then took a seat.

"Eyes to me," he said and Grace did so. "I'm going to give each one of you a spanking." Did he actually pause or did it just seem that time stood still for a moment as if to allow them to assimilate what he'd just said? "You'll each receive a dozen swats."

Okay, that's not many. Right? How bad could it be? Grace dared to relax until he continued.

"I realize you are all thinking that doesn't sound like much, and certainly not enough to be considered as a punishment. Let me assure you that you are wrong. You'll discover that quantity doesn't necessarily matter when the quality is delivered properly. You'll each take six with my hand and then six with the paddle." Grace's heart moved into her throat as he slowly untied the leather strap that held the paddle at his side. She then jerked and gave a small gasp when the sound of a woman squealing came from a different corner of the room. It took her only a moment to realize that the woman's voice had been joined by another, much closer this time. Her head turned to the left to see Master Conner's hand lifting to deliver another swat to the woman over his lap. She noticed Gretchen watching, her face looking a little pale.

"Miss Hensley, your attention is to be on me."

She snapped her eyes back and met his. "Sorry, sir."

He nodded and addressed the three. "A submissive is only to follow the commands of the

Dominant she is currently serving. In a club situation, you'll be surrounded by people in various activities. As much as you might want to watch, unless given permission or ordered to do so, you are to keep your eyes lowered and be ready to respond to any request given by your Dominant. Understood?"

"Yes, sir," they all answered, and Grace wondered if the other two were already resenting her for having to listen to a lecture.

"Good. In this situation, I want the two witnessing the spanking to observe. Miss Wilson, I can tell that this isn't your first experience in a D/s situation. Not only because you kept your hand raised with my question on spanking experience, but because you have not once stumbled in assuming either of the positions introduced tonight. Can you tell me why you felt a need to take this class?"

"I used to be in the lifestyle, sir. However, two years ago, the Dom I desired to serve disappeared. I took a break until I realized that my need to submit couldn't be denied. Though I've never had formal training, I've played here... I mean, in various clubs in New Orleans, and I've had friends who've trained here at *Plaisir.* Your reputation is one of excellence, and I decided to take the class before returning to the scene in order to be more appealing as a proper submissive."

"Thank you. Your experience will benefit your classmates. Please rise and come stand at my right side."

Talk about sucking up, Grace thought and then felt

instantly ashamed. The woman had been asked to explain her obvious experience. Grace was honest enough to admit to herself that she felt a twinge of jealousy as the brunette gracefully rose, immediately moved her hands to her back, and then took the few steps necessary to reach his side. God, even taking less than a half dozen steps she managed to appear as if she were gliding across the floor. She looked positively regal standing there. Not a muscle twitched and her eyes remained on Quentin until he spoke again.

"Lift your dress to your waist and then bend and place yourself over my knee."

The moment she lifted her dress, another glaring difference practically slapped Grace in the face. The woman was not only wearing high heels and lingerie far sexier than the panties she was wearing, but sheer stockings hugged her shapely legs, accentuating the defined muscles of her calves and thighs—stockings, not pantyhose. It wasn't until she heard her name being called that she lifted her eyes from her lap.

"Is there a problem, Miss Hensley?"

She desperately wanted to say yes and ask to be excused to go to the bathroom... not to use it but to rip off her hose. Unfortunately, even if she could grab her purse and run upstairs, she didn't own stockings, and she'd look ridiculous asking for those nylon footies after stating she didn't need them. Just barely managing not to sigh, she said, "No, sir."

"Then keep your eyes on me as you were instructed."

"Yes, sir."

She watched as Miss Wilson waited until Quentin's eyes moved to hers before bending forward without a single wobble, and only when her stomach was across his left knee did she move her hands and plant her palms flat on the floor, her toes touching the floor behind her.

The photographer in Grace noted that it was quite an erotic picture. Her tummy flipped again as Quentin reached for the waistband of the white, lacy thong, seeing the woman lift herself slightly to allow him the room necessary to pull the panties down to rest at her knees. Swallowing hard, she watched as Quentin lifted his hand and brought it down with a solid thwack that almost caused Grace's determination not to react fly out the window. A red handprint instantly appeared on the bare flesh and yet Miss Wilson made no sound. Swat after swat was delivered in a slow, deliberate cadence, alternating between her two buttocks. Grace didn't take a breath until the half dozen had been delivered and Quentin bent to the side and picked up the paddle he'd placed on the floor next to his chair.

The first stroke made a totally different sound than his palm had. It also caused the first movement from Miss Wilson as her fingers curled from their place on the floor. Again, each smack was delivered slowly but precisely, as if Quentin was making sure each one was not only accepted but had made an impression. It wasn't until the next to last that Miss Wilson's right foot lifted from the floor, and she gave a soft but audible moan. When at last the spanking was over, Grace took another breath.

"Very nicely done, Miss Wilson," Quentin said, resting the paddle against her now mottled bottom.

"Thank you, sir," she said, her voice sounding a bit breathless. After returning her panties to their previous position, Quentin helped her off his lap and she lowered her skirt and returned to where the other two were kneeling and sank into position, again, flawlessly.

God, will I ever be able to do that? Grace thought, and then watched as the woman next to her—Joanne, she thought her name was—rose with a slight hesitation at Quentin's order and was soon in the same position, skirt up and blue bikini panties at her knees. Even though Grace had just witnessed a spanking, every single swat of his hand and every stroke of his paddle were just as engrossing as the first time. Was it normal to find the scene spellbinding? Shit, was it normal to feel her panties dampen even more? Though Joanne was far more vocal and a bit squirmier when the paddle connected with her butt, when she was helped up, Quentin praised her as well.

Grace felt her heart skip a beat when his beautiful gray eyes met hers. "All right, Miss Hensley, it's your turn."

Praying she wouldn't embarrass herself or her classmates, she rose to her feet and though a bit wobbly, she did manage not to use her hands. Once she reached Quentin's side, she felt her face heat when she had to give her skirt a few hard tugs to get it up over her hips, and then wanted to melt into the floor when she saw Quentin's eyebrow lift at the revelation of her pantyhose.

"I'm sorry, sir. I didn't think about this... scenario happening when I dressed."

"A submissive should consider all scenes as possibilities. See that you do so as well in the future, Miss Hensley."

"Yes, sir," she said, not daring to shift her eyes to see the reaction of the two other women. She hesitated, not sure if she should push her pantyhose down, but when he gave a small shake of his head, she took a breath and laid herself across his knee. God, it was as solid as a tree trunk, the leather of his pants soft against her tummy.

"Hands on the floor, Miss Hensley."

"Oh, right," she said, reaching for the floor and realizing that doing so was a longer reach than she'd considered. Her feet no longer touched the floor behind her. She again cursed her short stature and wondered if she should apologize. Before she could, she felt fingers at her waist and when nothing further happened, she blushed and then lifted her hips as he pulled her pantyhose down.

Why didn't he take my panties down at the same time? It would have been a lot less embarrassing. With that thought, she understood it was intended as a lesson. If she'd worn the proper attire, she wouldn't be holding the awkward lift that required she wiggle back until her feet reached the floor to allow the leverage needed to lift herself. Finally, her very unsexy yellow briefs were at her knees, and when he lifted his leg a bit, she took the nonverbal hint and wiggled forward to return her palms to the floor. It was only then that she realized she felt something pressing against her hip. Her face heated when she understood that it was Quentin's cock, and another gush of moisture flooded her sex. Would he notice? Would he find it necessary to point out that it was abnormal for submissives to become drenched from nothing more than witnessing spankings? Her internal questions were interrupted when she felt him lift the hand that had been resting on her bare bottom.

Oh my God! From the very first swat, she understood that his hand was just as hard as the steel gray of his eyes. When the second blow landed on her right cheek, she whimpered, and the third had her biting her lip. Neither of the women before her had cracked within three strokes, and he hadn't even picked up the paddle yet. Forget the few swats her previous boyfriends had given her. With her ass quickly beginning to burn, she understood those had been nothing but little taps.

"Ow!" she yelped, not one but both feet kicking up, actually coming into contact with his lifted arm. When she felt a weight over her legs, she was mortified by the realization that he'd placed his right leg over hers. *Good lord, I can't even take a spanking without needing additional correction, even if it is silent. Bet you're wishing you'd let me swap places, aren't you?*

Another swat from his palm cracked against her ass, not only pulling her out of her thoughts, but reminding her that she couldn't even keep a correct count, having thought the hand spanking was done. Closing her eyes, she tried to breathe as deeply as possible when he once again bent to pick up the paddle.

Please, God, don't let me make a total fool of myself. Don't let me fail on the first freaking day. Okay, it might not have been very smart to add a curse word to her silent prayer but when she sensed his hand lifting, she hoped that God would understand.

She practically bit her tongue when the first stroke landed, the fire she'd thought was hot flaring into the inferno Quentin had referred to earlier. She couldn't help it, her hips jerked to the side as if trying to throw off his aim and yet, being the Dom he was, he delivered the next stroke, and the next, and the next, with unfaltering precision. By the time he'd given her the last of the 'mere dozen' strokes, she was desperately fighting back the tears that were threatening to spill.

Her heart hitched when she felt a slight touch on her sex. She almost moaned when it disappeared and he patted her blazing ass as if to get her attention. Had she really felt anything or had her mind just desperately wished for him to touch her? She appreciated his help as he held onto her arm, pulling her up until she was standing, her wobble causing him to keep his hand on her arm until she regained her balance. "Good job, Miss Hensley."

Why did his words cause her heart to swell? It wasn't as if he'd stated "very nice" or "nicely done" as he had with the others. Still, she couldn't help but feel proud—after all, she had survived. Tugging her clothing down gave her another reason to go shopping as soon as possible as the tight fit of her A-line skirt seemed to trap the heat of her well-roasted rear.

"Than-thank you, sir," she said and, at his nod, returned and only by the grace of God managed to sink into the kneeling position without falling flat on her face.

9

QUENTIN LOOKED at his three pupils and said, "Eyes down, ladies." He was pleased when each set of eyes instantly dropped to the floor, not missing the fact that one set, the green ones that reminded him of the swamp's living foliage, were filled with tears. He also didn't fail to notice that it hadn't been until he had Grace over his knee that his cock had hardened. He'd spanked countless women in his lifetime, and though each one had been an erotic experience in submission, very rarely did his cock instantly turn into a rod of steel before he'd even delivered the first stroke. Had the little artist even noticed? Had she been aware that his fingertip had grazed the seam of her sex, finding her so very wet? Shit, had the other two women noticed? His hand had seemed to move of its own accord, and it had been hearing her slight gasp that had him remembering where he was, what he was supposed to be doing. Forcing his mind away from the question of why this woman had him wanting to do far more than touch, he took the time to look around the room, noticing that every woman was kneeling and not a single one was whispering, much less giggling.

As he met the eyes of his staff, he nodded. He felt a surge of pride. Not in the men who were heading the class with him, but in every single woman who'd remained. He'd half expected to see at least one bolting for the door. Finally, feeling his erection subside, at least enough to allow him to stand, he did so. After returning the chair to its place, waiting as the other men followed his example, he spoke.

"Very well done, ladies. Please rise and form a line up front again." Soon, ten women stood, all in the proper position of attention before him and the other men. "Eyes to me." When he had their attention, he continued. "Ladies, I applaud each and every one of you. You not only survived your first spanking, you did so with dignity. I hope to see you all back in class tomorrow. Remember to practice moving from standing to kneeling, and please remember the clothing requirements." He managed not to grin when he saw Grace's face flush. He'd never even considered a woman might wear pantyhose. Then again, he was accustomed to experienced submissives who either wore stockings with or without garter belts, or simply went barelegged. He saw no need to add the qualification now, as he was sure if another woman had made the same choice, their trainer would have either told her to wear stockings the next time, or she'd have been just as conscious of her wrong choice as Grace had been.

"Before we dismiss you, are there any questions?" He half expected to hear from Miss Kennedy but she, like all the others, remained silent. "All right. If you have questions, we'll be glad to answer them as we go along. Again, good job, and it's nice to have you aboard. Dismissed."

He watched as Grace didn't wait to see if anyone else moved first. She practically flew to the table, where she grabbed her purse and was halfway to the door before he could speak.

"Miss Hensley, if you'll stay behind, please." She instantly halted but took a few seconds to turn and another few to walk back toward him. The other women slipped around her, some giving her looks of empathy and others simply keeping their eyes on the door. Despite his praise, he wondered if he'd see all ten back in class the next night. Once Grace was standing in front of him, he said, "Just a moment, please." He moved away to talk to his men, intending to not only thank them, but to ask them to turn their notes about their observations in before they left the building. Instead, he arrived in time to hear Conner.

"Evidently we didn't spank their asses hard enough. I would have sworn we'd lose at least a couple. I considered giving that mouthy Kennedy woman a few extras but with this flimsy fucking paddle, why bother? My girls barely even wiggled."

"If your submissives didn't leave your lap with a well-heated bottom, it's not due to the implement; it's how that implement was wielded, Conner," Quentin said, causing the man to turn in his direction. "Please remain in the hall. I'll see you in a moment."

"Listen, you can't send me out just because I was explaining—"

"I didn't ask for an explanation, Conner," Quentin said. "I'll be out in a moment, and expect you to be waiting. Understood?"

He saw Conner's eyes go to where Grace was standing, and didn't appreciate the look on his face when he turned back. "Sure thing, *boss*," he said with a shrug. "Take all the time you need to... well, to do whatever." Quentin wanted to slap the insolent tone right out of him but instead said, "Trent, Sloan, thanks. You can leave your reports with Sammy. He's got dinner waiting."

"Yes, sir," the men said, one after another, and then left. Neither one giving Grace a glance.

"Hey, I gotta eat..." Conner began but obviously he interpreted the look on Quentin's face correctly when he said, "Right, I'll be waiting for you out in the hall."

Once the room had cleared, Quentin returned to Grace, noting that she'd hung her purse so that it lay across her body, and had put her arms behind her. He couldn't fault her for her position but he did fault her for something far more important.

"Relax, Grace. I'm talking to you as just Quentin," he said and when she did, shifting her eyes to his, he walked to a table and pulled out a chair. "Please, sit."

"I'd rather stand," she said, though she did turn toward him.

It was a statement he could understand as he was sure her bottom was tender. "Why didn't you tell me you were in this class?"

"Why should I have?" she countered. "Did any of the other women personally inform you of their enrollment?"

"I wasn't asking about them, Grace. I have never even met any of them before tonight. You, however, I not only have met, but we also talked less than four hours ago, and yet you didn't think it might be appropriate to inform me that you'd enrolled?"

Her green eyes were no longer glistening with tears. Instead, if they were shimmering at all, it was with anger. "Again, I wonder at the question. First, I don't understand why you seem to be singling me out and second, why would I inform a practical stranger that I was going to spend my evening learning how to be submissive? I had no idea that you'd be the fucking teacher—"

"Don't cuss," he snapped.

"I'm not in your class now, Master Quentin, so I can cuss if I bloody well want to!"

Not missing the fact that though not in class, she'd addressed him as if she still were, he said, "Not unless you want to find yourself right back over my knee, young lady. If you don't believe me, say another ugly word." Quentin could practically see the desire to do so fighting with the fact that her ass was burning. He discovered he was a torn between being proud when her intelligence won over her stubbornness, and his desire to have that stubbornness give him an excuse to bare her heart-shaped bottom again.

"Yes, sir."

"Good girl," he said. "I admit, you have a point." When her chin lifted with what he considered a bit of unnecessary arrogance, he qualified his statement. "Not about singling you out. I treated you as I would have any of the others."

"Then why didn't you let me swap places with Gretchen?"

Quentin sighed and took a deep breath. "Exactly for the reason I stated earlier. No submissive, well, not one in my class, is allowed to direct the lessons. The proper terminology would be *topping from the bottom*. Deciding on what is going to happen and how the scene will proceed is the role of the Dominant. If you continue in class, you'll learn that a submissive definitely has the right to make choices about her service but, again, only so far, and not in this class. Imagine if all ten of you started making requests or arguing about what you've been instructed to do. It would not only create total chaos, it would make the entire point of the class moot. Do you understand that?"

She nodded, albeit a bit reluctantly.

"What I was saying was that you have a point in that you didn't have any responsibility to inform me of your enrollment, especially if, as you stated, you didn't know I was leading the class."

"I didn't," she said firmly. "And in case you are wondering, Laurie doesn't know I turned in the application. She knew I was considering a class, but I didn't actually submit the paperwork until a couple of days ago. So you don't have any reason to be pissed off at her." She paused, straightened her shoulders and then gave him a glare. "And you don't have any reason to spank her, either."

So, Laurie had evidently shared that tidbit with her new roommate. It didn't bother him in the slightest, and he had absolutely no thought that Laurie had done so with any intention other than discussing her evening with her best friend. However, he needed to continue as he had begun.

"What happens between me and Laurie, or between myself and any other submissive, is not your business, Miss Hensley. You've got enough to concern yourself with about your own choices. If you aren't happy with me leading—"

"Oh no you don't," Grace interrupted. "You aren't going to scare me off and, Master Quentin, don't you dare fail me simply because you have a thorn up your as—butt because you obviously don't approve of my being here. As you said, it is my choice, and I'm staying. Are we done?"

"Yes, we're done," he said. He waited until she'd twirled around and stomped toward the door, the motion of her ass in her tight skirt almost mesmerizing him before his gaze dropped down to her shapely legs. With a grin, he spoke again. "Miss Hensley?"

"What!" she snapped, turning around again.

"Your shoes?"

"My shoes?" Looking down, he heard her curse under her breath as she kicked off the heels and then stomped over to grab her flats. She didn't bother to put them on, just held them, yanked open the door, and disappeared.

"Well, that went splendidly, Quentin," he murmured as he walked to the door. With a sigh, he said, "Come on in." This time, when he gestured to a table, Conner didn't wait for an invitation to sit. He was seated with a cold look on his face and his arms crossed over his chest, and was already speaking as Quentin took a seat opposite him.

"Look, if you have a problem with my performance—"

"I don't," Quentin said, cutting him off. "But I do have a problem with your attitude—"

"What the fuck—"

"Interrupt again, and you can plan on picking up your last paycheck in the morning."

While his eyes flashed, Conner managed to hold his tongue.

"Every woman here deserves respect. You can, and are expected, to correct an infraction, but only if an actual infraction of the rules occurs. These women are making a difficult choice in choosing a submissive path. If Miss Kennedy had heard you belittling her, I can easily see her deciding that the choice to follow what her heart is yearning for should be ignored."

"That's easy for you to say," Conner said. "You have obviously chosen Grace as your class pet, though from the way she stormed out, it seems she might not agree. If you'd have allowed that hot little beauty to switch, I'm sure she would—"

"I don't give a rat's ass what *Miss Hensley* would have done. The choice is mine and mine alone, and I better not hear you refer to her or any other student with any disrespect again. In case you are too pig-headed to understand, listen to me very carefully. This is your last chance, Conner. Either get with the program or get out. Is that clear enough?"

Conner took a moment but then nodded. "Yes."

"Good. When you've finished your report, you can leave it with Sammy and then grab dinner."

"Fine, but I can just give it to you now, as I wrote it out in the hall while you were with Gra—Miss Hensley."

Quentin shook his head and stood. He walked across the room to pick up the heels Grace had kicked off. It might be a shitty thing to do, but if anyone needed to be taken down a peg, it was the man sitting with the obvious chip on his shoulder. Setting the shoes onto the table, he said, "Before you turn in your report or eat, sanitize these and return them to the cabinet." He saw Conner's mouth open and then close. Though he didn't verbally respond, Quentin didn't much care. He left the room and went to the elevator. Glancing at Brody's door, he almost went to it, but instead entered his own apartment only long enough to change before returning downstairs.

"Hey, how did it go?" Sammy asked from where he was preparing some sort of marinade.

"Good," Quentin said. "The men are going to be leaving some papers with you. I'll pick them up when I get back."

"All right," Sammy said, nodding to two large bakery boxes on the counter and a smaller container sitting on top of one. "Hannah left those for you. The little one is for Brody."

"Great, thanks," Quentin said, pulling out his wallet, ignoring Sammy's wave of his hand that was holding a chicken quarter. Placing two twenties on the counter, he picked up the boxes. "These should keep Brody in the nurses' good graces for a while."

Sammy chuckled and Quentin left. He'd have to take his truck as the boxes were too wide to fit into the bike's saddlebag. Arriving at the hospital, he grinned at the smiles that met him as he approached the nurses' station. He wasn't stupid enough to think they were for him; he knew they were practically salivating seeing the bakery boxes.

"Enjoy, ladies, and I wanted to say thanks for taking care of Brody."

"Oh, he's a doll," one nurse said as she reached for a pair of scissors to cut the string around the first box. Quentin was almost to Brody's door when he heard her squeal, "Oh, my favorite, pecan!"

Pushing through the door, he saw Brody lifting the arm that wasn't wrapped around Laurie into the air, palm out as if in surrender. "Before you go off, I had no idea that Grace registered for class."

"Shit, what did she say?"

"She didn't say anything," Brody said as Laurie

slid out of the bed. "I just got off the phone with Conner."

"Figures," Quentin muttered, crossing the room. "Though I can't believe the little shit called to tattle."

Brody chuckled as Laurie bent to kiss him. "You don't have to go," Quentin said.

"Yes, I do," Laurie countered. "As much as I'd love to stay and listen to some macho Dom talk, I'm only on my break." She moved to kiss Quentin's cheek. "And before you ask, no, I did not know either. I mean, I knew she was considering enrolling but she didn't tell me she'd decided to go for it."

"I know, she told me," Quentin said. He grinned and then chuckled. "In fact, she made sure I knew how innocent you were, and informed me that I'd be a total ass if I spanked you for it."

"She did?"

"Well, not in those exact words, but I didn't have to be a mind reader to get the message."

Laurie laughed as she went to the door. "I told you she was a great girl. Gotta go, I'll drop by later, honey."

After she left, Brody waved toward the box that Quentin still held. "That for me?"

"Yes, from Hannah with love," Quentin said, placing the box on the tray table and moving it over Brody's lap.

Brody opened it to reveal two slices of pie, one pecan and the other strawberry. "I gotta admit, that woman is my second love," he said. "Hand me that fork, would you?"

"You're not gonna share?" Quentin asked, passing him the fork.

"Hell no. All you have to do is walk downstairs to get pie."

Quentin dropped into the chair and after Brody had taken a huge bite, got up and placed his water mug on the tray as well.

"When you can talk again, tell me what Conner said."

Brody took a bite of the second slice and a drink of water before he did so. "He was questioning exactly how much authority you have. Seems he's forgotten that you have as much authority as I do, seeing as you own half the club." Taking another bite, he continued, "Look, I know he can be a bit abrasive, but maybe you could cut him a break?"

"Cut him a break? I was this close to firing his ass," Quentin said, rubbing his index finger against the pad of his thumb.

"I know, he told me you kept threatening him," Brody said, chuckling when Quentin practically growled. "Relax, if that is warranted, then by all means, cut him loose. I'm just saying that with my injury and Dave gone, he fully expected to step up to fill our shoes."

"That may be," Quentin said, running his hand over his face. "But I'm telling you, there is something off there. I can give him a little slack, but only a little. I won't have anyone on our staff, and especially not one training new submissives, denigrating the women."

"He certainly didn't mention that," Brody said, forking the last bite of pecan pie into his mouth. After swallowing, he grinned. "Though he did mention that a certain little artist seemed to capture your attention."

Quentin was about to protest and then shrugged. "Maybe, but only because she required a bit more attention and instruction than the others."

"Hmm," Brody said around the last mouthful of strawberry pie. "Far be it for me to judge not only my best friend, but my business partner and a master instructor. And just for the record, yeah, it pissed me off that Conner saw fit to call."

"Let it go," Quentin said. "He'll either come around or he won't." Looking toward the small couch, he said, "I'm a little surprised Grace didn't call and complain that I broke into your apartment and scared the crap out of her."

"Now, that's far more interesting. When did that happen?"

Quentin explained, including the fact that Conner might consider purchasing larger towels.

Brody chuckled. "Why in the hell would I want to do that?"

Quentin had to concede him that point and moved on to something far less stimulating but also far more important. "Have you had a chance to go through anything I brought? You were asleep when I dropped off stuff."

"I did," Brody said. "Grab the box, would you?"

Quentin did so and then moved his chair closer, setting up the computer on the tray table.

"I transferred your notes to a document," Brody said, clicking it open after entering his password. "It took some thought, but I remembered the temp hostess was named Marti Ansell. With her and Mike, I think you've listed all the staff." When he scrolled down to the next page, Quentin saw a much longer list.

"These are the names of the people we have checking in with rings," Brody said and scrolled down two additional pages. "However, since our security wasn't as intense back then, I'm afraid there are people who aren't listed. The fact that it was an open mixer doesn't help, as I can't swear that all the guests of members are even recorded."

Quentin had to agree, again thinking if he hadn't left that afternoon to drive to Texas, all of this would most likely not be necessary. "How can we ever have a complete list?"

"See these check marks next to some of the names?" At Quentin's nod, Brody continued, "I started going through the tapes. If I could put a face to a name, I checked them off. I didn't get a chance to go through the entire film loop—the club opened earlier and closed later than usual in order to accommodate the larger crowd. I'll continue tomorrow. Any I can't match to a name, I'll list their description and the time when they appear on screen. Even though you weren't there, you might recognize some." He paused. "I know we want to keep this as hush-hush as possible, but if there are still people we can't identify, we might need to consider asking the staff to take a look."

"Adam, and maybe Trent and Sloan," Quentin said.

"Any specific reasoning for not including Conner?"

"Nothing specific, just a gut feeling," Quentin said.

Brody nodded. "That's good enough for me. Besides, he was relatively new back then. You know it was Farraday who brought him in to interview."

"That's right, I'd forgotten. You've made a good start," Quentin said. "I'll come back tomorrow and help."

"That's fine, just leave the computer on the tray," Brody said, shutting it down. "Now, go home. I know you've got to be wiped."

"I am a little," Quentin admitted. "I've still got to pick up the guys' reports from Sammy."

"You never said how the class went."

"I think it went well. In fact, we only lost two so far."

"That's pretty impressive. It'll be interesting to see if that holds, but I won't be surprised if it doesn't."

"They all seem eager to learn," Quentin said and then shook his head. "Though having to pose fully clothed, or just have your bottom bared for a quick trip over a lap, is nothing compared to being told to strip and present."

"Or ordered to perform," Brody acknowledged. "Still, both Molly and Sarah came from one of our classes and they're not only great employees, they evidently love their jobs and keep our clients happy."

"Yes, they are and, as I recall, Laurie was another pupil. Hmm, how would her instructor describe her now, I wonder?"

"As near perfection as a woman can be," Brody said with a grin. "Thank Hannah for the pie."

"I will, you get some rest," Quentin said and then grinned. "At least until your little piece of perfection pops back in."

"Hell, if you gotta have your leg hanging in some freaking contraption, the least you deserve is a nurse who gives you such sweet loving care."

"Yeah, but unless you care to have every visitor see such devotion, I'd remind your little nurse to pull the curtain around the bed."

"You know Laurie. She's never been one to care about hiding her kink in some dark corner."

"Lucky you," Quentin said with a grin. "See you tomorrow." He made sure to throw away the evidence of the pie, even washing the fork in the sink and drying it before returning it to the table.

Once back at the house, he picked up the papers from Sammy, and lifting the cover off a pie, he cut a generous slice, placing it on a plate. Taking the stairs as a concession to the food he'd been recently consuming, he walked down the hall and knocked on Brody's door. When it opened to reveal Grace, he didn't get a chance to speak before she did.

"Checking up on your clumsiest student?"

"What?" he said, and only the fact that she began

to wobble had him almost dropping the plate as he reached out to steady her, forcing his eyes away from the soft mounds of her breasts He grinned when he realized she had teetered because she was now standing on one foot, the other extended to display the red stiletto heel.

"Not at all," he said, his eyes returning to her face but not missing the fact that her nipples were now pressing against the cotton of her pink camisole. She was wearing sweat pants that appeared about two sizes too big. He grinned, thinking the soft fleece had to feel better against her ass even though he truly hadn't spanked any of the women very hard. His cock had hardened just thinking of his hand smacking down against her beautiful little butt, drawing the softest mews and then louder yelps from her. Seeing her head tilt toward one side as if wondering whether he planned on qualifying his statement, he realized he'd been standing there like some kind of idiot.

"While I applaud your dedication, I thought you might enjoy a midnight snack." He held out the plate and was disappointed when she lowered her foot to the ground, giving him no reason to continue holding her arm.

"Oh, thanks, that looks delicious."

"It is. Hannah makes the best pies in Louisiana." She took the plate and he sensed that the door was about to shut... realizing he didn't want it to close. "Hey, I also wanted to say that if you'll look in Laurie's bathroom—"

"I don't invade other people's privacy," she interrupted.

"Well, we both know I don't have that same moral code," Quentin said. "May I come in for a minute?"

She hesitated but then nodded, stepping back to allow him to do so. He saw the slight grimace on her face as he entered and said, "I think that's enough practice for tonight."

"Thank God," she said, bending to remove the shoes. He smiled again at the look of relief on her face, and when he realized he was waiting to see the seat of her sweat pants tighten around her ass, he told himself to get a grip, shook his head, and moved past her. Returning to the living room, he caught her taking a bite of the pie without benefit of any utensil.

"I was just going to say that if you apply a bit of this, you'll sleep easier."

"What is it?"

"Arnica cream. It will help relieve both the heat and the tenderness." At her look toward her feet, he chuckled. "Not for your feet, sugar, for your bottom." The flush that suffused her chest and then her face had his cock protesting its confinement.

"Oh... um, thanks," she said, reaching for the jar only to find both hands currently full. Replacing the pie on the plate, she licked her fingers and again reached for the jar.

He had to bite back his groan when the sight of her tongue licking along her fingertips had his mind imagining it licking the head of his cock. While he knew that was an impossibility, he did seriously consider offering to demonstrate how to apply the arnica cream. Looking into her eyes, he saw that her pupils were slightly dilated. The Dom in him wanted to take her face between his palms and claim her mouth. The professional in him knew that move wouldn't be wise.

"Good night, Grace," he said instead, walking to the door and through it.

"Good night, Quentin. And thanks again, for the pie and the cream."

"You're welcome. Get some sleep."

"I will," she said and then giggled. "On my tummy, no doubt." He grinned and as she closed the door, he knew his shower wall would see a repeat of his cum splashing against the tile.

10

"Welcome to the club," Laurie said, lifting her coffee mug as Grace made her way into the kitchen the next morning. "Of course, it might have been nice to have known beforehand that you were applying for membership."

"Hmm, sort of like you let me know that Quentin was the leader of the class?"

"I didn't even think about that. When we discussed it, he hadn't come back yet. But, as I recall, he is quite the instructor. Would knowing he'd lead have you changing your mind about enrolling?"

"No, I don't think so. I mean, you know I've been waffling back and forth for months. It just seemed to be the perfect chance to take the classes since I am staying here with you, but I honestly hadn't decided until a couple of days ago," Grace said, pouring her own cup of coffee. "And I made sure that Quentin knew you had no idea."

"I know, he said the same last night. It was very

sweet of you to inform him that my poor rear didn't need his attention." She grinned and as Grace took her seat, unable to hide a small grimace that had nothing to do with the coffee she was sipping, Laurie spoke again. "So, I'm guessing you can you check off the 'sleeping on my tummy' box?"

"Ha-ha, very funny. I hadn't truly considered this class to be some sort of bucket-list, but, yes, consider that one checked in full."

"Oh, honey, you'll find that mark has a way of disappearing just as if you'd used invisible ink. Don't worry. If you truly embrace this dynamic, there will be countless more times when you can mark it off again."

"That's what I'm afraid of," Grace confessed, though she did so with a small smile. "You know, that would have most women running for the hills but— while that spanking wasn't for play and had me in tears—it just seemed... right, somehow. I can't explain it."

"You're don't have to explain it," Laurie said. "You just have to feel it in your very soul. I've gone through the same confusion, the same feeling of being considered strange or deviant. Once you let all that go, you'll be free to discover what makes you feel whole. I'm here to answer any questions. Sometimes it's easier to talk to another submissive than to wonder." After taking another sip of her coffee, she leaned forward and placed her hand over Grace's. "The important thing is, how are you really?"

Grace took a few minutes to mull over her

response. She'd been doing so since she'd found herself actually sitting in the dining room with eleven other women last night, determined once and for all to learn if becoming a submissive would be anywhere near as enticing as the erotic books that filled her Kindle made the dynamic appear. "Actually, I'm pretty damn good and, by the way, I owe you for a jar of that magical cream. Quentin insisted you wouldn't mind."

This time it was Laurie who grinned. "I don't mind, and you don't owe me. Consider that one a gift. I've got several more. That is one item that I keep well-stocked. Did he bother to mention the soothing relief of arnica to the entire class?"

"No, he just mentioned it when he came over..." Pausing, she met Laurie's gaze and shook her head. "It's not what you are thinking. He just came over to bring me a piece of pie and—"

"And turned all compassionate even though he was the one who roasted your rump?" Laurie said, her eyes twinkling.

"Be careful," Grace said. "He catches you thinking it was about anything other than seeing that I was okay and you'll be needing a gallon of the stuff."

Laurie waved her hand as if she had no concerns. "Whatever. But, now that your best friend has shown proper concern for your wellbeing, I want to hear every single detail about the class."

Glancing up at the clock on the wall, Grace said, "Shouldn't you be getting ready for your shift?"

"Nope, I have the day off, and Brody told me that

if he saw me at the hospital before this evening, he'd have Quentin tend to my hide again."

"Seriously?"

Nodding, Laurie sat back again. "I've told you that the two men are not only best friends, but, duh, they are both Dominants, though I guess I might have left out the fact that I've lost count of the times I've been across Quentin's knees." She gave Grace a look and then smiled. "In fact, just to be totally transparent, I've been between his knees as well."

It took Grace a moment to absorb what Laurie had said and she still could feel her face heat. "If you mean what I think you mean... um, wow."

"Wow is one way to describe it," Laurie agreed. "Then again, erotic, fulfilling, hot, worthy of an award, sexy as hell..."

"Okay, okay, I get it. But again, wow. Wait, are you talking about when you were in the class?"

"Yes, then, as well as right before he left New Orleans. The great Doms, the ones who truly believe in fulfilling their sub's desires, don't get all stingy. I don't mean that Brody would force me to accept another Dom's attentions, but neither does he deny me the experience. Until you have more than one man at a time, or are submitting to another man knowing your Dominant is watching, well... there is really no way to understand the feeling. I've had the most incredible orgasms in the scenes I've shared with Brody and other men. Forget wow—think more woozer!"

Grace swallowed hard, remembering the feel of

Quentin's erection pressing against her hip and his hand resting on her bottom. What would it be like to kneel before him, not in the position she'd learned the night before, but between his legs, waiting for his command to open her mouth? What color would his eyes turn when she obeyed, when she concentrated on nothing other than pleasuring him? What would it be like for him to have him ask another Dominant to join him in pleasuring her?

"Hellooo..." Laurie's voice brought her out of her fantasy and reminded her that she would be mortified if either one of those scenarios happened until she completed her very vital mission.

"Since you are off, how about we go shopping? I don't dare show up in class again until I do."

"Only if you promise to explain that statement," Laurie said, her eyes twinkling.

"One word that had me wishing the floor opened up and swallowed me whole," Grace said, and when Laurie's nose crinkled in puzzlement, she leaned forward and whispered, "pantyhose."

"Oh no! Don't tell me... oh, Grace."

"Oh yes, and talk about humiliating."

"Get ready! I know exactly where to go." Laurie stood and bent to give Grace a hug. "I guarantee that by the time we are done, you'll feel so sexy that you'll want to prance around in nothing but your new lingerie!"

"And high heels," Grace added with a mock groan.

"Agreed. It's been ages since I've done some 'me'

shopping, and a girl can always use a new pair of shoes. Meet back here in half an hour?"

"That'll work," Grace said, standing and giving her bottom an unconscious rub. Laurie's giggle had her dropping her hand and then shrugging. "Just make sure I don't do that in public, promise?"

"Promise."

The two women got ready and then traipsed down the stairs. They stopped in the kitchen so that Laurie could express her thanks to Hannah for the pies. "There wasn't a crumb left of either one by the time I clocked out. And Brody said to..." She paused and bent forward to kiss Hannah's cheek.

"That boy," Hannah said, her smile showing her pleasure. "How's he doing, by the way?"

"Getting very tired of being in bed."

"Hmph," Sammy said with a chuckle. "You tell him that Sammy is ashamed of him if he can't think of a way to entertain himself in that bed... especially when he's got a gorgeous, willing nurse to kiss his little—"

"Mr. Sammy, you are so bad," Laurie said, her face coloring.

"What?" Sammy asked, his eyes widening as if to advertise his confusion. "I was just saying to kiss his boo-boos."

"Oh, is that what you call it," Hannah said, rolling her eyes. "Ignore him, girls. A nice plate of shrimp etouffee and hot garlic bread will lift Brody's spirits." She paused and lowered her voice, "And lifted spirits have been known to lift other things, if you know what I mean."

"Hannah, you are just as bad as Sammy," Laurie said. "Not to say that I won't be happy to test that theory when I take it to him tonight. Right now, Grace and I are going girl shopping."

"Well, hell's bells. If I'd known you could actually shop for a girl, I'd have—"

"You'd what, you old geezer?" Hannah asked, her hands moving to rest on her wide hips.

The two younger women left when Sammy grabbed his wife, lifting her off the ground, causing her to squeal as he nuzzled her neck.

"Oh, yes, that is a definite buy," Laurie said an hour later as Grace stepped out of the dressing room.

"You don't think it's a little too... well, little?"

"Absolutely not. Turn around." When Grace did, she felt her face flush to match the pink color of the matching demi-bra and panty set. "Girl, if I didn't love you, I'd be jealous. I've read about heart-shaped butts, but yours is perfect." As Grace turned again, Laurie continued, "Oh, did Master Quentin give his 'don't think wearing a thong will save you' speech?"

"Yes, though I don't really see why a thong would have to come down." Looking into the mirrors that were arranged for customers to be able to see the full picture, she shook her head. "I mean, my entire ass is hanging out."

"It has to do with that whole humility thing, I suppose," Laurie said. "Besides, every time Brody hooks his fingers into my waistband and starts pulling them down... I feel just like a naughty girl about to get her heinie spanked. Go put on the other set."

The next time Grace stepped out, she felt more covered, and yet just as sexy in the black lace set as she had in the pink. This set seemed to set off her breasts as the soft pillows were pushed up, their pale color so contrasted against the inky black satin and lace of the bra. The panties were high cut on the legs, and though her cheeks were totally covered, the sheer lace seemed to be almost teasing you to remove them to see what they only barely hid.

After an hour, she had five new sets of underthings and three garter belts, as she just couldn't decide between the red, white and black ones she'd tried on. She'd also picked up several pairs of stockings and had to admit, their tops clinging to her thighs, the garter belts almost acting as a frame for her panties, well... who in the world would continue to wiggle into pantyhose that never seemed to fit correctly.

"Brody is gonna love that purple set," Grace said as the women moved out of the store, the distinctive pink bags swinging from their hands. "And, might I say that your ass is just perfect the way it is."

"Why thank you," Laurie said, giving an exaggerated pat to her behind. "Lunch now, or shoes?"

"I actually wanted to get a couple of skirts or even a dress. Besides the pantyhose, I was probably the only one in the room who had to actually tug and yank to get my skirt up before my spanking." The moment those last few words left her mouth, she slapped her hand over it. A man who'd been passing them as they walked in the mall, turned and gave her a grin. Though he didn't say a word, his lifted brow and wink had her blushing and Laurie giggling. When he turned away and continued walking, Grace shook her head.

"God, I can't believe I said that out loud. What would people think?"

"I'd say that guy was thinking he wouldn't have minded at all how long it took you to pull your skirt up."

"Gee, thanks." The two shared a bout of giggles and then entered another store. As if to make sure she wouldn't have the same problem as she'd had the night before, anything she tried on, she lifted to her waist. Grace fell in love with a skirt that was layered and swished around her legs. Since it was black, she could pair it with any number of tops, including the white camisole she bought. A dress with a fitted bodice but with a skirt that flared after nipping in at the waist was her final choice.

"You know, we're pretty close to the same size," Laurie said. "Feel free to raid my closet while you are here."

"Are you sure?"

"Of course. I'd offer my shoes but my feet are a size bigger."

Grace groaned at the thought of their next stop. "I'll need sustenance before shoving my poor dogs into heels. I'm not sure they've forgiven me for last night. I couldn't believe they just happen to have heels on hand for those who didn't come in any. Don't men know that high heels are painful?"

Laurie laughed. "Honey, I don't think dominant men consider them 'high heels'. They like to think of them as 'fuck me' shoes. All you need is to find the right pair. Get ones that fit perfectly and not only will they be easier to wear, but once you are standing before your Dom in nothing but them and any of that lingerie you just bought, I promise you'll understand the appeal."

They ate lunch at the Starbucks attached to the mall. Once seated in a corner table, Grace took a sip of her latte but just toyed with her sandwich.

"You okay?"

"Yes, I was just thinking about what you said." She leaned a bit closer. "What do Doms think when they pull those panties down and find them... um, damp?"

"Ah, they consider that a sign of a natural submissive. And, if they find you becoming even *damper* during the spanking they are delivering, then, my friend, they consider that a huge success."

Grace knew she was blushing and yet it wasn't due to Laurie's answer. It was because she was wondering if that was truly what Quentin had thought. Though she wasn't sure if it had been intentional or not, she still could almost feel that featherlight touch of his finger against her sex, and she knew she'd been dripping.

They returned to their apartment two hours later. "Okay, go change into your new lingerie and stockings. Put on your high heels."

"Why? It's too early to get dressed," Grace said.

"Because we are going to practice," Laurie said. "And, if you want, I'll show you the next position you'll be learning."

"Isn't that cheating?"

Laurie laughed. "Not if you consider it as being a proactive student who takes her classes seriously. Besides, won't Master Quentin be shocked when you move flawlessly into position right beside that snooty Miss Wilson?" She'd barely finished her statement before Grace was flying down the hall to the guestroom. Laurie took her purchases into the master bedroom and changed as well, returning to the living room in her new purple bra and panties, a pair of thigh high stockings, and her new purple heels.

"Now I know why you didn't bat an eye when I mentioned purple shoes won't go with many outfits. They are stunning now."

"Aren't they?" Laurie said, looking down at the purple suede. "There is a very good reason women have a lot of shoes. It is not because they are hoarders, it is because shoes are just as much an accessory as earrings. And I must say, you make quite the erotic picture yourself, Miss Hensley."

Grace smiled and didn't protest the compliment.

She felt quite sexy. She'd chosen to mix it up. Her bra was red but had a tiny black bow in the center. The black lace panties felt almost nonexistent over her ass and the red garter belt and sheer stockings completed her clothing. She had on her new, very expensive heels. She'd been very surprised when Laurie insisted she try them despite the fact that they were at least an inch higher than any she'd worn before. Once the salesman had slipped them on her feet and she had stood, fully expecting to wobble, she'd been shocked to discover that the shoes had to be magical. Her toes weren't instantly screaming, and when she'd walked a few steps to look into the floor length mirror, she had an idea of why the high heel had been invented.

"All right," Laurie said. "Show me what you learned last night."

Grace moved into the standing position and Laurie walked in a circle around her and nodded. "That's good. But you don't have to stand so stiffly. Yes, you are at attention, but you aren't in the army."

When Grace relaxed just a bit, Laurie moved in front of her and when Grace saw her hand, the fingers pointing to the floor, she carefully sank to her knees, only tilting a tiny bit, though it took her a second to remember to move her hands from her back and cross them on her lap.

"That was pretty darn good," Laurie said.

"Well, I practiced last night until my thighs were killing me."

"Just another price of submission," Laurie said,

waving it off. "Okay, now, I'm expecting them to teach you the basic variation of this kneeling position. It can be given with the word, 'Nadu', or it can also be given silently. Look at my hand."

Grace did so and noticed the signal was the same, except that the two fingers that had been pressed together were now spread apart.

"If you see the fingers spread, then you are to spread your knees apart." As Grace shifted, Laurie shook her head. "'Fraid not, hon. Wide apart." A moment later, she nodded. "Better. Now, put your hands on your thighs, palms up. Some Doms prefer palms down but as that allows a submissive to perhaps grip her thighs, we're taught to turn them up." Again, Grace obeyed. "Okay, rise and we'll run through them together. I won't use hand signals as I'll be doing them with you, but remember, rise, kneel or Nadu, okay?"

The two women spent the next half hour running through the three positions. Though her thighs were once again burning by the time Laurie called a halt, Grace felt far less clumsy. Throwing her arms around her friend, she thanked her.

"You're welcome," Laurie said. "Of course, these are the easiest positions, and the less revealing ones."

"Quentin said that we'd be doing them in the nude."

"You will, and let me tell you, the first time you do, don't be shocked to find that your inner thighs are glistening."

"Ah, another sign of success for the Dom?"

"More like a sign that you are born for this dynamic. After all, if you just wanted to serve a man drinks, you could work in some bar wearing a sexy uniform. What women like you and I want is to serve in a far more primal, intimate way. Never be ashamed of that need, Grace."

"I'll try. Now, if I don't sit down, my legs are gonna collapse. Remind me to take the stairs from now on. I've got to build up some muscle!"

Laurie laughed. "Deal. I've got to change and run off to the hospital. We'll talk after your class. Good luck and have fun."

When Laurie left a half-hour later, Grace was curled up on the couch with her sketchpad, but she noticed that Laurie still had on those purple 'fuck me' heels and had changed into a dress that would, as Master Quentin had said, "Be easy to remove."

11

QUENTIN bent closer to the computer screen. "Wait, run it back a little."

As Brody manipulated the mouse to do so, Quentin suddenly said, "Stop!" Reaching out, he tapped his fingertip against the frozen image of a man. It didn't show his face fully, as he was turned to the side. Still, there was something about him, maybe his pose or his physical shape that was pulling at Quentin's gut.

"Who is that?"

Brody lifted the laptop from the table and brought it closer to his face.

"Getting old?" Quentin quipped, in an effort to ease his sudden tension.

"I'm not one of our subs, you ass. While they may be able to bend and contort their beautiful bodies for hours at a time, you try doing it with your fucking leg hanging up in the air."

"Sorry," Quentin said.

"To answer your first question, I can't identify him from this frame but something about him seems familiar."

"That's what I was thinking. Shit, we've got to find a better shot."

"We will if there is one. We've still got the outside footage to go over. Maybe he's caught on tape entering the building." Brody returned the computer to the tray table.

Quentin stood to move the chair he'd occupied for the past few hours back where it belonged. "I'm thinking we need to call someone to see if they have better luck tracking Mike down."

"I agree," Brody said, making a note on the pad. "We still have a few faces to identify, but the film shows Farraday as being there that night. The fact that he up and quit the next day is something I feel needs explaining."

"Especially since he quit before we even knew Beth was truly missing," Quentin agreed from where he had moved to look out the window but not really seeing the scenery. Instead, his mind was running like a loop through the security tapes he and Brody had just finished poring over. "Add Marti's name as well. I know she just stepped in to help out, but I still want to see if perhaps she remembers anything out of the ordinary that might have happened that night."

"I've got them both down. I'll contact Peter Zinger tomorrow. He's not the cheapest, but he's a member of the club so knows about the importance of discretion."

Quentin nodded as he turned back. "While that's important, I still want him to turn over every rock and probe every cranny. I don't really care about the cost. I've got enough saved to cover expenses."

"You mean *we* have enough saved," Brody countered. As Quentin began to protest, Brody shook his head. "Don't piss me off, Quentin. We are partners and Beth disappeared from our club. I'm not going to let you shoulder the blame nor all the expense. Discovering who killed her will be worth whatever the price."

"Thanks, man." Quentin wasn't surprised to hear the comments, and yet they still had him remembering just how close the two of them were.

The door swung open and the men turned, both giving long wolf-whistles as an ethereal creature swept into the room, the familiar scent of White Diamonds perfume wafting along the air with her entrance.

"Well, thank you, gentlemen," Laurie said, as she moved slowly toward the bed, using every step to the best advantage. Her skirt swished around her legs at mid-thigh, her freshly washed and curled blonde hair swung enticingly around her shoulders. When she stepped in front of Quentin to bend over to kiss Brody, Quentin grinned.

"Bend over any further and I'll be able to swat that pretty ass of yours without having to lift your skirt." She didn't answer, as her lips were pressed to her fiancé's, but he had to chuckle when she wiggled her hips as if to provoke him into action. He shook his head, wondering why instead of taking her up on her silent dare, he was picturing another lovely bottom. Looking at his watch, he said, "While I'd love to stay and visit longer, I've got to run."

Laurie pulled away from Brody and straightened. "Before you do, would you help me?"

"Ah, so you do feel the need to get your tushie tanned?"

"Not at all," Laurie countered. "I have Brody's dinner in the car. Hannah insisted she send along a big pot for the nurses, and it's too hot and too heavy for me to carry."

"I was rather enjoying my appetizer," Brody said, his hand reaching to caress Laurie's arm.

"Oh, babe, I promise there are many more courses for you to enjoy this evening. Now, be a good boy and I'll be right back. Jennifer is going to come take your vitals a tad early so that we won't be disturbed for a while."

"In that case, Quentin, get the woman's pot. I want to keep the nurses both happy and occupied."

Quentin chuckled and bowed. "After you, my lady," he said, sweeping his hand toward the door. Laurie took a moment to drop one more kiss on Brody's lips and then the two left.

"In case I haven't told you recently, you're good for him," Quentin said as they crossed the parking lot. "That man thinks you walk on water."

Laurie pressed the button to unlock her car and smiled. "That man is my life. I can't tell you how terrified I was when Connie called and told me they were bringing him in. He looked so pale and was in such pain..." She paused and shook her head. "I'll be eternally grateful that he is going to be all right."

Quentin gave her a hug before reaching into the trunk to lift out the heavy stew pot. "Just keep doing what you're doing and he'll be back up in no time."

"That's what I'm counting on," Laurie said, taking the smaller covered plate and shutting the trunk. As they begin to walk back to the hospital, she grinned. "Back *up* being the operative word tonight."

"Hence those killer heels and short skirt?"

"You are so astute, kind sir. Hannah practically guaranteed that after eating a plate of shrimp etouffee, he'll be ready for a bit of, shall we say, intimate physical therapy?"

Quentin chuckled again, happy for his friends and yet, for the first time in a long time, acutely feeling the loss of such a deep connection with a woman. Again a picture of a petite beauty with the most expressive green eyes crossed his mind and stirred his cock. Well, he might not have the connection, but at least he'd be seeing Grace in a short while.

He delivered the pot to the nurses' station, receiving smiles all around as one lifted the lid and moaned. "Keep feeding us like this and we might just have to break that man's other leg."

"How about you wait for at least a couple of hours?" Laurie asked. "I've got some other plans right now."

Jennifer joined them after taking Brody's vital

signs. "Consider that room as secure, hon. I'm afraid all of us will be far too busy to respond to any calls for a while."

The other women and one male nurse all laughed as Laurie said, "A good *long* while."

Quentin left the hospital to head for his bike. It had been both a frustrating day in that they still hadn't finished making a complete list, but it had also been one of action. He felt they were getting closer. For now, he put the investigation aside. He needed to eat, shower and change before meeting his students. With a grin, he rode toward the club, wondering how many of the lovely ladies would be leaving class early after discovering what was on tonight's agenda. He truly hoped that Miss Hensley would not be one of them.

GRACE CONSIDERED BREAKING her recent vow to take the stairs as she exited the apartment. It wasn't that she didn't think she needed both the tiny bit of exercise it would provide, or because she knew she needed the practice in her new heels. The fact was that she was more than a little pissed off, basically at herself. She'd been finishing getting dressed for class when her cell phone rang. Instead of ignoring it and not even bothering to look at the ID, she had reached to press the receive button on her phone lying on the coffee table.

"Hello."

"Good evening, Grace," a man's voice she didn't instantly recognize said in greeting.

"Who is this?" she asked, reaching for her shoe.

"I'm a bit disappointed you don't recognize my voice."

With the shoe in one hand, she'd picked up the phone, which did no good as the display read *unknown number*. "I'm sorry, but—"

"You can make it up to me. Are you free for dinner tonight? We never did get the chance to discuss your future."

"My future? Look, I don't want to be rude but—"

"This is David Brooks," the man said, a bit of exasperation in his tone. "Since we were rudely interrupted at the show, I thought I'd give you another chance to speak about your genre of choice in your artistic work. What time can you be ready?"

Grace rolled her eyes. The man was not only presumptuous, she'd thought he'd understood she had absolutely no intention of meeting with him. "Mr. Brooks, I'm sorry if I gave you the impression that I'm open to anything you have to offer. I sell my art, not myself."

"Are you sure?"

"What is that supposed to mean?"

"You may be a newcomer to New Orleans, Grace, but I find it hard to believe that after your little tête-à-tête, you have no idea what sort of lifestyle Doucet practices. I finally remembered where I'd seen that blonde before, though seeing her with Doucet threw me for a moment. She's his partner's eye candy... or perhaps the stories I've heard are true and they share her. All I know is that you really need to rethink being seen with either of them."

Grace wanted to slap the man but instead used as cold a tone as she could muster. "Mr. Brooks, I don't appreciate you maligning my friends. I don't have to know what you have against Quentin because I really don't care. He's been nothing but a gentleman—"

"Gentlemen aren't arrested for murder."

That was it. No more Miss Nice Guy. "Look, even you should know that slandering a person can lead to a lawsuit. I suggest you remember that he was never arrested. He was questioned and released. I don't care for your—"

"You might care after tomorrow, Miss Hensley," he said, this time with no attempt to disguise the rancor in his voice. "I'll give you one more chance. Meet with me tonight and we can clarify your mistaken illusions."

"Mr. Brooks, I'm trying to be polite but you just aren't listening."

"I'm afraid, Miss Hensley, it is you who isn't listening. Ask yourself this. Can you afford not to meet with me? While I need only to write about your naughty paintings, I am not averse to providing my readers a far more in-depth report. Imagine what they'll think when they discover that while you might not be willing to *sell* yourself, you are obviously quite willing to *give* your body away to any man who kotows to that scum Doucet."

Grace felt her heart skip a beat. She actually

looked up and around the apartment, as if expecting to see Brooks' face looking through the window. How did he even know where she was staying or... no, there was no possible way he knew she was taking lessons in submission. Remembering that Laurie had stated he'd been involved in the reporting of Beth's murder, she thought he was simply using prior knowledge in his bluff. From what she understood, the club had taken a hit, and yet Brody and Quentin had managed to not only keep it open, but to increase its membership, obviously not with any help from reporters like Brooks.

"I seriously urge you to remember there are consequences for libel, Mr. Brooks."

"Look, I'm not interested in destroying your career. As I said the other night, I find your work quite... stimulating. Come out with me."

"No, not tonight nor any other night. Please don't call me again, Mr. Brooks."

"You'll be very sorry—"

"Too late. I was sorry the moment I answered the phone." Without further thought, she pressed the end call button. She told herself that if she was trembling, it was because she was furious, not because his words had unsettled her. How dare he disparage an innocent man and basically threaten her? Looking at the heel she was still holding, she shook her head. There was absolutely nothing wrong with what she was doing. She was an adult and perfectly capable of making her own decisions, her own choices. Putting her shoes on, she stood and purposely left her cell phone where it lay.

Still, standing at the top of the stairs, she took several deep breaths. It would be a shame to tumble ass over teakettle. Purposely pushing the call from her mind, she thought of how excited she'd been when dressing. She'd chosen the tiered skirt and paired it with a silk t-shirt. It had taken her at least a half hour to decide whether to wear the garter belt or just the thigh hugging stockings. Standing before the full-length mirror, she'd changed in and out of both until she decided to go all in. Though she'd had plenty of opportunities to dress up during her life, she had never felt so... well, sexy. She wore minimal makeup, concentrating on only accentuating her eyes and applying a pale lip-gloss, not bothering with any blusher. If tonight's lessons were anything like the previous evening, her cheeks would be pink enough. Thinking of what she might learn that evening had her smiling. With her hand on the railing, she began to carefully descend.

Reaching the bottom of the stairs without breaking her neck, she smiled and moved down the hall off the back of the kitchen toward the dining room.

"Hey, Grace, wait for me!"

Turning, she saw Gretchen walking toward her, realizing the woman had come through the restaurant. Suddenly an unpleasant thought grabbed her attention even when Gretchen caught up to give

Grace a hug. "God, if I had been this excited about class in college, I might have graduated with honors."

Grace realized she was attempting to look past Gretchen into the restaurant. Could David be there, waiting for her?

"Hey, are you all right?"

Seeing that Gretchen's smile had slipped, Grace again reminded herself that she had every right to take classes in anything she wished. "Yes, I'm great. Just wondering what's in store for us tonight."

"I just hope that I remember to keep my mouth shut," Gretchen said with a sigh.

"Why would you say that?"

"Because, as Master Conner told me, 'if you'll shut your mouth and open your ears, maybe you'll learn something instead of disturbing the entire class.' I was just asking if I was positioned correctly, but I guess he didn't approve."

Grace was instantly annoyed. "That's not only rude, it goes against what Master Quentin said. He encouraged questions."

"Well, I didn't get him, I got Conner." Shrugging, she looped her arm through Grace's. "Still, I am excited about tonight so I'll just try to be quieter." Forgetting her wish that she'd chosen a different seat, Grace didn't hesitate to take a seat beside Gretchen.

"Hey, great shoes!"

"Thanks. I love yours as well."

Gretchen stretched her leg out and then apologized when another woman had to stop abruptly to keep from tripping over it.

"Oops," Gretchen said when the woman's face showed her irritation though she didn't speak. Once she'd moved to a different area, Gretchen sighed. "Well, so much for trying not to disrupt the class. I bet Julie thinks I was trying to trip her."

"I'm sure she didn't," Grace reassured her, though seeing the woman speaking with Starla Wilson, she wasn't so sure. In fact, as she watched the two women sweep their gazes over their classmates, she had the distinct feeling both considered themselves to be far above any other soul in the room. Okay, it might have been cheating, but suddenly she was very glad that Laurie had worked with her that afternoon. "Did you practice last night?" she asked Gretchen.

"Until I had to force myself to get up off the floor when I collapsed. Believe me, I seriously considered just sleeping right in the middle of the living room."

"Me too," a woman who had just joined their table offered.

"Grace, this is Penny. Penny, Grace."

Grace shook hands with the woman and instantly liked her. She had a mop of short curly hair and freckles sprinkled across the bridge of her nose. More importantly, she had a ready smile, and when she asked sotto voce if their asses still ached, Grace and Gretchen both nodded and giggled.

"From what I've read, that wasn't even a real spanking," Gretchen said.

"Well, if it wasn't, I'm not too sure I can survive a real one," Penny said and then sighed. "I was so sure that Master Conner had left bruises all over my butt, but not a single mark was visible." She paused and lowered her voice even further. "If anyone had bruises, it would be you. He seemed to be harder on you."

Before Gretchen could speak, the door opened to admit all four of the instructors. Grace almost kicked herself when it took Starla and Julie rising and striking the proper pose to remind her of what was expected. She had wanted to tell Gretchen that she didn't have to stay with Conner. Master or not, the submissives had choices. She stood with her tablemates and came to attention.

"Good evening, ladies," Quentin said as he strode to the front of the room. "Well done." Grace felt a thrill as his eyes swept the room and seemed to pause when they reached her. Had his eyebrow lifted to see that she was not only standing properly, but had on high heels and a proper skirt? When he turned to confer with the other Masters, she decided it had been a figment of her imagination. After all, she was only one of nine—wait, nine? Their table was toward the rear so even without turning her head, she could count the other submissives. Yes, there were only nine. What were the consequences for arriving late?

"I'm glad to see that most of you decided to continue your journey," Quentin said. "Miss Landers has decided not to join you. Before we begin, does anyone have any questions about what we covered last night?"

Grace saw Penny drop her hand from behind her back and then return to its proper position, as if unsure if she should risk raising her hand. Evidently Quentin saw the move as well. "Please, Miss Stoneman, you may speak freely."

"Sir, I was just wondering if, well, if this room is secure. I mean, not secure, as I can see the door is closed but um, I walked through the restaurant and suddenly wondered if anyone could have heard... um, anything last night."

Grace was impressed not only by the fact that Quentin had known her name without looking at the folders he once again held, but that Penny had given thought to something she'd not even considered. She felt her cheeks heat at the thought of an unknown stranger or, God forbid, some asinine reporter, sitting out front suddenly pausing in dining, tilting his head, and wondering where on earth that whimpering and yelping was coming from.

"I assure you that this room is entirely soundproof. When we go upstairs to the club, you will be able to stand outside and hear nothing but silence as well. We want you to be free to voice all your emotions, both those of discomfort and those of pleasure." After a moment, he continued. "All right, if no one has any other questions?" Evidently no one did as he gave an instruction, "Please come line up."

Once they had, he looked down the line and when Grace saw his hand signal, she instantly sank to her knees, proud to see his approving look. Though not positive she'd beaten the two experienced subs, she was happy she'd done so without faltering. Her wrists were crossed properly, and her toes were pointed against the floor.

"Very nice. I can tell that you all practiced last evening. That tells me you are dedicated to not only your lessons learned, but are anxious to learn more. Is that correct?"

"Yes, sir," the line chorused.

"Very good. Eyes to me." Once every pair of eyes lifted, he went on. "Before we go upstairs, I want to go over a few things. Yes, you are submissives, but don't ever believe you don't have a choice. As Miss Alton questioned yesterday, there are safety measures put into place. If you ever go to a club where there are none, please do not stay. The D/s lifestyle is built upon trust and if you feel unsafe, follow your instincts and leave." He paused and Grace hoped that every woman was taking each word he uttered as seriously as she was.

"That said, when you are in a committed relationship with a Dominant, you will need a safeword. And, ladies, you won't be choosing *no*, *don't* or *stop*." He gave a small grin and then said, "Miss Wilson, could you share why none of those is a good choice?"

Starla instantly answered, "Because, sir, when something feels really wonderful or even bordering between pain and pleasure, you might say, 'No... don't... stop,' when what you really want is for the action to continue, especially if your Dominant is skilled enough to have you but a breath away from climaxing."

Her answer was evidently the one he was searching for because he nodded. "Exactly. For the purposes of this class, and standard among most clubs, *Plaisir* uses what is often termed the stoplight system. Green means all is fine, yellow means you need a break or for the action to slow down, and red, ladies, means that everything stops immediately. You and you alone can really know what you are capable of, or desire to experience. That's not to say that as you continue along this path and gain experience you won't be tested, especially if you are in a one-on-one relationship with your Dom. It is his duty to pay attention to your words as well as your body, but he will at some point began to push you to explore your limits. Even then, once you utter your safeword, the action should instantly halt. Any questions?"

Again there were none, every eye on him. "Tonight, as I said, we will be going upstairs. Doing so will give you some real experience as what to expect. You will be expected to be respectful at all times. Before we go, you will be learning a new position. Please rise."

As she rose along with the others, Grace wondered if their pulse rate had also increased with the combination of nerves and excitement his words had evoked.

"You learned to stand at attention and how to kneel at attention. Tonight, you will learn how to kneel in a way that depicts you are available to serve intimately." Grace listened as he explained what was expected, and once he demonstrated the hand signal, she tried not to grin. Laurie had been right. He was showing them the silent signal for the Nadu position. When he changed his hand signal to the original kneeling one, the class sank as one, hands crossed at the wrists, legs together. Since he'd instructed them to keep their eyes on him, when his fingers spread apart, the women moved as well. From the moment Grace spread her legs, wider than she'd done in practice, she felt her face heating with the natural blush she'd known to expect. Thinking about the fact that if she were nude in this position, there would be no concealing either her sex or her arousal, she could feel her nipples tightening.

"Eyes lowered." Even as she obeyed, Grace saw the instructors moving to circle the women, and heard soft corrections being given.

Quentin squatted slightly behind her, his hand on her lower back. "Shoulders back and a bit straighter if you are able."

Instead, she almost moved to slouch a bit more, having looked down to see that her thin t-shirt did nothing to hide the fact that her nipples were indeed poking against the fabric. So much for deciding that padded bras would be cheating. An inch or so of foam would certainly have helped keep her instant arousal hidden. With his instruction, she remembered what Laurie had said. Never be ashamed of who she was or what she needed. Straightening, she was rewarded with a softly uttered, "Very, very nice, Miss Hensley." Just those few words had her wondering if the other women's panties were anywhere as damp as hers.

The instructors returned to the front. Quentin ran them through all three positions a few more times before he seemed satisfied that his pupils understood them and could perform them with relative confidence.

"Eyes to me. Ladies, we are going to take a small break. This is the time to make use of the facilities if you need, as well as to consider whether you are prepared to do as instructed once we go upstairs. You'll be instructed to assume the positions you've learned. However, once we enter the club, you will remove your outer clothing."

"You mean we're going to be naked!"

"Miss Kennedy, what did I tell you yesterday about speaking without permission?" Conner snapped, his irritation evident in his tone.

Grace felt sorry for her new friend when she saw her cringe at the chastisement.

"I'm sorry, Master Conner, I-I didn't..."

"No, not tonight," Quentin said when Gretchen stammered, and Grace saw that there was no trace of a smile on his lips and the vein at his neck seemed more prominent. She was worried that he was also upset with Gretchen, until she saw his eyes cut to Conner before looking again at his class.

"You will remove only your outer clothing. If you are naked, it will be because you didn't pay attention to the instructions about underwear being required." He allowed a smile as a couple of women nervously tittered. "One step at a time, ladies. Now, since we are now at nine, I'm going to ask one of you to move to Master Trent's group. I'll have the new assignment when you return from your break. Take this time to decide if you are ready to take that next step. If not, let one of us know you won't be continuing. Otherwise, be back here in fifteen minutes."

"Yes, sir," the women said and at his addition of "dismissed," they rose and Gretchen immediately scurried from the room.

12

QUENTIN SAW Trent's nod and turned to see that instead of heading for the restroom, Grace was approaching them. "Um, Master Quentin?"

He hoped his disappointment didn't show as he asked, "Are you leaving us, Miss Hensley?"

"Oh, no, sir. I just wondered... might I speak to you, um, in private?"

Pleased to learn she was staying, he nodded and, taking her arm, led her to the other side of the room so they could speak without being overheard.

"I know it's not my place, sir, but I feel compelled to ask you something."

"Please tell me you aren't going to volunteer to leave my group?" Though he knew he shouldn't care, he did.

"No, but I would like to ask a favor, sir." He gave her a nod and didn't miss that she glanced back toward the other men.

"Gretchen... I mean, Miss Kennedy, please don't tell her I told you—"

"Relax, Grace. I'm not going to bite. Just tell me what's on your mind."

He saw her relax and give a small nod. "All right. It's just that she, Miss Kennedy, told me before class that last night, Master Conner, seemed to... well, belittle her in front of the other women in their group. If there is any way you could allow her to be the one to move? I'm sure she would appreciate it." She paused, and then added almost as an afterthought, "Another woman validated her statement, saying she thought Master Conner was much harder on Gretchen than the others."

"I see," Quentin said, wondering what Conner had said, as he certainly hadn't volunteered that information the evening before. "And Master Trent?"

"Oh, he's nice," Grace said with a smile. "I mean, even when he corrects you, he doesn't do it in a way that makes you feel stupid or... well, embarrass you in front of the rest of the class."

Quentin didn't give her an answer, simply said, "Thank you, I'll give your request serious consideration."

"Thank you, Quent—sir."

"You're welcome. Go take a break. We'll start again in ten minutes."

"Yes, sir."

He watched as she walked away without a single wobble. He'd have a few questions of his own when class was dismissed. Walking back to his staff, he was pleasantly surprised when Trent spoke.

"I know you're the boss, but if you don't mind, I'd like to ask that you allow Miss Kennedy to join my group."

Knowing there was no way the man had heard Grace making the same request, his respect for Trent increased. Obviously the man also remembered the derogatory tone in which Conner had spoken of Gretchen the previous evening.

"Hey, I didn't get to pick—" Conner began but Quentin cut him off.

"Consider it done. Conner, give the file to Trent so he can go over it before we resume. And remember, every one of these ladies is putting their trust in our hands. Do not in any way cause them to wish they'd chosen not to." With the decision made and the none too subtle warning given for Conner's benefit, he left the room to take his own bathroom break.

On his way to the restroom, he saw Gretchen, and noticed that the pep in her step was definitely missing. "Miss Kennedy, a moment please?"

"Yes, sir?"

"I just wanted to inform you that Master Trent has requested you join his group."

"Really?"

"Yes, do you have any objections to moving?"

"Oh no, sir. I-I'd like that."

"Very good. Now, let's see that enthusiasm back, all right?'

He walked into the men's restroom as Gretchen ran back into the ladies' room.

"GUESS WHAT? Master Trent asked for me!"

"Sure he did," Starla said, dropping the towel she'd been using to dry her hands into the bin.

"He did, Master Quentin just told me he had," Gretchen said. "Why would he lie?"

"Oh, I'm sure he's not lying. But if he is really allowing you to move, I guarantee that some little redhead had something to do with it."

"What are you implying?" Grace said, stepping out of the stall. "Every one of us, including Master Quentin, heard Conner speaking harshly to Gretchen. I'm sure he understands that it is difficult for a submissive to progress if she is uncomfortable with the Dominant supposedly giving the lesson."

"Neither one of you will ever be a true submissive," Starla said, fluffing her hair with her fingers. "Submissives do not wheedle and whine. They do what they are told. I suggest you both get with the program or do us all a favor and get out." Once she'd pushed through the door, Gretchen turned to Grace.

"What a bitch. Just because she has some experience, that doesn't mean we aren't able to learn."

"Especially when you'll now be able to learn from Master Trent," Grace reminded her. They left the bathroom just as the men's room door opened behind them.

"That's right, isn't it great? You just have to adore Master Quentin, don't you?"

"Yes, I suppose you do," Grace said.

FIFTEEN MINUTES LATER, Quentin wondered if adoration was what was in the forefront of the women's minds as they were led into the club. Though it was a Tuesday, the club was not deserted. A few couples were either engaged in activities at various stations or were sitting with others, chatting.

Turning to his men, Quentin nodded and the men quietly instructed their individual groups to move down the wall, leaving a small amount of space between each group. Turning to his own pupils, he said. "All right, ladies. You'll find that there are lockers in the ladies' room where you'll be able to remove your clothing when you come as guests, but since we have a larger group tonight, please undress and leave your clothing against the wall." Though they'd been warned, he noticed that besides Miss Wilson, who already had her skirt unzipped, both Grace and Joanne gave each other a glance before reaching for their own clothing. He didn't step away, didn't turn his back. In fact, he made sure he kept his eyes on the women. They needed to understand that the request was a common one. If they chose to continue in this dynamic, they'd more often than not be wearing nothing but lingerie, if that, as they played in the club.

Despite his control, when Grace turned and bent to place her t-shirt and skirt onto the floor, his eyes widened at the sight of the plump globes of her heart-shaped ass bisected by nothing more than a thin strip of white lace. If that wasn't heart stopping enough, sheer stockings hugged her legs, the tops held in place by the hooks of a white garter belt that rode low on her hips. When she turned to face him again, immediately going into the attention pose, he had to stop himself from repeating the wolf whistle he'd given Laurie earlier. The cups of the bra she wore barely covered her nipples which were puckered tightly, straining against the thin fabric, just as his cock, which had jumped to attention the moment she'd bent over, was now pressing against the leather of its confinement. He tore his eyes away and saw that though the other women were indeed beautiful, Joanne in red and Starla in black, the purity of the white that Grace wore outshone them all. *Yes, you ass, I'm sure that's the only reason she stands out. Get a grip, Doucet.*

The instructors had met before class and knew the rotation they were to take. Every group would be given a tour of every station. They'd also be required to kneel and, at a given instruction, rise and go to the bar, where Adam would take their order on behalf of their Master for the evening. They would also be given the opportunity for a hands on demonstration of the various stations. By the time they were dismissed, it was his hope they'd be more comfortable in an actual club environment, as well as further educated on what to expect in future classes.

"You will follow me and observe. Please save any questions until later. It's not that I don't wish to answer them, it is to show respect for anyone currently in a scene. At some point, I will ask you to choose one of the various apparatus. At that time, if you do not wish to submit, you may say so." When he saw what looked like concern on Joanne's face, he added. "Do not be afraid to say no. Though you are training to be submissives, we realize you might be in an environment that is foreign to you. If you aren't ready to experience what you've observed, I ask that you consider the reasons when you return home and decide if you'll be able to do so when asked again. Remember, ladies, submission is not an easy choice. But, I promise, if you do participate, I will not harm you in any way." He gave them a moment and qualified his statement. "I will spank you, but never ever will harm you. Understood?"

"Yes, sir," they all said in unison.

"Very good. Follow me."

He led them to the right, knowing that Trent would start on the left and Sloan would begin with the innocuous areas of the dance floor, the location of the restrooms, and introduce them to Adam, and that Conner would begin with his group touring the private rooms in the back, as well as the few rooms that had been outfitted for specific fetish play.

When his group reached the first apparatus, he

stopped several feet away, as it was occupied. A Dom was applying a wooden paddle to his sub's bottom while she lay prone over the spanking bench. He'd seen the couple earlier that weekend and had asked if they'd be willing to attend this night to demonstrate one of the apparatus. In fact, most of the Dominants in the room had been asked. Quentin had been very pleased when not a single one had even hesitated, all stating that their own subs, now many of them their wives, had all needed to learn, and that doing so by observing had always made the second most profound impression. Actually having the apparatus or equipment demonstrated on their bodies had, by far, been the experience that would last a lifetime.

By the condition of the woman's rear, she hadn't been there long. Her skin was still pale, and though restrained, she wasn't pulling in the least on the chain that had been attached to the cuffs on her wrists. Her feet weren't kicking even the few inches the chains would have allowed, either. Quentin turned to watch the reaction of his students, pleased to see that all three were watching with nothing short of fascination as the man began to increase not only the rapidness of his strokes, but the intensity. When his sub began to squirm, he softly instructed her to settle. The cracks of the wooden paddle filled the area around them but were soon joined by the submissive's soft moans. Quentin had to bite back a grin when he had to repeat his soft instruction to follow him in order to pull his students' attention away from the erotic tableau.

They visited the next station, where another submissive was being spanked, this time with a crop as she bent over a barrel that was rigged to roll her forward a bit with each stroke and then back again in time for the next. He saw Grace's head tilt to the side, as if she was trying to determine what kept the woman from rolling forward until she face planted on the other side. He moved to her side and pointed at the floor to show her how the barrel had been mounted in a depression only slightly larger than its diameter. It would never go further than was safe while always causing a sub's tummy to flutter, wondering if she'd be tossed off. Though Grace's gaze followed his finger, she immediately lifted her eyes back to the action.

The next station, where an apparatus that resembled a gymnast's vault stood waiting, was currently unoccupied. Quentin hadn't failed to notice that all three of his ladies had nipples straining against their bras.

Since the station was free, he spoke softly. "This is commonly referred to as the horse. You'll notice that there are restraints available for use around each leg. In addition, if a Dominant so chooses, there is a leather strap that can be buckled around a sub's waist. Go ahead and look more closely." Both Joanne and Grace instantly stepped forward, running their hands over the butter soft leather. While Joanne bent to examine the chains, Starla looked as if she'd not only seen one, but most likely had been bent over something similar. He wasn't surprised when Grace gave him a quizzical look after running her hand over what appeared to be a patch.

"I appreciate your respectful silence but now I'll answer any questions you might have so far," Quentin said, drawing their attention back to him.

"Only one of the women we observed was naked," Joanne said. "The other was wearing clothing."

"Yes, clothing or lack thereof is at the Dom's discretion. As I mentioned yesterday, lingerie is also an aphrodisiac. Did you notice that though the first woman wore a skirt, she wasn't wearing panties?"

"Um, yes, sir."

"Did you also notice that her Dom's pocket had a bit of pink lace hanging out?"

"Really? No, sir, I didn't."

Quentin smiled. "Leading a woman to a station and only then removing her underwear often helps her sink into her submissive role."

"I can see how that would work, sir," Joanne said, a soft smile on her face.

"Miss Hensley, did you understand that I was attempting to reassure you that the barrel won't pitch a sub off?"

"Yes, sir, but..."

When she hesitated, he moved to reassure her. "But what? Please, now is the time to ask questions."

"Well, I really didn't have a question. I suppose I just assumed that, as you assured us, the club and its equipment are safe. I was actually watching her face."

Quentin was surprised but intrigued. "I see, and what did you notice?"

"Though the crop was leaving a red stripe every time it landed and the barrel rolled forward, even though she gasped and I could see her bottom quiver, when the barrel rolled back, she was lifting her bottom... as if she wanted another stroke."

He was impressed and then realized he shouldn't have been. After all, Grace was an artist and was looking at things with an educated eye. "What does that tell you?"

"That she was enjoying the session even though it was obviously painful, sir."

"Very good. Submissives often say that when the pain reaches a certain point, it morphs into pleasure. For the Dom, delivering the spanking is only the first part of his own pleasure. There is nothing more satisfying to most Doms than to watch their submissive find her pleasure under his hand, whether it be wielding an implement or just by his touch." When she nodded her understanding, he turned to Starla. "Do you have any questions, Miss Wilson?"

"No, sir."

"May I ask another, sir?" Grace asked.

"Yes."

"What is the patch covering?" she asked, pointing to the horse.

"Come, I'll show you." The three followed and watched as he removed the patch to reveal a metal threading. He walked a few steps away and opened a cabinet to reveal a shelf where various sized dildos were available to be chosen. Picking one that wasn't the smallest, nor the largest, which was quite long and very thick, he returned to the horse. Within a minute, he had it securely twisted onto the threading.

"Ah, now that has definite possibilities," Starla said, showing the first true interest in the tour.

"A submissive can be instructed to simply bend over the horse to be spanked, or, as you can now see, she can be told to mount the dildo. Her Dom might request she simply ride until she comes, or he might have her bend forward a bit and ride as he uses an implement on her bottom. And, if he so chooses, she can be instructed to lean back, riding while he flogs her stomach and breasts."

After a few moments of silence, Grace spoke again. "How does she know the dildo is, well... clean?"

"Good question," Quentin said. He stepped away again to pick up one of the condoms in a bowl. "Not only are any attachments thoroughly cleaned after use, every station is equipped with a bowl of condoms as well as sanitizer. In fact, unless you are in a committed relationship, every Dom is expected to use a condom for any sexual activity where penetration is part of the play, excepting fellatio, of course." He tossed the condom back into the bowl, looked around and then said. "Do you see that woman in the black halter dress at the bar?"

They all nodded. "She is one of our staff. Her position is that of what we term a 'floating submissive'. That means she's chosen not to commit herself to any one Dom, but rather serve many. She is also responsible for making sure that every piece of equipment is sanitized after use. On the weekend, we have three women serving as floaters. In fact, we are actively looking for at least two more." Unscrewing and returning the dildo to the cabinet, replacing the patch and making sure they didn't have any additional questions, he moved them to the next station.

Again, Grace stood in respectful silence, watching as a statuesque woman strained against the chains holding her arms above her head, her toes barely able to touch the floor beneath her. Quentin heard Grace's soft gasp as she recognized the couple. The chains would give an occasional rattle as a particularly hard stroke was delivered and received. Her body was glistening with a layer of perspiration. Her head was arched back as Keith walked around her, giving an occasional flick of his wrist, sending the tail of the whip to snap across a breast, her stomach, a buttock that already bore the marks of previous strokes, or the back of a tender thigh.

Though he'd told the women to remain silent, he stepped closer and whispered, "Watch very closely." None answered but they didn't need to as their eyes were glued to the scene. Quentin noticed that they didn't even move when Trent and his two students joined them, the women moving to stand beside his three.

They'd arrived at the perfect time. Keith twirled the whip above his head and, as he delivered the next stroke, he spoke softly but clearly. "That's right, my love. Come for me." Another stroke and then another, the whip becoming a blur as the speed of the strokes increased until Jessica arched and screamed, her entire body clenching and unclenching as she came, softer blows continuing to land until the orgasm seemed to have subsided. Only then did Keith coil the whip and attach it to a loop of his belt before moving to stand behind her, his fingers running gently over the wheals he'd placed upon his wife's body.

"Beautiful, you are such a good girl," he said, bending to press his lips against a few of the raised lines. Quentin smiled, not at watching a Dom take care of his sub, but watching prospective subs mesmerized by the scene before them. When Jessica stopped trembling, Keith undid her restraints and the students watched as she turned, her face showing her pleasure as he lifted her into his arms.

"Her jewelry is incredible," Starla said softly, evidently forgetting the request to remain silent. Quentin saw Grace smile but since she remained quiet instead of informing the woman she had made the set, he did the same. Still, he had to agree. The flowers that served as clamps were missing tonight; Jessica's nipples protruded from the gold leaves of the vine. He also noticed that the cluster of leaves at her sex had disappeared, her swollen labia evident as Keith lifted her into his arms and carried her toward a partially screened sofa where Quentin knew he would make sure she was all right. He saw Molly stop and hand him two bottles of water before she moved toward the group, standing a bit apart to allow Quentin to finish describing the station.

Giving them a moment to glance around, he smiled, moving to the wall to press a button and watching as their heads tilted back to see the chains descending from the pulley mounted on the ceiling. "This is a hoist," he explained. "As you saw, a submissive's cuffs are attached together to one chain, or to separate ones. Her ankles can also be restrained to those bolts on the floor. Her Dom uses the control to stretch her arms above her head and pull her legs apart. Some Doms prefer to leave her legs unrestrained in order to lift her completely off the ground."

"Isn't it a little dangerous? I mean, that woman was basically hanging by her arms. Couldn't that cause a serious strain?" The question came from one of Trent's students.

"It could be, which is another reason to make sure that any club you play in has safety measures in place, and that any Dom you submit to knows what he is doing. As I've said before, a Dom's responsibility is to make sure that every activity is safe, sane and consensual. When Master Trent, Sloan and Conner are not instructing, they are monitoring the room, as well." He paused and nodded toward the bar and then to another area where a man stood, looking relaxed and yet Quentin knew he was on alert. "See those men? The ones with red bands around their arms? They are also monitors. The floor is never without two at any time, and as many as six on weekends. They are yet another layer of security in keeping a submissive safe from harm." He gave them a moment to digest his words.

"I assure you that if Master Keith thought his sub was having difficulties, he'd have lowered her a bit." He grinned and then added, "Or, perhaps instead of whipping her into climax, he'd have simply lifted her legs around his waist and joined her in ecstasy."

"Oh, my," Grace said.

"Ready to continue?" Quentin asked, loving that her face had turned a beautiful hue of pink as she looked at the dangling chains again, no doubt imagining the scene he'd offered coming to life. Nodding at Molly, he led them toward the next station as Trent led his group to the horse.

Quentin wondered if the three women would even be able to tell him what the next station contained. It was another spanking bench but this one was adjustable, able to be positioned at various angles. Currently, it had been angled so that the sub was bent almost in half, her cheek resting on the leather in front, her knees behind her, and her ass perched directly on top. Her Dom was using nothing more than his hand, and yet her skin was a mottled crimson and her moans were those of pleasure rather than of pain.

The next station was a set of stocks where a woman had been placed, her head and hands held in the half-moon depressions of the lower bar. The upper bar had been locked into place, ensuring she had very limited movement. Her ankle cuffs were attached to D-rings on the floor that held her legs wide apart while her Dom used a leather paddle. Quentin wondered if his students noticed that each implement they'd seen used made a different sound as it connected to bare flesh. He didn't have to wonder if they were aroused. Their eyes were slightly glazed and the pattern of their breathing had changed.

The last station was again unoccupied. It was one that was often described in spicier romance books. Just the mere presence of the massive wooden 'X' was normally enough to have a submissive flushing at least, and her pussy gushing as her Dom positioned her spread-eagled, her wrists and ankles securely held with straps of leather.

"This is the St. Andrew's Cross. A sub can be positioned either facing away from her Dom or facing toward the front. It seems to be an ongoing debate which is worse—not knowing when the next stroke is coming, or being unable to keep from watching your Dom's every movement. If you ever find yourself secured to the apparatus, you'll be able to cast your own vote."

"And what would your preference be, Master Quentin?" Starla asked. "Do you prefer watching your sub watching you, perhaps pleading with her eyes to be released, or turned away, accepting all that you care to gift her with?" She smiled as she ran a hand across the smooth wood.

Quentin saw Grace turn her gaze to him and knew that not long ago, he'd have assured Starla that he had no preference. Now, imagining Grace's green eyes focused on his as he wielded a whip, waiting, wondering where the stroke would land, he knew he couldn't answer the question with complete honesty. Instead, he said, "Every sub is different, every scene, as well."

"Yes, I suppose, but I'd not want to trust any Dom without the level of experience you must have."

"Submissive classes are not the only ones taught, Miss Wilson. *Plaisir* also offers classes and hands-on training for Dominants. Believe it or not, we aren't born knowing everything. We learned just as you are doing now."

Before Starla could ask another question, Joanne broke in. "How do you know? I mean, how can you be sure that you are a submissive?"

Quentin gave her a smile. "You've seen the stations and witnessed submissives in play, right?" At her nod, he continued. "Answer me this, then, are your panties wet?"

She blushed but nodded and, as if in support, Grace nodded as well.

"Then, ladies, just listen to your body. If it makes you wet, if your nipples are aching and if you are wondering how quickly class will be dismissed so that you might go home and relieve that ache, I'd say that you are well on your way to being a submissive." He gave them a moment before he asked, "Ready to continue?"

He showed them the rooms that had been set up to live out specific fantasies. One looked like an old fashioned classroom, right down to the slate board, and a large oak desk at the front with a rack of canes mounted on the wall behind it. In a corner sat a tall stool, and he heard Grace giggle at the sight of a pointed dunce hat. "Seriously?" she whispered.

"Don't mock it," he said, pleased at her enjoyment. "Nothing quite says I've been a very naughty girl than having to sit on a hard wooden stool on a well caned ass while wearing that hat."

The other room had all three women practically squirming as they observed the full medical exam table, complete with stirrups. The tall pole from which hung an enema bag had each one turning a beautiful shade of red, and he noticed that Starla seemed very interested in a rolling table with a tray on top holding a pair of latex gloves, some cotton swabs, and row after row of capped needles.

"I've heard of this," she said. "I've even seen photos on the Internet, but I didn't think clubs condone needle play, sir."

"Various clubs have various rules. I can assure you that no such play is allowed until a Dominant has proven his ability and been certified and recertified on a yearly basis. As I've stated, safety is our main concern... even before pleasure. One of our floating subs attends in the role of nurse and a monitor is either in the room or right outside, depending on our past experience with the players."

"Are you certified?" she asked, her eyes going from the tray to him.

"Yes." After that one-word answer, he led them

from the room and, after briefly seeing one of the rooms available for private play not requiring specific equipment, they stopped at the bar to meet Adam before moving on to see the dance floor. Quentin was pleased to see Keith holding his wife, who appeared to be almost melted against his body, the golden chain around her waist glowing under the soft lights. When the music stopped, Keith looked up and gave the students a smile.

"Hello, Grace, ladies," Keith said. "I hope you are enjoying your tour."

When the women just nodded, her two classmates both looking at Grace, Quentin gave them another lesson. "When a Master speaks to you, you need to verbally respond. In this club, if you wish to speak to a submissive who is with a Dominant, you need to ask him for permission. If his submissive speaks to you first, she will have received prior permission from her Master to do so..." Remembering how this very woman had run across the room without thought the other night, he grinned and added, "Unless, of course, she forgets, in which case there could be consequences for breaking protocol." At his words, Jessica pushed away from Keith, turning to face the group but remaining in his arms. Her smile was soft as her husband chuckled.

"I'm enjoying the evening very much, sir," Grace said. "Your demonstration was extremely moving."

"Oh, it sure was, sir." Joanna said.

"Your sub's jewelry is incredible, sir," Starla said. "If you don't mind saying, where did you get it?"

"From an incredibly talented artist," Keith said with a smile.

Jessica contributed, "Thank you. My husband worked with Grace to have it custom made so it fits so perfectly that I forget I'm wearing it sometimes. Well, unless my Master has added various attachments." Her words had Keith moving his hand to cup one of her breasts, his thumb running across her bare nipple, causing it to peak instantly. Jessica arched a bit as if offering him more even as she smiled beautifully. "Thanks again, Grace. It's amazing how I feel when wearing the full set."

"You are the one who makes it come to life," Grace said and then quickly added, "Oh, sorry. May I speak to your submissive, sir?"

Keith chuckled. "Seems you already have, little one, but no worries. You all will learn that the rules can be bent a bit, especially among friends." Quentin gave a soft chuckle of his own and was about to turn his group away when Keith added, "I do hope to see you all again. Listen to your instructors and remember that everyone starts somewhere. You are lucky that you've chosen to start your exploration in *Plaisir*."

"Nicely said, Master Keith," Quentin said. "And I have to agree with the ladies. Your demonstration was very nicely done."

"It's all due to the whip. It's balanced so perfectly it's like an extension of my arm."

"That helps, but as I was telling my students, it also takes a willingness for a Dominant to learn and practice a skill in order to become truly proficient. Your demonstration is a perfect example of that fact." He saw Jessica tilt her head back to give her husband a smile that bordered on worship and he added, "And you were stunning, Jess."

"Only because my Master is so incredible himself."

Quentin led his students away as another song started to play and Keith turned his wife to face him, his head dipping to kiss her as they began to sway together again. Returning to the center of the room, Quentin asked, "Now, have all of you selected the station you'd like to experience?" Seeing Starla turn to look at the specialty rooms, he qualified his question. "You may choose from any of those in the main room. The fetish rooms are reserved in advance in order to make sure that every safety rule is understood and can be monitored." He ignored the look of disappointment he saw on the experienced sub's face and had no doubt that some day in the future, he'd find her submitting to having needles piercing her skin, and also had no doubt that she'd enjoy the experience. To make sure the others understood tonight's purpose, he added, "Last night, you were spanked to give you a taste of how a punishment could be delivered. Tonight's lesson is to allow you to experience a spanking that is given for pleasure."

"I'd like to try the spanking bench, sir. The flat one, I mean," Joanne said.

"I think I'd like to try that barrel," Grace said, her answer not surprising him.

"Is having a dildo attached to the horse a choice?" Starla asked.

"Sorry, not this evening. Tonight is about only a spanking being given to allow you to ascertain the difference between last night's discipline and tonight's pleasure." Quentin saw her slight frown but added nothing more until she made her choice, a bit surprised when she picked the stocks, having thought she'd request the St. Andrew's Cross.

"Very good. Shall we?"

13

GRACE PACED UP and down the hall, her heels tapping a staccato beat against the wooden floors, and yet she didn't hear it. Instead, she was hearing the soft swishing sound of the flogger, and the whap as each strand of the leather landed against her bottom, causing her soft moans to join the exquisite chorus of the experience she'd been given over that remarkable barrel. Lord, she was hot, though her skin pebbled in goose bumps as she ran her hands up and down her bare arms. Her soft sigh as she sank down on the top step of the stairs changed into a low groan. Though her bottom was tender, it was not like it had been after her spanking of the previous night. Squirming just a bit, she felt her nipples grow even tighter, wondering how that was even possible as they'd been hard points throughout the entire evening. The heat she felt seemed to be internal and burning the hottest between her legs. The first ember had been ignited the moment she and the others had entered the club, and every minute since had that ember flaring into sparks. Replaying her last session of the evening in her head, she felt the sparks shooting into flames.

———

SHE WATCHED Joanne as she approached the spanking bench she'd chosen. Master Quentin instructed her and Starla to kneel with the additional command to keep their eyes on the scene. Grace wondered if Joanne would actually go through with the spanking, and was impressed with the way Quentin guided her through her hesitancy. He softly spoke with her, letting her know what to expect. By the time he instructed her to remove her panties, Joanne did so, her face flushing, and yet the thrust of her nipples beneath her bra easily told of her arousal.

"Good girl," Quentin said and, taking her hand, helped her lie down on the bench. She only gave a soft mew as he placed cuffs around her wrists and ankles and then he squatted beside her, speaking too softly for the others to hear. Grace saw the woman give a small nod and her soft smile was followed by a slight relaxation of her body. Quentin stood and turned to his other pupils.

"Joanne has chosen to have her spanking given with a paddle," he informed them. "You all experienced a leather one last night. I'll be using a wooden one now." He went to another cabinet and when he opened it, Grace could see that he had a wide variety of implements to choose from. He returned to the bench with a paddle that was by no means the thickest, widest or longest she could see hanging from hooks or lying on shelves before he'd shut the door.

He set the paddle against Joanne's bottom and then asked if she was ready. Her soft response indicated she was, and yet he didn't yet lift the paddle.

"Relax, Joanne. Remember, this is not a lesson in punishment but one of pleasure." He gave her a minute to process his words and when her hands unclenched and her body softened, he began.

Grace had witnessed spankings the evening before, as well as scenes played out earlier in this very room, and yet from the first stroke on, she was captivated. Her pulse seemed to sync with the steady cadence of the paddle meeting flesh, though she wasn't watching the strokes fall. Instead, she was watching Joanne's face, seeing what should have an impossibility but smiling as she thought she could understand how the woman seemed to relax further instead of pulling against her restraints. Joanne's eyes were closed, and though soft mews issued from her throat, her smile told of her enjoyment of the spanking. When the paddle fell for the last time, her eyes fluttered open as her instructor once again squatted near her head.

"Wow. I don't really understand how that works, but... um, thank you, sir," she said.

"My pleasure," Quentin replied, working slowly to

remove her restraints, obviously giving her the time to recover at least a bit of her senses.

Grace was slightly surprised; not when Quentin helped Joanne off the bench and then bent to hold her panties as she stepped into them, but at how red her bottom was. The cracks might not have been as loud as she'd expected, or given as hard, and yet there was no denying that they'd done a very good job of covering every inch of a previously pale canvas. Looking at the evidence, Grace believed it definitely gave credence to Joanne's confusion about how she could have derived pleasure from the scene.

"Rise," Quentin instructed and then led the group to the barrel. It was only when he addressed her as Grace, instead of Miss Hensley, that she realized he'd done the same with Joanne. Was that a subtle sign that giving pleasure even through a spanking, was more—what? Personal? Intimate? Feeling her pussy spasm in anticipation of her own turn, she stepped up to the barrel and began to lean forward only to have her eagerness rewarded with a question.

"You do remember that I said wearing a thong doesn't mean you won't be removing it, don't you?"

His question pulled her out of her thoughts. "Oh, I'm sorry, sir. No, I-I was just... um, yes, I remember." She moved back and was suddenly very conscious of the fact that his eyes were on her as she stepped out of her panties. She felt her face heat as he held out his hand. He'd know for sure that she was aroused, but then again, hadn't she and Joanne already admitted as much earlier?

He placed the thong on the small table that held the bowl of condoms and the bottle of sanitizer before moving to the side of the barrel and offering her his hand. As her upper body pressed into the surface, she could feel her nipples protesting being flattened by the unforgiving wood, and yet she could also feel another rush of moisture flooding her sex. The moment her wrists were cuffed and attached to the hand holds on the barrel, she felt submission running through her and didn't allow herself to be ashamed when her ankles were also secured, her legs spread open, even though she knew that her thighs must be coated with a sheen of her own cream.

"Remember, you are perfectly safe," Quentin said, not needing to squat in order to look down and speak to her. "Your choice of implement?"

"I'd like to try a flogger if that's an option, sir."

"Very good," he said, moving away, and she heard the sound of a door clicking open behind her, thinking that the club truly catered to its clients. She only knew he'd made his selection when something that felt like many soft fingers slid across her ass, caressing her skin. "Ready, Grace?"

"Absolutely, sir," she said and then blushed, wondering what he'd think of her obvious eagerness to begin.

Though prepared, she still gave a soft yip when instead of feeling the first stroke land, she felt the barrel move forward. It became obvious that he was allowing her to become accustomed to the movement when he repeated the motion a few more times. She'd just settled into the rhythm, her body molded to the curves of the barrel, when her head lifted with the first stroke.

"Oh," was all she said before settling again and closing her eyes to block out everything but the feel of the individual falls of the flogger striking against her body. It was the most erotic experience she'd ever had. The irony of being rocked as if to be soothed only to have her bottom struck with a blow that wasn't delivering true pain but was still sharp had her body spiraling toward a pinnacle that surprised even her. She wished it never to end and yet the moment she felt her body begin to tense, her hips lifting as if to beg for another kiss of leather, she was denied as Quentin stopped the barrel.

He moved to her head and she had to bite back a needy whimper when he reached out to tuck a strand of hair behind her ear. "Nicely done, Grace."

"Thank you, sir," she whispered, though she desperately wanted to inform him that she was perfectly willing to take just a few more strokes as he'd stopped just before she could come. With that thought, the knowing look in his eyes, and that incredibly sexy little lift of the corner of his mouth, she felt her face heat. She had absolutely no doubt that he was exactly aware of the state he'd left her in.

When she'd knelt again, her pride in her ability to withstand a flogging diminished as Starla requested the cane.

"The cane is one of the severest implements, Starla. Have you any prior experience with one?"

"Yes, sir. It is one of my favorites."

"Very well, but remember the safewords. Yellow if it becomes too uncomfortable and red if you've reached your limit."

"I won't be needing them, and ask that you don't hold back. I find a session is rather useless if a Dom is simply going through the motions. I assure you that I can accept all that you give me, sir."

"This is a lesson to allow you to experience the various apparatus and implements, Miss Wilson, not a session," Quentin informed her, and Grace wondered if Starla heard the same tone in his voice that she had. She watched as Starla was secured in the stocks and noticed that she didn't wait for Quentin to ask her to spread her legs. She had her soles planted as far apart as she could and had also arched her back to lift her ass high. God, she was gorgeous. Bent over at a ninety-degree angle, and nude except for her demi-bra, stockings and heels, it was evident that it wasn't only her form that was flawless, her body was as well. Her stomach was perfectly flat, her breasts ample. Her arms were supple with the cut of muscles visible beneath her skin. Grace also noted that the woman was completely bare, nothing hid her sex from view. Though she herself kept her pubic hair neatly trimmed, she had to wonder if men did prefer it when a woman was as smooth as Starla was.

Quentin had returned with a cane and at the sight of it, Grace heard Starla sigh. "Isn't that a beginner's cane?"

"Excuse me?"

"I just mean that I can take a real caning."

"Miss Wilson, even though you are obviously more experienced than some of your classmates, let me remind you of a few things. First, you are the submissive and, as such, are not allowed to top from the bottom. Second, you are to remember to address a Dom with the proper respect. Lastly, while I did give you the choice of implement, it is not your call to question which one of the canes I've decided upon, nor is it your choice as to how many strokes you may expect. As you've been instructed, use your safewords if you find it necessary, as this is not a punishment. Understood?"

"Yes, sir. Forgive me, sir."

"Are you ready?"

Grace almost gasped when, from her position, she could see the woman roll her eyes, and had a good idea Starla wanted to answer with a, 'duh, don't you see my raised ass?' Grace told herself not to be so catty but, when Starla said, "Yes, sir. I'm all yours," what she really wanted to do was grab the cane from Quentin's hand and give the woman a swat herself.

Grace had to admit, she'd read about caning in her various books, and even thought she understood the difference between what were commonly called 'nursery' or 'junior' canes and 'senior' canes. However, seeing the line that immediately began to appear on Starla's uplifted bottom at the very first stroke, she couldn't help but wonder who on earth would want a 'real' cane applied to such a tender area. Though the scene had her stomach tensing and her heart beating faster, by the time Quentin was removing the locking pin on the stocks and helping Starla to her feet, it was evident that the woman wasn't too pleased. She tossed her hair and then looked over her shoulder to see her bottom before turning to look at her instructor, pausing for a moment before she said, "Thanks, sir."

Quentin nodded, and even though Grace thought he had to be holding himself in check at the mocking tone in her voice, her respect for the man grew as he held her panties so that she could step into them. She also had to bite back a grin when she noticed that while he'd eased both her and Joanne's panties back into place, giving their bottoms a little pat after doing so, this time, once Starla's panties were at her knees, he released his hold and after a moment, she reached down and pulled the black lace back into place. It might have been subtle, but she knew it was also a lesson to remind Starla that, experienced or not, she had a lot to learn about proper respect.

The evening's lesson ended after Quentin led them to an area where Trent and his students were already seated—well, he was seated, his students were kneeling in the service position at his feet. Quentin had his own group kneel and after they'd done so, he asked Joanne to rise and go to the bar and order a beer for him, reminding her the bartender's name was Adam. She instantly rose and moved away, and only then did Quentin instruct Starla and Grace to rise and told them that they might choose either a bottle of water or one of juice. He also asked that they inquire of Joanne which she'd like.

"Hell, how am I supposed to show him that, unlike you, I'm a serious submissive. I told him I wanted a real caning but because you were gasping with every stroke, he held back," Starla hissed as the two women made their way to the bar. Grace was rather surprised the woman was even speaking, much less to her, and Starla turned away with a huff before she could even think of an answer. As they stood in line, waiting to place their order as several of their classmates had also been sent for service, she asked Joanne what she'd like.

"Oh, water would be fine, thanks."

Thanking the bartender for her glass of cranberry juice and a bottle of water for Joanne, Grace turned to discover Starla was waiting for her.

"I suppose you can't wait to repeat what I said?"

Grace was slightly offended and yet this time made a verbal response. "Despite what you might think, if Master Quentin held back, it was because he chose to, not because of anything else. And, for your information, I don't appreciate you insinuating that I'm one to tattle."

The woman didn't respond, just stepped ahead of Grace and sashayed back to the group, sinking gracefully into the required pose. Grace didn't miss the fact that she'd done so as close to Quentin's legs as possible.

HER TRIP down memory lane ended when Grace heard footsteps and looked up, her eyes not traveling far, as they were instantly frozen at the sight of black leather molded perfectly against a rather impressive bulge. It took his voice to have her tilting her head back and meeting his eyes.

"Are you all right?"

"Um, yes, sir," she answered, wondering what the penalty was for lying.

"We're not in class. You don't have to address me as sir."

"Oh, um, okay." Despite his words, she almost had added a *sir* to her response.

"Is there a reason you are sitting on the stairs?" His grin had her squirming just a bit, as if her rear had awakened to remind her of the delicious experience she'd just had.

"I forgot my keys," she admitted. "Laurie isn't back, and I was hoping that if you came up before her, you'd let me in again."

"I can do that," he said, offering her his hand.

The moment she took it, she realized she didn't particularly want him to unlock the door. Her arousal was instantly increased ten-fold by his mere touch. Though he was much taller than she, her position on the last stair from the landing had her at face level to him when he pulled her to her feet. She didn't know if it was the fact that right before she'd been lifted, she'd seen his cock swelling, or if it was the look in his gray eyes, one she'd not seen before, that had her speaking.

"Fuck me, Quentin."

His eyes widened and yet turned a smokier gray as he began to shake his head. Before he could speak, she shook her own.

"I remember what you said that night. I'm not asking for anything else. But, God, I need you to fuck me. Please?"

She held her breath even though she needed the oxygen, waiting to hear his rejection. Instead, he climbed the last few stairs and when he turned to the left instead of the right, she felt a sense of expectation that would have stolen her breath if she'd dared to take one.

It only took a second for him to unlock his door, and the moment they'd stepped inside, he kicked it shut and had her pinned against the door with nothing but the cage he made with his palms planted against its surface on either side of her head. Her nipples hurt so badly she thought they'd burst, and she could feel her juices sliding down her thigh, the gusset of her thong way too ineffective in trapping her arousal.

His mouth descended on hers in a kiss that stirred every molecule in her body. He didn't kiss her softly. His tongue gave a single pass along the seam of her lips before pushing inside. Her moan was trapped by his mouth when he dropped one hand to cup her breast.

She arched against him, wanting... needing to be closer, to offer him whatever he desired. He pulled away only long enough to pull her t-shirt over her head, tossing it aside. She gasped again when he flicked open the front closing of her bra, freeing her breasts.

"Oh, God," she moaned as both hands cupped her breasts. His fingers briefly caressed the skin before he took her mouth again, his thumbs and fingers closing around her nipples, rolling, twisting, and tugging until she was pretty sure she'd just come from the combination of pain and pleasure. Her hand moved to his crotch, her fingers stroking along his cock beneath the leather. Her knees threatened to give way as she felt the growing length.

When he pulled back, dropping his head to nip along her neck, she groaned. "Please, I need you inside me." She knew it sounded as if she was whimpering but didn't give a damn. She had never spoken a truer statement.

His growl had her sex spasm as one hand went south to push beneath her skirt. Fingers shoved aside the sodden silk of her underwear to slide into her and she threw her head back against the door at the incredible sensation as he filled her. "Oh, God, yes," she mewled, her muscles clamping down on his fingers in an attempt to keep them inside, but again, he proved why he was the one in control as he pulled them free.

Her pussy spasmed as he lifted his hand, two fingers glistening with her own essence, but her heart actually fluttered when his eyes locked on hers, as his tongue appeared, broadening to take a long, slow lick along each finger. His eyes darkened as he bent to kiss her, and she eagerly pressed her mouth to his. She could not only taste herself on his lips, she felt another gush of that very cream flood into her panties.

She wasn't aware that his other hand had left her breast until his lips pulled away to hover a mere centimeter from hers. "Wrap your legs around me," he said, lifting her easily. She instantly obeyed, the feel of his cock at her entrance making her wonder how on earth he had managed to not only free himself, but magically pluck a condom from thin air and don it, all while continuing to pleasure her. When she felt her thong being ripped off, she almost came with the primal feel of it all. He was as needy as she. He began to push inside and though he'd given her several thrusts with his fingers, she gasped, her eyes flying wide open as he slowly filled her.

"I-I don't think... oh, God!"

"Shh, you'll be fine," he said, a moment before he silenced any further protests by kissing her again.

Grace discovered he was more than correct. She wasn't just fine... she was absolutely perfect as he thrust and withdrew, only to thrust again until he was fully buried inside her. He pulled his mouth away and lowered his head to suckle a nipple. Her hands clung to his shoulders as his hands cupped her ass, his fingers kneading the recently spanked skin, driving her arousal higher and higher with every squeeze of the punished flesh. When he bit down on her turgid peak, she screamed and came, her body jerking, and yet he easily held her, keeping her in place as he increased the intensity of his thrusts.

Lifting his head, he spoke, "Good girl, come again." He didn't seem to expect an answer as he moved to lave and suckle her other nipple. She had never been multi-orgasmic and yet, when he tilted her just a bit, pounding into her, stretching her, filling her so completely, she could feel herself climbing toward the crest again. Another sharp bite, a few more deep thrusts and she obeyed, her scream louder, her climax prolonged, and yet he still hadn't reached his own. By the time he sank as deeply as possible and she felt his body jerk, she came for the third time, joining him in pleasure she'd never truly imagined as possible.

He continued to hold her, his head dropping to rest against her own. She didn't once fear he'd drop her, though she could feel a slight tremble run through his shoulders as she continued to hold on. Dropping a hand, she pressed it against his heart, wishing he'd taken the time to remove his own shirt. As they regained their senses, the artist in her wondered what sort of picture they made. Without benefit of a camera or even a mirror, she had no doubt that in her own eyes, it would be one of erotic pleasure... pleasure she already wished to re-experience—and yet, she'd told him she remembered his statement after her show.

He didn't do relationships. He didn't make love. He *fucked*. God, did he ever. He fucked like no man she'd ever been with. He fucked with a power and control that already had her nipples forgetting their slight tenderness from his bites and pebbling again.

He slipped from her and she reluctantly allowed her legs to slide from their clasp around his waist. She wobbled as they took her weight and she knew it had nothing to do with the fact that she was still wearing heels.

"All right?" he asked softly, not releasing her fully.

"Perfect," she returned, looking up and seeing the softest gray yet reflected in his eyes.

"I'm going to dispose of the condom, but need to know that you aren't going to collapse if I let you go."

She really didn't want to be released but nodded. "I'm fine."

He bent forward and gave her a quick kiss. "Sugar, you are far more than fine." She leaned against the door as she watched him walk away. God, what she'd give to see him walk away naked. The flex of his muscles and the pull of those incredible pants against his ass had her mouth watering. Thoughts of his clothing had her thinking of her own. She clasped her bra and, seeing her shirt on the floor, bent to pick it up and pulled it on. She couldn't help but grin at the fact that her brand new panties were now useless. Granted, they hadn't been much help before, and yet, feeling the fabric that had been torn lying against her skin, she reached beneath her skirt and pulled them off. She'd read of such things and now knew that it was a total turn on to have a man... a wonderful, dominant man, want you so badly he didn't take a single second to remove your underwear.

"Sorry about that."

Looking up, she saw he'd returned. "Don't be," she said. "It was one of the sexiest things I've ever had the pleasure of experiencing." She was pleased to see his brief grin but wasn't pleased when it disappeared just as quickly. Now that he'd fulfilled her request, she wondered if he were already regretting doing so. Unlike the expectations of the classroom, she was torn as to what to say next. Should she just thank him or say what she really wanted, which was to ask if they could do that again.

"Ready?" he asked, solving her dilemma. She nodded and stepped away from the door so he could open it. Neither spoke as he walked her down the short length of the hall. After unlocking her door, he pushed it open but reached out to take her arm before she entered. He seemed to hesitate but then gave her a smile. "Sleep well, Grace."

Her smile wasn't the least bit forced, nor her response a lie. "I will. Thanks, Quentin, and sweet dreams."

She lifted herself onto her toes and kissed his cheek before ducking inside, and after gently closing the door, she leaned against it with a smile still on her face.

14

QUENTIN RAN UP THE STAIRS, barely managing to stop himself before plowing into Laurie. "Sorry," he said and then took a closer look at her face. "Hey, honey, are you okay?"

She met his eyes and shook her head. "No... I mean, I'm all right."

"No, you're not," he countered.

"You're right, I'm not. I'm really pissed off but can't do a fucking thing about it because if I don't get going, I'm going to be late for my shift."

Quentin was a bit surprised at the anger in her voice. Yesterday when he'd last seen her at the hospital, she'd been practically giddy. Had her expectations not been met? He rather doubted it, as he knew that Brody was the sort of man to make sure his submissive was completely sated, and the fact that the two were now engaged only told him that if Brody hadn't, then something was seriously wrong.

"Is it Brody?" he asked.

"Brody? No, Brody is fine." When her glance darted toward the door to her apartment, Quentin got a sick feeling in his stomach. Shit, he should have known better. Though he'd been expecting to mentally kick himself ever since he'd returned to his apartment after unlocking the door for Grace last night, he'd enjoyed their encounter too much to do so. He knew he was an ass, and evidently, Laurie knew it as well. He opened his mouth but she spoke before he could.

"Poor Grace, she's trying to be brave but I know she is devastated."

Okay, he was not only an ass, he'd been a fool to believe her when she'd insisted that she didn't care... all she wanted was to fuck him. From the encounters they'd had, he knew she wasn't the one-night stand sort of woman. Regardless of that fact, he'd let his cock lead the way.

"Look..." the two said at the same time.

"Go ahead," he said.

"I was just going to ask that you go talk to her. I know you can't be held accountable but, shit, maybe just talking will help her."

Not accountable? Her words were making absolutely no sense.

"Please? I've really got to go."

"Sure," he said, not positive what she expected but hoping his assurance would remove at least a little of the tension he could see in her body.

"Thanks, Quentin, you're a doll." She bent to give him a quick kiss and then ran down the stairs. "I'm sorry I cussed," she added right before she turned the corner.

"You're welcome," he muttered, resuming his ascent. The fact that he hadn't at least given her butt a smack in passing had him pausing outside the door. Hell, he had planned on returning to the hospital and continuing the investigation. Now he was about to be raked across the coals by the guest of a woman he admired, and found he couldn't blame Laurie for her attitude. He had to repeat his knock before the door opened.

His first thought was how very different this woman appeared from the one he'd been with only hours earlier. At some point, tears had obviously caused her mascara to run and yet she wasn't presently crying. Instead of a sexy tee and cute skirt, she was wearing a flannel shirt and another pair of sweat pants. No pretty red heels were on her feet, as they were bare. Her auburn hair wasn't floating around her shoulders but was pulled back into a high ponytail, and from the look of the pencil stuck into the sloppy bun, she hadn't given a single thought to anything but getting it out of her way. But it was the look on her face that tugged at his heart. He'd never felt like a bigger shit than he did at that moment.

"Grace, I shouldn't have..." Even though he shouldn't have fucked her, he couldn't honestly say he was sorry he had. He settled on, "I didn't mean to hurt you," as at least that was honest. Her obvious despair had him opening his arms, wanting to give her more than a poorly worded apology.

She stepped into them, her arms wrapping around his waist, her cheek pressed against his chest. Without her heels she was so much shorter and felt so tiny in his arms. When he realized that he could feel her trembling, he scooped her up and walked to the couch. Taking a seat, he arranged her on his lap, not speaking as she gave in to a fresh bout of tears. It was several minutes before she began to quiet.

"What a goddamned bastard."

He winced but accepted the accusation. It didn't help him any remembering that he'd told her not to expect anything from him. He still felt like a jerk for taking advantage of her. Hell, he'd known she left the class aroused. Before he could say anything, she saved him the trouble.

Pushing up a bit, she swiped at her eyes. "How can a man be so fucking cruel? I mean, who the hell does he think he is?"

Quentin was about to automatically chastise her for cursing when the pronoun she'd used replayed in his head. *He?* She hadn't said, "you." Deciding there were more important things to discuss, he let the curse words slide... at least for the time being, he qualified, a bit surprised that he did so.

"Grace, I'm not sure who you are talking about."

"Him!" Her answer didn't help him but seeing her hand sweep toward the floor, and noticing for the first time that the newspaper appeared to have been shredded, a glimmer of understanding began to flicker. It flared to life when she continued.

"David shithead Brooks. How dare he. Just

because I wouldn't go out with him. Just because I told him off when he called. Just because he is a world-class asshole, I still didn't believe he'd follow through with his threat."

"Wait a minute," Quentin said, every protective instinct going into overdrive. "What threat? Are we talking about the night of the show?"

She seemed to nod and shake her head at the same time. "That might have started it, but I'm pretty sure he wanted to make it clear that I understood that artists who didn't accept his offers could kiss their fucking careers goodbye. God, Charles is going to kill me. He warned me, and... oh, God, I don't know how I'll be able to face him. He took a chance on me and now I've done nothing but draw negative attention to his gallery."

Quentin understood she had to be talking about the review of her show. While he was sure he wouldn't enjoy reading it, he knew he needed to. However, he didn't take the paper, and the one on the floor was totally useless. Making a decision, he patted her knee. "What we need is not only a plan but to fortify ourselves. Go put on some shoes. We'll get some coffee."

"Laurie made a pot," she said, sinking against him again instead of rising to find her shoes.

"Well, I suppose it's coffee, but I was thinking a bit of fried dough and about a pound of powdered sugar would—"

She cut him off with a slap at his chest. "I don't eat an entire pound!" With a smile, she shook her head.

"Wait, is that why you started calling me Sugar? Because of my sweet tooth?"

Quentin knew he could just say 'yeah' and she'd most likely not give it another thought. However, he also realized he'd come to use the endearment with a far deeper meaning. "As I recall, your teeth aren't the only part of you that tastes sweet." Her flush showed what he hoped was pleasure. "But it you aren't in the mood to go—"

"Are you kidding? I'm always in the mood for Café du Monde!" Sounding far more like herself, she bent forward, pecked his cheek and then jumped off his lap. "Don't go anywhere, I'll be right back!"

He chuckled as she ran down the hall. While he waited, he gathered the torn paper from the floor and even attempted to piece some parts together. As he had thought, it was a useless endeavor. She returned and he had to smile. She'd not only found her shoes, she'd taken the time to change. She now wore a pair of jeans and a green t-shirt, her ballet flats on her feet.

"I'm ready."

"Though I think you look adorable, maybe you want to run a washcloth over your face?"

"Oh, geeze," she said, running down the hall again. The next time she appeared, she said, "Please tell me you weren't going to let me go outside with a pencil in my hair!"

"Actually, I found it rather becoming. Sort of how I'd picture a bohemian artist." He liked seeing her smile, even though it was a quick one. Wanting it to return, he opened the door and led her down the stairs saying, "We could walk in deference to the calories we are about to consume, or we could say fuck it and take the bike."

She tilted her head and her smile was much wider. "I definitely vote for fuck it. I'm so mad that my body is burning like a furnace. I'm sure not a single gram of sugar or fat will survive."

He chuckled, squeezed her hand and said, "Then let's ride."

HE AGAIN SENT her ahead to pick out a table while he placed their order. On his way toward her, he saw a man leaving and that he'd left the newspaper on his chair. Snagging it, Quentin took it and their tray to the table Grace had chosen. Removing the items from the tray, he grinned as her hand reached out to snag a beignet off the plate before it reached the table.

"Hungry?" he teased, setting down the plate and then her coffee mug before her.

"Starving," she said around a mouthful of pastry. Once she'd swallowed and he'd taken his seat, she said, "Good thing you were smart enough to order your own plate. I'm not exactly in a sharing mood right now."

"I promise you won't leave until you are satisfied," he said.

She paused in her chewing and smiled, tilting her head slightly. "You never do."

Her words and the look in her eyes had his cock stirring. Shit, he wasn't supposed to be so easily aroused, and yet he didn't deny that with just her statement, he was remembering the absolute heaven that he'd felt with her legs wrapped around him as he sank into her warmth. It took her reaching for her coffee for him to snap back to the reality they were here to discuss.

"Do you mind?" he asked, lifting the paper.

"Ugh, if you have to," she said, replacing her cup and reaching for another beignet. He reached for one as well and saw her grin as he took a big bite. "Good?" she asked.

"Unbelievably so," he admitted, finishing it in another bite. He could practically feel the sugar molecules coursing through his system and grinned at her smile. Opening the paper and finding the column, his grin slid from his face. She had been right. Brooks was a definite bastard. He read every line and then read them again.

"What a son of a bitch," he said, closing the paper and reaching for his coffee.

"Told you. Have another. Perhaps if we consume enough sugar, we'll be able to think sweeter thoughts."

"I doubt that," he said, knowing that no matter how many pastries he consumed, he'd never forgive the man. "I'm really sorry, Grace. It wasn't a good idea for me to stay that night."

"It wasn't that night that caused him to write that load of crap," she said. "Well, not just that night."

Quentin remembered what she'd said earlier. "Tell me, exactly what did he say to threaten you?"

The tip of her pink tongue licked along the corner of her mouth to gather the powdered sugar before she answered. "He didn't actually say, 'you better do what I want or else,' but he didn't have to."

Forcing himself not to think about how it would be to clean her with his own tongue, Quentin shook his head. "What exactly did he say?" When she hesitated, he reached across the table and covered her hand with his.

"Grace, don't feel you have to spare my feelings. No matter what you say, I know that I'm at least partially responsible for the review. I'm a big boy, I can handle it."

She shocked him by giving a soft giggle and squirming on her chair. "You are," she said with a smile. "A big boy, I mean."

He couldn't help the grin that pulled at his lips. "The paper, remember?" he gently reminded her, giving her fingers a squeeze before releasing her hand.

"Oh, right. Um, when I once again refused to meet with him, he told me that I was risking my career and, well, he insinuated my reputation as well by being friends with you, Brody and Laurie. He acted as if he knew I was taking your class but I really can't see how he could. I mean, I didn't even know I was going to until a couple of days earlier, and I know that none of you make a habit of informing others about the membership of your club. I can only imagine he is making assumptions based on what he learned when he was covering your girlfriend's death."

"I'm rather surprised he didn't warn you that your life was in danger," Quentin said. He noticed that her eyes drifted to the side, and she didn't immediately answer. "Goddamnit, he did, didn't he?"

"Not in so many words, but, yes, it was implied." Straightening in her seat, her expression changed. "I told him that I didn't appreciate him maligning my friends, and if he wasn't very careful, I'd be more than happy to sue him and his paper for libel. Unfortunately, well, I suppose that's not much of a threat since he didn't actually print anything that wasn't true. You can't sue someone simply because he gives what he clearly states as his 'opinion' about my show or my ability as an artist. It is his right, and I suppose he sees it as his job, to write what he thinks."

"It's still bullshit," Quentin said, impressed that though she had to be deeply hurt, she was putting on a brave front. "I hope you understand that you are not only an incredibly talented artist, Grace, you are a remarkable person. I've never seen anyone who takes the time to look at the world through different eyes. You not only capture moments of pure beauty, you seem to capture the very essence of your subjects' souls. I also hope you understand that Brooks is not only a bastard but a liar. Honey, if he truly thought what he wrote was true, if he thought you were 'some stuck-up girl who is attempting to draw attention to herself by vomiting up vulgar works of so-called art,' then I promise he never would have picked up that phone even knowing you knew me."

She sat back in her chair and he saw a sheen in her eyes. "Ah, sweetie, don't cry. Don't give him the satisfaction."

"I'm not," she said, swiping at a tear that escaped. "It's you. You reminded me why I paint and... you are an amazing man."

He wondered how she could even consider that. He wasn't amazing. Hell, he wasn't even a good man. Why then did he suddenly desire to prove her words true? Why did he know that if Brooks appeared before his eyes, he'd not hesitate to rip him limb from limb? Not for anything he thought about Quentin or his chosen lifestyle, but because he'd attempted to hurt Grace where it would cut her the most deeply. He'd attempted to plant doubt about her incredible talent into her very soul.

"How can you do that?" she said.

"What?" he asked, having to take a moment to understand she'd asked a question.

"You know, in class, I saw you only studying those folders once and then you knew everyone's names. And just now, how could you quote his words back verbatim?"

Quentin shrugged. "I suppose it's like you in a way. You see things with a different perspective. I see faces or words and they just seem to stick."

"I bet that helped in school," she said.

"Let's just say that I didn't have to hit the books as

hard as others. I remember Brody staying up all night cramming for some test while I could remain calm and work on my hobby. Man, he used to get pissed." Quentin chuckled at the memory and felt a bit of his anger dropping away.

"Um, are you going to eat that?" He looked down to see her fingers hovering over the last beignet.

"No, feel free."

"Thanks," she said, snatching it quickly, as if worried he'd change his mind. As she took a bite and asked, "Wanna share?" he had to wonder if she knew she often spoke with her mouth full. Shit, thinking of her mouth being full had his cock jerking again. This woman had a way of pulling at him even when she wasn't doing anything remotely sexual.

"No, babe, I'm afraid I might lose a finger or two. Besides, you are really cute when you eat."

"Sorry," she said, swallowing and then giggling. "Your fingers are safe. I didn't mean the beignet. You said you had a hobby. Would you share what it is, I mean, if you don't mind telling me?"

"Leather," he said and couldn't help but see her mouth open a bit, and was a bit shocked to see her nipples lift to poke against her t-shirt. His pants became even more uncomfortable. "I'm guessing you like leather?"

Her eyes followed his and she turned a pretty pink. "No, I love leather. You made those paddles and that whip that Master K..." He was proud to see that she didn't continue, remembering that members names were not to be bandied about.

"I've made several different things," he said. "I'm presently working on something for Brody and Laurie as a wedding gift."

"Oh, will you show me?"

He nodded and realized that he'd be happy to do so. He also noted that she was no longer tense and that the lines across her forehead had disappeared. The pain in her eyes was gone, their green color now clear, no tears in sight.

"Now?"

"You aren't interested in plotting revenge against Brooks?"

"No," she said, draining the last of her coffee. "My parents taught me that you might not be able to choose the people you encounter in your life, but you do have the choice to walk away from them. I'm just pissed off that I gave him so much thought. It irks me to have to admit that I also owe him a thank you."

"How in the hell could you think that?" He bit back a groan at her next action.

She wet the tip of her finger with her tongue and pressed it against the empty plate, coming away with white powdered sugar, which she promptly popped into her mouth, and his cock threatened to burst through his jeans as her cheeks hollowed with her suckling. Popping it out, now free of any sugar, she said, "Because, if he hadn't written his article, you wouldn't have come to comfort me and we wouldn't be sitting here now. Thank you, Quentin."

"No, thank you, Grace." He didn't elaborate and she didn't ask. She simply took his hand when offered and clung to him as they mounted the bike. At every red light, he put his foot down onto the pavement and dropped his hand from the handlebars to give hers a squeeze. One day soon, he'd take her on a longer ride, and perhaps show her the part of Louisiana that he truly considered his home.

It seemed like the most natural thing in the world to walk hand-in-hand up the stairs and into his apartment. If she was remembering the night before, she managed to hide it pretty well, her cheeks only flushing a little.

"Would you like something to drink?"

"God, no. I made an absolute pig of myself. Another single thing in my tummy will cause me to burst."

"We can't have that," he said, opening the fridge as he continued to speak, "the only bursting allowed is when you explode in pleasure." His hand closing around an ice-cold bottle of water had him wondering what in the hell had possessed him to say that. Straightening, he turned back toward her to see her head tilted a bit. Well, shit, the words were true but he didn't need to have her wondering why he'd said them. "But, come to think of it, I would like to discover if you put anything but coffee and fried dough in your mouth." Her quick grin and glance down at the zipper of his jeans had him kicking himself. Fuck, what was the matter with him? He wasn't some green teenager who uttered innuendos to check out a woman's interest.

Her smile reached her eyes, which were

twinkling. "I think I'll keep that a secret until you decide to show me what else you'd like me to taste."

He uncapped the bottle and took a long drink before lowering it from his mouth. Maybe the chill would allow his cock to at least go to half-mast?

"Oh, is that it?"

It took him a good second or two to understand she was no longer talking about... well, eating. He finished the water and joined her where she was standing in front of his couch, looking down at the coffee table. He sat and pulled her down beside him before bending forward and picking up the bundle of leather that would be the falls of the flogger. Handing it to her, he watched as she ran her fingers through the individual strips.

"It's so soft," she said, looking up at him. "Did you make the one you used on me last night?"

"Yes, I made most of the leather items in the club. Some of the wooden ones, as well, though that requires items I have in my shed at home."

"You don't live here? I mean, I know you just came back but I thought..."

"I have a cabin as well. There's a shed, well, actually, it's probably bigger than the house, but it's where I do most of the work. I can do the finishing touches on some items here but it takes special equipment to work the hides, and to cut and shape either leather or wood."

"I can understand that," she said, again running her fingers over the leather. "I remember my first roommate was always complaining that I took up more than my share of space because I had so many canvases and different paints. It takes more than talent to be an artist, it takes a lot of room."

He chuckled and bent again, picking up the braided handle he was working on. "I'm almost ready to attach the falls to the handle."

"Is that what this is called?" she asked, lifting the section he'd given her.

"Yes, as you can see, there are a great many individual pieces. A Dominant can actually make it feel as if they all land in one area or, with various twists of his wrist, can cause the strands to fall across a wider area."

"Like you did last night," she said with a small squirm. "Um, is it okay to tell you that I really enjoyed the barrel? I mean, I know we're not in class, but—"

"It's not only okay, I'm glad you told me. I enjoyed watching you enjoy it so much." He saw her flush again and though it might not be proper, he couldn't help himself. He cupped her cheek with his palm and bent toward her as she lifted her face. A breath away from her mouth, he continued, "The next time I have you over the barrel, I won't stop until you come, Grace."

"Promise?" she whispered, right before his lips met hers. He didn't totally understand it, but he knew he definitely hoped to keep that promise one day.

When he released her and allowed her to catch her breath, she smiled. "I just thought of something."

"Babe, if you could think, then obviously I didn't kiss you thoroughly enough."

"No, no," she said with a giggle. "Believe me, any more thoroughly, and I'd be nothing but a puddle of submissive goo at your feet. I didn't think about it until I saw that handle again. I'm thinking that, since you said your gift was for both of them, then Laurie must enjoy flogging as much as I do, right?"

"That's really yet to be seen, about your enjoyment. There's a big difference between being flogged for pleasure versus punishment that often includes feeling the leather striking on areas far more sensitive than your ass. But, yes, Laurie will tell you that flogging is one of her absolute favorite experiences."

Again, that slightly tilted head and those green, expressive eyes were doing a number on his cock. He could practically hear the gears turning in her head but didn't know if she was picturing how the impact of the leather on various parts of her body would feel, or perhaps wondering how to ask for a tangible demonstration of the difference.

Perhaps neither, as she said, "I wonder if they'd like a painting. One that shows their pleasure using your gift."

"If you are talking about a painting like those in your show, I not only think that's a great idea, I think they'd be incredibly honored."

HIS ANSWER HAD her flushing with pleasure. "I know Brody is incapacitated due to his leg, but, um, I know you spanked her and, well, to be honest, she told me that you've done so in the past. Do you think there is any way that Brody would permit you to flog Laurie and let me photograph the session?"

She watched as he seemed to consider her question. "I think so. Brody enjoys giving her pleasure, and he knows there is only so much he can do right now. Still, I'll need to ask."

"I know, I wouldn't expect you just to grab her and start whaling on her." She cringed a bit at the rudeness of that statement but relaxed when he grinned.

"No, the only one I might grab and whale on without prior permission is a sassy little artist I know."

"Okay, now that's another image I won't be able to stop thinking about. If you'll..." Seeing that he had not only sat back but that his brow was furrowed, she paused. "What? Did I say something wrong? I didn't mean..."

"No," he said, suddenly sitting forward again. "You said something I believe might be very important." He placed the handle back on the table and reached for the bundle of leather strips. "I'm sorry but I really need to get to the hospital."

"Oh, no, that's fine. In fact, would you mind if I tag along? I haven't been to see Brody in a few days." When he hesitated, she added, "That's okay. I can go later."

"I need to go over something about, well..."

"Your investigation into Beth's murder? Laurie

told me about you and Brody going through files. That's why you came to get the laptop that day, right?"

"Right. Okay, if you're sure you don't mind knowing the topic of what I need to discuss, then I don't mind you going with me."

"I don't mind. I wish I could help in some way."

"I think you might have already. Come on. I'll see if what I think could help, and after we visit, we'll grab some lunch. We'll be back in plenty of time for class."

She didn't hesitate as he helped her to her feet. She didn't totally understand what he was talking about but she had been truthful. If they could bring the person who'd killed Beth to justice, she knew it would go a long way toward healing the hurt that had sent him away from the people who loved him. She also knew that she needed to be extremely careful because she was frightened... not of Quentin, but of the fact that she knew she was falling in love with him.

15

"To what do I owe the pleasure?" Brody asked when they entered his room.

"Hi, Brody. We came to see how are you feeling," Grace said, moving to his bedside and bending to give him a kiss.

"Better now," he said, reaching out to palm her cheek. "I must say, I'm very glad to see you smiling. Laurie told me what Brooks said in his article."

"It doesn't matter," she said, giving his hand a squeeze. "Life is too short to worry about things you have no control over." She stepped back and when Quentin offered her the only chair, she shook her head. "No, I know you need to sit close to discuss the investigation. I'll be fine over there." He nodded and bent to kiss her before she moved to sit on the window seat.

"Well, well," Brody said softly, "Laurie did not see fit to mention that you two seem to be getting along rather smashingly."

"Probably too scared I'd smash a paddle against her ass," Quentin quipped as he took the chair.

"Yeah, I'm sure that's it," Brody said. When Quentin tapped the pad of paper that Brody had been writing on, he turned serious. "Okay, what's really up?"

"Grace said something that jarred my memory. I remember something that has always bugged me. Something has always seemed off but it took her mentioning images before it clicked into place."

"Okay, what image?"

"I called Detective Stewart before we came over. He said that though it wasn't really proper, seeing as how the case was considered a cold one, he didn't particularly give a damn. Anyway, can you log on to your email from here?"

"I'm not sure if the hospital has Wi-Fi," Brody said. "Since we've been working off flash drives, I haven't needed it."

"Shit, Jason said he'd send you the file. It won't do any good if you can't access it."

"You can always use a cell phone," Grace offered. Both men turned to look toward her. "I mean, unless you have some antique phone plan? I have a smartphone and plenty of data so if you need, you can access my hotspot."

"Learn something every day," Brody said, moving the mouse to click on his search engine, pulling up his email account. When he shook his head after trying to open it, Quentin asked for Grace's phone.

She brought it to him and soon had the connection working.

"Just keep the phone on the table next to the computer and the connection will be fine."

"Thanks, babe," Quentin said. "Okay, pull up your email. You're looking for a file of jpeg images." Turning slightly, he said, "You might want to go back to the window." He noticed her hesitation. "These aren't going to be pretty." With a nod, she returned to the window though kept her attention turned toward the men.

"Shit, man, are you sure you want to see these again?" Brody said when the first photo appeared on the screen.

"Hell no, I don't want to but I need to. Just click through them until I tell you to stop, all right?"

"Sure."

The clicking of the mouse was the only sound in the room for several minutes until Quentin said, "Right there." With the photo frozen on the screen, he leaned forward and then sat back. "Goddamnit, how could I have missed that?"

Brody's eyes went from the photo to him and then back again. "Missed what?"

"Look at her hand. She never wore a ring on her left hand. In fact, I remember her specifically telling me that the only ring she'd ever place on that finger would be a wedding band. The photo shows the club ring on the ring finger of her left hand."

"Holy shit, you're right," Brody said. "But that would mean..."

"It would mean that she didn't use her ring to gain entry into the club. She was left-handed and wore the ring on her other hand. It made it easier for her to press it into the depression and reach for the doorknob when she entered the building or the elevator by herself. Someone took that ring off her hand and put it back on the wrong finger."

"Fuck, that changes things," Brody said, closing the image. "We've got to identify every single person who was there that night."

He clicked back to the flash drive. "Hey, would you mind getting me some more water?"

"I'll get it," Grace said, standing and taking his mug off the table.

"Thanks, there's ice down the hall in a little room next to the nurses' station."

"Can I bring you something, Quentin?"

"I wouldn't mind a cup of coffee if it hasn't turned into sludge already. Black is fine." He smiled, watching until she left the room. Turning back, he noticed that Brody's eyes were on him and not the screen.

"Welcome back," he said softly. "She's good for you."

Quentin didn't bother to deny his words. "The question is, how good could I possibly be for her? You said Laurie told you about the article, did you read it?"

"Yes, the nurse brings me the paper every morning. I gotta admit, I was worried. Laurie was spitting mad when she got here."

"I know; she was the same when I saw her."

Brody grinned and nodded. "Yeah, she even admitted she deserved a few smacks for her cussing."

Quentin wasn't one to miss an opportunity. "Speaking of which, how would you feel if I gave her a session? Not for punishment but for pleasure. Grace wants to photograph her being flogged and, well, I won't tell you everything as I don't want to ruin the surprise."

Brody grinned. "I think I can guess, but let's try to keep it a secret from Laurie. She'd be absolutely thrilled if it's what I think it might be. As for your request, yes. Not only would that clear my girl's conscience, it's been damn hard to give her all she needs with me in this bed. Though I don't think she has any complaints about last night."

Quentin chuckled, and the two were bending over looking at the frames from the club when Grace returned. When they both looked up and took their respective beverages, she said, "Well, that might explain it."

"Explain what?" Quentin said, puzzled at her comment.

"That photo," she said, pointing to the screen. "If I'd known Brooks was a member of the club, I might not have freaked out yesterday when he seemed to know what went on upstairs."

"Brooks isn't a member," Brody said.

"Then why is he in the club?" She bent forward and tapped a fingertip at the image of the man they'd attempted to identify.

"You think that's David? You can't see his face."

"Yes, but look at the way he's standing. He stands sort of like we are required to do. I mean, his feet are apart and his hands are behind his back. Can you make it any larger?"

Brody made a few clicks of his mouse, enlarging the photo. Though it turned a bit grainier, she nodded. "That's his watch. I remember thinking I hadn't seen a man wear a watch with such a band before."

Brody leaned forward, almost bumping heads with Quentin as he did the same. "Shit, she's right. I haven't seen another band like it. Most men don't even wear a watch anymore as they depend on their phones for the time. And, if they do, they are either solid gold or silver. When was the last time you saw a brown band, and a cheap one at that? See how it's frayed along the edges?"

"Fuck that," Quentin growled. "How the hell did he get into our club? We've never accepted an application from a reporter and, even if we had, I'd never have approved him. Even before Beth's murder, I questioned his journalism, and I wasn't the only one."

Brody nodded and sat back again. "All right. We've got to tell Stewart what we've discovered and get Peter started on digging deeper into Brooks' background."

"You don't think he killed Beth, do you?" Grace asked, her voice shaky.

Quentin wrapped his arm around her and pulled

her close to his chair. "We don't know, but the very fact that he was there sets off warning bells. We need to find out who let him in as a guest. If no one did, then he definitely needs to answer how the hell he got in. Until then, if he calls you again, don't answer the phone... no, forget that. If it won't worry or frighten you, answer but record the call. However, if he actually approaches you, get away." At her nod, he set his coffee down on the table tray and pulled her into his lap. "Fuck, babe, I'm sorry."

"For what? You didn't do anything."

"Only brought you to his attention in a negative way," Quentin said. "And just the thought that he might have anything to do with Beth's death and the fact that she was in a relationship with me, I fear that Brooks might take out some sort of anger he had toward me on you. Hell, he's already started with that review."

"I'm not afraid of him," Grace said. "If he knows anything and pretended to know nothing all these years... if he had anything to do with hurting Beth, then, don't worry about me. You get him, Quentin."

"We can't jump to conclusions," Brody warned. "I know we are tempted to do so but we need to be positive before this goes any further."

"I agree, but until this is settled, I want both Grace and Laurie to be extra careful. No more going anywhere alone. Laurie needs to tell either you or me when she is leaving for work, and call when she arrives," he said to Brody.

"I'll tell her when she comes in. And, knowing her,

she'll agree and forget. The first time she does, she'll need her ass blistered to drive home the importance of obedience on this matter."

Quentin could feel Grace squirm a bit but he agreed and said so wholeheartedly. "As for you, young lady, perhaps it would be safer if you left..."

"Don't ask me to leave, Quentin. I won't go, no matter if you threaten to spank me, too. Besides, you just said we aren't to be alone. If I go, Laurie will be in that apartment alone, and I won't abandon her. And don't think about telling me I'm out of the class. You can't fail me just because of Brooks. That would let him win and I will be damned if I'll allow that."

He hesitated but couldn't deny he'd just voiced that concern. "Fine, but from now on, I'll be escorting you to and from class. You aren't to leave the apartment unless you go with Laurie or me. Is that understood?"

"I need to go see Mr. Westing—"

"We'll go together."

"Okay, I understand, though I'm hoping you are overreacting."

"Be that as it may, I'd rather overreact than fail to protect you or Laurie." Quentin had never spoken a more truthful statement. He'd failed one woman; he'd rather die than fail a woman he'd seen fulfill his best friend's every dream, or the one on his lap... the one he'd been determined not to need and yet, she'd managed to wiggle her way into his heart.

He kept her on his lap as he called Jason, putting the phone on speaker as he filled him in. He assured him that he had absolutely no doubt about either of the two things they'd discovered.

"We've going to put Peter Zinger to work," Brody provided.

"I've heard of him," Jason said. "Good man, but I'm not going to sit around and wait for his report. I'll pull the ring from the evidence and have forensics go over it with a fine tooth comb. I'm not sure it was ever considered anything other than jewelry Beth wore. Perhaps there is something they can pull that can be analyzed."

"Isn't it pretty small for a fingerprint?" Quentin asked. "I think it's like a size six or something. Much smaller than the one I wear."

"I'm aware that it's smaller, but I'm talking more along the lines of DNA."

"Oh," Quentin said, "I didn't think of that."

"That just shows that you don't stay glued to the television," Jason said. "You can't even guess how many people think all they need to do is watch those series to become forensic scientists. And, unlike those shows, it is highly unlikely we'll have any answers quickly. After all, we don't have the luxury of solving the crime in a one-hour time frame. Hell, it's been two years and we haven't solved it."

"But we will," Quentin said.

"Yes, I believe we will. Every stone overturned gives us something. I'll get started on the requests for the ring and, just so you know, I'll be interviewing Brooks."

"You don't think that might tip him off?" Brody interjected.

"Why? Are you worried he might pull something?"

"I admit, neither of us would put it past him, but we can't let our concerns keep us from finding out what we need to know. But I need you to promise you won't let him know that it was Grace who recognized him from the film," Quentin said.

"That I can do. Hell, I don't have to even give him any explanation. It's my job to investigate, and until the case is solved, he and anyone else will just have to put up with being inconvenienced."

"All right, thanks, Jason. We've already told the ladies they aren't to go out alone."

"Well, if they are anything like my Anna, it might take a trip over a knee to drive that request home."

"No worries, they'll both understand that they won't like the consequences if they forget." He thanked the detective again and then disconnected the call.

"Wow, does everyone you know use spanking as a deterrent?" Grace asked, her head swiveling between the two men.

Brody chuckled and Quentin answered, "Come to think of it, I'd have to say yes. Even Hannah knows that her butt isn't truly safe when she mouths off once too often."

"Oh, my," Grace said, her squirm definitely more pronounced. "I'm not sure I'll ever be able to look Sammy in the eyes again. He is just so..."

"Big?" Brody offered.

"No, I mean, yes, he's big, but both of you are as well. No, it just seems that Hannah has him wrapped around her finger."

The men's laughter had her crossing her arms over her chest, looking a bit wounded.

"We're not laughing at you, babe," Quentin said. "But you've gotta admit, the image of a huge linebacker wrapped around a little finger is amusing. Besides, I promise that while Sammy has loved Hannah practically since infancy, he will tell anyone who bothers to ask that the secret to their long marriage and the reason why they are both so ridiculously happy is that he knows when to step up to the plate and take control."

"The plate? You boys do know the man played football, right?" Grace said with a grin, and then gave a squeal when Quentin easily turned her toward him and popped his palm across her rear.

"Ouch!"

"What I know is that's just a small example of what happens to sassy little girls," Quentin said, and then bent to kiss her.

A few minutes later, Quentin and Grace left, running into Laurie at the elevator. She stepped off and they let the elevator go so Quentin could talk to her.

"Brody will fill you in on what's going on, but I wanted to ask when you've got a few hours free."

"I'm pulling a double shift today, and come back in tomorrow. How long are you talking about?"

"More than an hour or two."

"Hmm, may I ask why?"

Quentin lowered his voice. "I do believe that if you'll give that just a bit of thought, young lady, you'll be able to answer your own question."

He saw the acknowledgement bloom in her eyes. "Oh, um..." He watched as she gave a pointed look to where his and Grace's fingers were entwined and saw the smile appear on her lips.

"So not going to matter," he said, effectively cutting off any thought of leniency simply because she might have been right about her belief the two would enjoy each other's company.

"That's not really fair," she said, despite his assurance.

"Oh, honey, when have you ever known a Dom to be concerned about fairness, especially when it comes to reminding naughty girls that ugly words have no place coming out of their mouths?" He let her stew a moment longer, very aware of Grace's slight shifting of her feet, as if remembering she'd spewed a few of those words herself.

"However, since I can understand the reasoning for your lapse in judgment, perhaps I can be enticed to deliver the required strokes with an implement of your choice," he added.

Her eyes lit up and she practically bounced on her toes. "The flogger? Oh, Quentin, thank you!"

He chuckled and shook his head. "God help me. How am I supposed to deliver a proper lesson if you are so thrilled to be receiving it?"

She shrugged, her smile never dimming. "How should I know, sir, I'm just a good little submissive."

Grace giggled and he grinned. "In that case, I guess it will be up to a Dom to answer that question, now won't it?"

He pushed the button and Laurie took the chance to escape. Once in the elevator, he looked down at Grace. "You, however, have no time constraints that I'm aware of."

"Oh, um..."

"Watch it, sugar. Subs who fib find the amount of strokes increased."

"In that case, sir, I'm ready whenever you are."

QUENTIN WAS OBVIOUSLY in no hurry, or believed that having to stew over the upcoming event would serve to keep a naughty sub's mind focused. He was right. It took until she was seated in a booth at a hole in the wall restaurant for her to change the course of her thoughts.

"You let Laurie choose the implement, that's not normal, is it?"

"No, so if you're thinking along the same lines, don't."

"Oh, I actually wasn't," she confessed, wondering why she hadn't. "I just wonder if that means that you've talked to Brody about my request."

"It does, and he's on board. I didn't give him the

full picture, as I wasn't sure if you intended to fill him in on the final product."

"No, I'd love for the painting to be a surprise. I'm not sure how I'm going to explain my presence."

"I don't think you need worry about that. Laurie is a bit of an exhibitionist and will probably be pleased to think she is simply enhancing your lessons in submission... or should I say continues to." She wondered at his grin until he continued, "You seriously didn't expect me to believe you could perform perfectly the second night of class when you were wobbling all over the place before."

"Oh," she said and then grinned back. "Instead of considering it as cheating, I decided to think of it as being a proactive student who is dedicated to her education."

"That sounds suspiciously like something Laurie would say, leaving out that entire cheating part."

"You know her well, don't you?"

"I know her well enough to know that she has this wonderful ability to twist things around so that you at least give the situation a bit more thought." He smiled. "I'm also a man who definitely approves of dedication, and yours was apparent the moment you opened the door that first night. I must say, seeing you wearing heels while you practiced made me proud. And, watching you move flawlessly into new positions last night... well, let's just say I definitely noticed."

"So you aren't upset?"

"No, I'm sure there will be things I'll be teaching you that Laurie has yet to even consider."

She felt her body responding simply from his tone and his words. Hell, she was open to absolutely any lesson this man offered. When the waitress placed a bowl of steaming linguine and clams in front of her, she gave the dish a puzzled look.

"What's wrong?" Quentin asked, reaching for the loaf of garlic bread as the waitress walked away.

"I guess I didn't expect there to be shells in my food. How am I supposed to eat this?"

"Here, sugar, let me show you." He plucked one of the black shells from her bowl and grinned at her. "Do you want me to demonstrate how a proper Cajun would eat, or how some delicate little wuss would?"

She couldn't help but smile. "Why, sir, since you are one of those Cajuns, I, of course, need to learn how you like to see a woman eat." Delighted with the sudden flare that sparked in his eyes, she felt her panties dampen.

"Watch it, little one," he said, not dropping his glance from hers. "I'm not sure you are quite ready to progress to the lesson on how to slide beneath a table... yet."

God, that vision alone made her nipples go rock hard and left her questioning if his cock was doing the same. Blushing, she wondered what he'd do if she decided to prove him wrong. The waitress returning to refill their tea glasses reminded her that they were in a public place. Good lord, was she wired to be an exhibitionist as well? His chuckle had her considering he was most likely pondering that same question.

"This is how we do it," he said, letting her off the hook as he took another of the shells and used it like a spoon, sliding it beneath the plump clam, detaching the flesh from its hold. He lifted the mussel to her lips and, when she opened them, he tilted the shell so that the clam slid out and onto her tongue.

After eating it, she smiled. "Wow, that's really good. I think I'm going to really enjoy playing with my food."

"Babe, I promise you aren't going to enjoy it half as much as I will." He bent to lightly kiss her and when he leaned away, she wondered what was steaming more... their meals, or the heat that she could feel flooding through her body.

When he tore off a huge hunk of bread and handed it to her before tearing off another and dipping it into the broth of his court bullion, which he'd explained was a spicy Cajun fish stew, she smiled. If they both ate the bread, generously smeared with a thick garlic layer, well, then neither would have to worry about their breath now would they?

After she'd eaten all she could, truly enjoying using a shell as a spoon, and making a show of sucking a long linguine noodle off her fork, she giggled when he said he had always loved that scene in *Lady and the Tramp* where they had shared a spaghetti dinner. Just imagining him watching a classic Disney movie had her going all soft inside. "I love all of them, but my favorite is *Beauty and the Beast.* There is just something about seeing how he could turn from such a frightening powerful beast into a gentle creature with Belle."

Quentin accepted her bowl when she stated she couldn't eat another bite. "I haven't seen that one. Maybe we can pull it up on Netflix one night." She was about to respond how much she'd like that when he continued, "If this Belle is anything like an artist I know, I'm quite anxious to see what she offered that had the power to soothe her savage beast."

"I-I'd love that," she managed, her mind definitely no longer on films.

TRUE TO HIS WORD, after lunch, Quentin took Grace to the gallery. He was rather disappointed to see that the walls that had held her paintings were empty. "Shit, I was hoping that Westing had bigger balls than letting Brooks' review make him decide to remove your art."

"Oh, no," Grace said. "My show was only for the weekend. Remember, I spent the next day helping remove what didn't sell? Charles is a wonderful man..."

"I'm flattered."

They both turned to see the gallery owner walking toward them, and Quentin's respect for the man grew when he pulled Grace into an embrace.

"Don't you let that douchebag bother you, my

dear. It's quite obvious he wrote that ridiculous piece of malice from an entirely different perspective than that of an art critic."

"Thank you, Charles," Grace said. "I just wanted to make sure that the article won't have a negative impact on you or your gallery."

Charles released his hold and smiled. "I'd be quite surprised to learn that anyone who read it isn't questioning not only his taste but his infantile behavior. It's apparent that not only was your show a success, but that you are smart enough to cut the man off at the... knees?"

Quentin chuckled and enjoyed Grace's quick giggle.

"More importantly, when are you going to have additional pieces to showcase? I know we went over the sales from the show, but since then, I've had more calls about commissioning you for both your jewelry as well as requests for photo sessions." Charles looked about, as if making sure the gallery was as empty of people as it was art before continuing. "I must admit that though I am very well aware of your talent, hearing that George Mathias wishes you to paint his wife... well, my dear, you are well on your way."

At her pleased but puzzled look, Quentin said, "Mathias is a bit of a legend in New Orleans. He can make women weep simply by playing his instruments. Hell, I've known men to tear up when he plays. George can pull emotion out of a piece of jazz like you can pull it from your art."

"It will be nice to meet another man who loves his craft," Grace said. "I'd be thrilled, Charles, but I do have another session planned with a friend of mine."

"I believe he would be willing to give you whatever time you need to do the painting as long as you don't postpone the photo session for too long."

"I'll give him a call and talk to him."

Quentin waited while Charles took Grace back to his office to get her the contact information. He grinned, wondering if there would be any way that he could go with her. Not to sit in on the photo session, but just to actually meet the man whom he really respected. He was totally unprepared when she returned and Charles said, "Grace tells me that you are quite the artist yourself, Mr. Doucet. I'd be interested in planning a show around your leather work."

Quentin gave her a look and then shook his head. "It's really more of a hobby than art, Mr. Westing."

"Don't let him fool you. His pieces are not only beautiful, they are quite, shall we say, able to evoke all sorts of emotions? That is what good art should do."

Charles nodded. "Absolutely. Anyone can go to the museum to see paintings or pottery crafted hundreds of years ago. They go to galleries to see what is being created in today's time frame. And, might I add, to be moved by works that evoke emotions that may have lain dormant for years. Just as Miss Hensley's art is both beautiful and seductive, I fully believe that an exhibit showcasing implements that can both give pain and pleasure would be highly successful. Please tell me that you will at least give it some consideration."

Quentin honestly didn't know what to say. He created his pieces because he hadn't liked the ones he'd found in other shops or on the net. He'd actually never considered them as art and yet, seeing Keith wielding the whip he'd made, he had to admit that the entire scene had been not only stimulating, it had been artistic and extremely sensual.

"Thank you, I'll give it some thought," he said and after the two men shook hands, he and Grace climbed back onto the motorcycle and returned to the house.

As they ascended the stairs, she said, "You're not upset that I shared your art with Charles, are you?"

"No," he said, not bothering to even pretend he intended to let her into her own apartment quite yet. "It was just a surprise." He unlocked his door and escorted her inside. "I am flattered that you consider my hobby anywhere near worthy."

"Quentin, it is more than worthy. I agree with everything Charles said about it being able to move people, to evoke emotions..."

"Good, because it will be quite interesting to see what sort of emotions the heat of your spanked ass can evoke when I put you on your knees between my spread ones."

He grinned when her mouth formed a little 'O' and her eyes dropped to his crotch, pleased to see that he had just given her a surprise as well.

16

WHILE BETH HAD PLAYED at being a submissive, Quentin had always wondered if she was truly following her heart, or if she was simply willing to assume a role that she knew pushed his buttons. He couldn't deny that they had shared amazing sex but when it came to discipline, she always balked, and while she did submit, he'd never felt that she wished to relinquish control to that level, reluctantly allowing him to assume a role he'd always considered he needed as part of a truly fulfilling D/s relationship even outside the confines of the club.

Though he'd never done so before, he felt the irresistible urge to do things differently with Grace. He'd seen the look in her eyes with every instruction given, every new experience, not only during class, but the way her eyes lit up with any innuendo they'd shared, and definitely with anything having to do with spanking. He'd been extremely aware of her responses at both the paddling he'd given her that first night, as well as the flogging the previous evening. This woman was either the most consummate actress he'd ever encountered, or she was a natural submissive who truly desired to allow a Dominant to control her outside either the bedroom or the club. Granted, he'd yet to have her in his bedroom, but God, he'd had her against the door and had felt her come apart in his arms, not once but three times. He'd told her he had no interest in a relationship and yet, with every moment they spent together, the mortar in the wall he'd been building for the past two years was crumbling, and he knew it would only be a matter of time before the stones began to fall from his very soul.

Holding her hand, he led her not to the sofa where they'd sat earlier, but to a corner across from it. She looked up with surprise on her face, and yet she didn't attempt to pull her hand away or even to question his intention. Instead, her eyes seemed to burn a bit brighter, and the soft flush that crept up her neck to suffuse her cheeks had his cock twitching.

"You'll stand facing the wall and contemplate your behavior. When I call for you, you'll come to me, ready to confess your transgression." He saw her tilt her head a bit and he wondered what she was thinking of his instruction, but didn't ask. They were taking steps toward something that would, if he were as lucky as he suddenly desperately wished he'd be, define their roles. Instead of speaking, he released her hand. When she immediately began to turn toward the wall, he took hold of her arm. "Not yet."

He watched her flush turn darker as he unsnapped her jeans and could see her breathing quicken when he lowered the zipper. "Naughty girls who deserve to be punished think better with their bare bottoms on display." His words were demonstrated as he began to pull her jeans down to her knees. Another twitch of his cock proved how arousing he found it when she drew in a breath and held it as he hooked his fingers into the waistband of her panties. They reached her knees as well, though at a much slower rate. There was just something about baring a woman for punishment that made his own breathing quicken and, at the scent of her arousal, his cock going to full attention.

Once he was sure she was very aware that he'd noticed not only the damp gusset of her panties, but had inhaled her scent, he moved a step away. "Nose to the wall and keep your hands locked behind you."

"O-okay," she murmured.

"That's yes, sir, Daddy," he corrected.

Her eyes widened and he briefly wondered if his did as well. The word wasn't one he'd expected to slip free, but now that it had, he wasn't about to pull it back. Still, he kept his eyes locked on hers, watching as her cheeks flushed and her mouth opened, closed, and then opened again. "Yes, sir, Daddy," she parroted, but it took him twirling his finger for her to remember what he'd instructed her to do. She took the step past him that was necessary to reach the corner. Though not in heels, she still shuffled a bit, her clothing at her knees restricting her stride. Once her nose was touching the juncture of the wall, he reached out and patted her bare bottom, loving her little gasp of surprise.

"That's my good girl."

Oh my God! I called him Daddy, Grace thought to herself as she closed her eyes. Not to shut out the paint on the walls, but to attempt to get herself under control. She'd read about 'corner time' in countless erotic stories but had never considered that men in today's age actually still voiced the order. Upon arriving upstairs, she'd felt her sex moistening when she'd realized their destination, and felt it threatening to flood her underwear when he'd unsnapped her jeans. And, oh sweet lord, the look in his eyes when he ran his fingertips over the damp gusset of her new pink bikini panties before actually inhaling what she knew without a doubt had to be the scent of her arousal, had her trembling. But his instruction to call him Daddy... now that almost had her coming without so much as a single touch. How could a word have every cell in her body quivering? Hell, how could standing half-naked, nose to the wall, make her feel both like the naughty little girl he'd called her and yet be so incredibly sexy at the same time?

"Grace, hands behind your back."

"Oh!" She quickly moved her hands to her back, only to feel him guide them so that each palm cupped an elbow. When she felt her jeans begin to slide, she was about to panic when he gave another soft order.

"Legs apart far enough to keep your clothing in place. Stand up straight and push your naughty little ass out."

She did so, feeling heat move through her body as she wondered what he was thinking about... well, the view. Were his eyes that delicious smoky gray color they'd been when he plunged into her the night before? Feeling another dribble of her own cream, she forced herself from that memory. A girl was probably not put into the corner to think about how wonderful it felt being filled by this man. When she heard a chuckle, and a slightly harder pat landed on her left buttock, she didn't have to be verbally reminded why she'd been put nose to the wall. Still, it wasn't until he moved away that she turned her mind to considering her behavior. It took effort to stifle the giggle that threatened to erupt when she wondered what his reaction would be if she turned around and stated that whatever it had been, it was worth it because, hand to God, she'd never been more aroused.

Honestly, why on earth would those girls in the pages of her books complain about corner time? When she heard Quentin's voice, it seemed as if she'd only been standing a few seconds, every one of those spent thinking about how arousing it was to be nose to wall, bare butt displayed to the room. Turning to obey his order to 'come to me,' she did give those girls a bit of credit, as walking with her clothing basically hobbling her steps, she felt a bit of embarrassment for the first time since they'd come down. It seemed to take longer to reach the sofa than the time spent facing the wall. When he spread his knees, she automatically stepped between them. Even with him seated and her standing, he seemed to loom over her, and yet she didn't feel even a modicum of unease. Well, not until he spoke.

"Tell me why I'm going to spank you."

Seriously? Evidently, just like corner time, men actually did ask that question and really, what sort of question was it? Then again, just hearing it had made her stomach do a somersault. Okay, it was a question that made a girl feel even naughtier.

"I used naughty words?" Oh, geeze Louise, what adult used that phrase instead of simply stating "I cussed?"

"That's right. You said several naughty words."

His repeating the phrase and another somersault had her realizing that there was far more power in what she now considered 'spanking foreplay' than she'd ever imagined.

"You are an adult, young lady, and an educated one. There is no need for you to lower yourself by using vulgar words, is there?"

She opened her mouth to ask if the *fuck me* she'd uttered last night counted toward that vulgarity but managed to catch herself. She also briefly wondered who spanked him when he uttered such words but decided that was not only a ridiculous question, but one he'd consider a moot point, as he was definitely the one in charge. It would surely behoove her to take the safest path, right?

"Um, no, sir."

Gray eyes remained locked on hers as his right brow lifted. "Excuse me?"

"What?" Grace said then instantly remembered his earlier instruction. "I meant, no, sir, Daddy."

"That's better and is also correct. I'm going to spank your little bottom so that the next time you feel the desire to spew out filth, you'll remember that there are consequences for doing so."

"Y-yes, sir, I'm sorry, Daddy."

"This is where I could state that you *will* be sorry, but I believe actions speak louder than words." She gave a startled squeak as he reached for her arm and guided her down over one knee. Her face was pressed against the cushion next to where he was sitting, her feet remaining on the floor behind her.

Her hands had come from her elbows as she'd been pulled down, and her breath hitched when she realized that she had been positioned not so she was lying over his thigh, but so that his leg was between hers, her pussy basically riding his knee. He took both wrists in one of his hands, pinning them to her lower back. When his free leg crossed both of hers, instead of feeling trapped, she felt secure... as if he were making sure that she would be safe, that she wouldn't feel the need to flail about, that she was... well, protected. That feeling increased as his hand began to rub across her ass.

"I realize that you still have class tonight, but that

said, I am not one to be lax in making sure that you receive what you need at all times. In other words, Grace, though you will be removing all of your clothing in class this evening, I am not concerned that doing so might reveal that you've been a naughty girl. After all, who's fault is it that you got your ass spanked?"

She'd not given any thought to what the evening held since he'd entered her apartment that morning. Did she care that the other women might see her red rear and wonder what she'd done to deserve a spanking? Quite pleased that the answer that instantly popped into her mind was 'not particularly', when another popped in immediately after, she had to fight the urge to ask exactly how hard he was planning on spanking her. It took her a moment to understand that it didn't matter. She'd offered herself and relinquished control of the situation the moment she'd addressed him as Daddy and turned to face the wall. She bit back a grin thinking he now had two roles. He was the Daddy when he disciplined her. He was the Dom when they played. And she... well, she was the happy and naughty submissive.

"It's my fault, Daddy."

"Yes, it is." His hand lifted and the spanking began. Yes, she'd been over his lap before, and yet from the first swat, she wondered if she'd ever become accustomed to it. Her breath caught and though her bottom was no longer tender from that first time, it quickly became clear that it would be by the time he released her. And forget trying to guess the amount of strokes. When the count passed the six he'd given her with his palm that first time, and then passed the dozen he'd considered proper to demonstrate how a punishment spanking felt, she was squirming and attempting to pull herself forward only to discover there was absolutely nowhere to go.

"Ow, please... ow, I'm sorry!" she wailed, only to feel two swats delivered with uncanny precision to each of her nates. Two more quickly followed and with each crack of his palm, her ass burned hotter until she was soon a writhing mass of contrition.

"What happens to naughty girls?" he asked, swatting her again.

"They get punished!" she yelped.

"Excuse me?" Two more cracks sounded before she could grasp her error.

"They get punished, Sir Daddy!"

He actually chuckled before saying, "That's really cute, but I've not yet been knighted by the queen. When being disciplined, Daddy will suffice. Understood?"

Funny that despite a hot ass, she instantly nodded. "Yes, Daddy."

"Then let's continue. Tell me, sugar, how do naughty girls get punished?"

"They get spanked, Daddy."

"That's right. Naughty girls get their bottoms spanked until they are nice and red and hot." She didn't know how red her butt was but was sure if it got any hotter, she was going to spontaneously combust.

"Please! I won't ever cuss again!" Her promise earned her nothing more than the feel of his leg lifting and her torso being pressed at a more acute angle onto the couch cushion.

She understood the change in position the moment he popped his hand against her ass.

"Owww!" Her head arched back as those two landed on that poor, untouched, and obviously extremely sensitive area where her cheeks met her thighs. "I'll be good, I swear!"

"You are good," he informed her, and yet two more strokes caused her to buck. "You were naughty, but you are a very good girl. And, young lady, after this spanking, I think you will be a very good, sweet talking girl for a nice long while. What do you think?"

"Yes, Daddy, I will. I have learned my lesson!"

"Not yet, but I do believe you are learning it." With that, his hand began to fly at a pace she wouldn't have believed possible. There were no longer individual cracks; it was as if one of those tommy-guns she'd seen in old Western movies was discharging in the room, every round hitting the target of her blistered ass. She had teared up in class, but with this barrage, she burst into tears and went totally limp.

"That's my good girl. You submitting to your spanking tells me that you are also submitting to the needed lesson. Just a few more."

They were delivered while she continued to cry, and when he pulled her up, sitting her burning bottom on his denim covered thigh, she felt not only very well punished, she felt cared for. Burying her head in his neck, she sobbed and then surprised herself when she choked out a rather strangled, "I'm real-really so-sor-sorry. Thank you for-for spank-spanking m-me."

"You're welcome, honey."

He held her until her sobs quieted, replaced with a few sniffles, and when she hiccupped, he held her as he bent forward and reached for something on the coffee table. She tensed for a moment, the thought that he might be reaching for an implement making her breath catch. When he sat back and sat her up, pressing a tissue to her nose, she didn't know whether to be embarrassed because her sobs had caused her face to be all wet and evidently snotty, or to be eternally grateful that he wasn't about to tip her back across his knee. Deciding to be grateful, she allowed him to help her clear her nose and felt a surge of arousal when he bent to kiss the tip of her nose after doing so. It was only when he moved to help her off his lap that she saw the wet spot on his jeans. Oh dear lord, forget the kiss, evidently the entire spanking had caused her juices to flow so copiously that he'd know without even having to look between her thighs.

"Like I said, you are a very good girl," he said, causing her face to heat as he gave a pointed look to his leg where she'd been perched before giving her a grin. He turned her from him, patted her butt, which caused her to yelp, and said, "Back to the corner. Remember, stick that beautiful red ass well out."

"Ye-yes, Daddy," she managed, though she'd never

know how. This time when her nose hit the sheetrock, she discovered that not only did men in today's world give real spankings like those in her books, Quentin delivered ones that made far more than her bottom burn.

GOD, *she is absolutely perfect*, Quentin thought as he watched her from across the room. Unplanned as it had been, he'd taken a chance, revealed a desire he'd not even shared with Beth, and was rewarded far more than he'd ever felt possible. Grace's obedience was freely given without a hint of falseness. Her acceptance of his wish to be addressed as Daddy, a gift he most humbly received. If looking at the red globes of her heart-shaped ass wasn't enough, running his fingertips over the large wet spot on his jeans was all that was required to have his cock throbbing. What had his fingers stilling and his heart skipping a beat was the realization that though he'd spanked a hundred bottoms, had seen every shape and size, heard every possible variety of cry or plea, not a single one had affected him as Grace just had. Forget not wishing to become involved. It was far too fucking late for that. He did give a little grin thinking that if she'd just said that word, scarlet rear or not, she'd be right back over his knee. Then again, he would certainly enjoy that. But, for right now, he had plans on enjoying something even more.

"All right, sugar. Come here."

She turned and once more hobbled back to him. Perhaps the next time, he'd pull her clothing totally off. But he couldn't deny she made a precious sight with her jeans and panties at her knees. Still, when she reached him, he did bend forward to pull her clothing to her feet, and she automatically lifted first one foot and then the other. Setting her clothes aside, he didn't speak. He simply spread his legs apart and gave her a silent hand signal. He waited until she was kneeling, her legs spread wide, her hands on her thighs, her head up but her eyes lowered. He watched her face as he unzipped his jeans, taking his time, and seeing the acknowledgement of his action when she tucked her lower lip between her teeth. Freeing his cock, he fisted it in his palm, stroking its length until he was as hard as a rod of steel.

Keeping one fist wrapped around his shaft, he reached for her with the other. Caressing her cheek with his fingertips, he said, "Eyes to me." When they lifted, he felt his cock jerk in his hand seeing the desire reflected in the emerald depths. He ran his fingertip over her lips, gently disengaging her bottom lip from her teeth. "Beautiful," he murmured, loving the fact that her eyes never once attempted to drift from his. "Open."

She obeyed, her lips parting. "Good girl." He moved his hand to the back of her head, drawing her forward. "Keep your eyes on me." He paused and then issued a one-word command. "Suck."

The moment her lips closed around the head of his cock, he felt his world shift. For the first time in as long as he could remember, he wondered at his control, fearing he might reach his end long before he desired. The silk of her tongue as it licked across the surface of his cock and then dipped into the tiny slit had him praying that he didn't embarrass himself by coming within mere seconds of her attention. She didn't just suckle the fluid of his pre-cum, she seemed to savor it, the sound of the soft moan she gave vibrating around his cock, causing it to jerk yet again. When her hand lifted, he removed his own, allowing her to take his erection in her fist where she began to squeeze gently, her fingers lifting individually to massage and press as she took more of his length into her mouth. When she took enough that he could feel the tightness at the back of her throat, he prepared for her to pull away, and yet she continued to surprise him when, instead, she took a deep breath and then moved lower, allowing him into the confines of her throat.

Good God almighty, he wasn't going to last much longer. She was magnificent in her control, her focus completely centered on his pleasure, on obeying her Dominant. At that thought, he felt his balls tighten. Any doubt, any hesitancy he had, evaporated. He wanted nothing more than to be exactly that, *her* Dom. Before he could spill inside her throat, he pulled back and then bent forward, lifting her from her knees and holding her above his lap. "Spread your pussy lips," he said, his voice husky. Seeing her hands move to spread the outer labia of her sex open was incredibly hot, and watching her fingers come away glistening with the proof of her readiness to receive him, fulfilled every fantasy he'd ever had.

"Good girl, now put my cock inside." She obeyed and then broke eye contact for the first time since they had begun as her head arched back and she moaned as he began to lower her onto his shaft.

"Oh, God, yes," she groaned, reaching for his shoulders, her face showing that she was experiencing both discomfort and pleasure as he continued to lower her until every inch of his impressive length was buried inside the heaven that was her pussy.

He released her, leaving her in place, loving her soft whimper that protested being still, signaling that she wanted to move, to feel him thrusting. It took him but a moment to strip her t-shirt over her head and to unhook and toss her bra aside. The sound of her protest changed as he bent forward and ran his tongue across first one peaked bud and then the other. Her back arched as she attempted to press more of her breast into his mouth, her fingers tightening on his shoulders when he gave her nipple a bite.

Her soft moan of pleasure changed into the most delicious gasp when his fingers moved to her sex. Taking a few of the auburn curls between his finger and thumb, he gave them a sharp tug as he gave her other nipple a bite. She arched, unseating herself for the bare inch she could before realizing that by doing so, the tug became more intense.

"Oh, God," she moaned, her head dropping to his shoulder.

"Color?" he asked, relaxing the pull and yet not releasing the curls.

"Wha... what?"

"Green for good, yellow for..."

"Green, definitely green."

"That's my girl," he said, returning his lips to the delectable treat that was her swollen peak of raspberry-colored nipple. He continued to twist, tug, and pull until she was breathing hard, little gasps that had his cock demanding that he move. Releasing her pubic curls, he slid his hand lower and felt the stretch of her lips that accepting his cock's girth required. Her clitoris was easily found, and the moment he rubbed his fingers over it, she whimpered and pushed down against them. A single nip of the slippery bud was all it took before he felt her tense and then shudder with her climax. He could feel her cream flooding around his cock, and with the knowledge that she'd found her pleasure, he began to thrust up into her, now ready to seek his own. It was only when he felt her walls gripping him that he realized he'd forgotten to don a condom. Shit! He'd made it a fucking point in the class that condoms were required for penetration. When he gritted his teeth and began to lift her off, she whimpered.

"No, oh, God, please don't stop."

"Just for a minute, baby. I need a condom."

"I'm on the pill, please—"

"Grace..."

"Please, Quentin, I want to feel you and only you inside me."

Her assurance and her plea had him lost, and the tightening of her muscles as they attempted to keep him seated made the decision far too easy. Pulling her back down, he began to move harder and faster up into her. Her breasts bounced with each thrust, but he wanted to watch her face as she came. And when she did, her eyes wide and her mouth open with her cry of bliss, he erupted into her with his own bellow. When she collapsed against him, her cheek pressed to his shoulder, her hand moving to rest against his chest, he wrapped his arms around her and laid his cheek on the top of her head, realizing that he was in absolutely no rush to move.

17

GRACE AWAKENED to find herself enveloped in Quentin's arms, his head laid back against the couch and her head on his shoulder. It was a heavenly feeling until she realized that the light from the window appeared far dimmer than afternoon sunlight would provide. It was her squirming and twisting to see if there was a clock within sight that had him stirring. Of course, it wasn't his entire body that was twitching. It was his cock, which was still buried inside her. Forget the time, this was something that had her nipples puckering and her sex moistening as he continued to harden inside her.

"Hey," he said, his eyes opening to reveal that smoky gray color she so loved to see.

"Hey," she said with a grin, leaning forward a bit to kiss him lightly. "I've heard of morning wood, but this gives that an entirely new definition."

She squealed when his hand cupped her ass and gave it a squeeze, the flesh still tender from her spanking. However, when he lifted her off his cock, she barely stopped herself from reaching for it, as if to tuck him back inside. He chuckled and then stood before turning around and releasing her carefully so that she wound up bent over the arm of the couch.

"Spread your legs," he said.

Her nipples tightened and her sex convulsed at the tone in his voice, as if there was no question that she would obey. She spread her feet apart, not caring at the image she made—only anxious to have him back inside her. The head of his cock nudged at her opening and yet, when she felt something thrust inside, she knew that it couldn't possibly be his cock. Confusion clouded her mind until she felt him spreading the globes of her buttocks apart. As he withdrew from her pussy, she understood instantly that he'd lubricated a finger in her juices and that finger was now pressing against her anus.

"Ever had a cock in your ass?"

"N-no, I've never had anything in my ass, sir."

"Ah, then very soon, you'll have a new definition of what it feels like to be completely filled."

"I-I don't think... oh my God," she half yelped and half gasped as she felt his finger pushing into a place she'd never truly considering being breached.

"Easy," he said, slipping his cock into her pussy just the tiniest bit but enough to have her instantly wanting more.

"Please..."

"You've got safewords, but I'm hoping you'll trust

me enough to allow yourself to experience something new."

His finger slid in another inch, followed by his cock pressing forward into her sheath. "I-I do trust you, but—"

"No buts, sugar. I'm not saying you're ready today, just that someday soon, I'll be fucking your ass."

She moaned, her face heating at both the taboo of anal sex and the fact that he hadn't said he'd be asking if he could, he'd been *stating* that he would. The absolute certainty that he meant exactly what he said affected not only her body but her very soul.

"Relax. Don't clench. Let me show you the pleasure you aren't even aware your body can give you."

Submitting meant obeying, something she had craved to offer a Dominant. Learning positions and being spanked were one thing. This man, this man she wanted to give far more than just her heart to, was asking for her absolute submission. Taking a deep breath, she forced herself to relax, allowing her body to press down onto the support of the couch's arm, and mentally and emotionally allowing herself to accept the support of his experience.

"Good girl," he said, sliding yet further into both orifices. "Just feel."

Considering it an order, she did so, and when he began to slowly thrust, his finger matching the strokes of his cock, she felt a blooming of pleasure she'd never expected. After several repetitions, she even whimpered a bit at the loss when his finger left her ass, only to gasp when the pressure of reentry was greater than it had been at first.

"Quentin..." she moaned.

"Color?"

"Um... um..." Her mind didn't seem able to keep up with her body, as she couldn't seem to decide if what she was feeling was pain or pleasure. It wasn't until he'd breached her anus' ring of muscles to sink what had to be two fingers inside that she answered, "Green... greenish-yellow." His chuckle had her blushing, but his actions had her hips pushing back in an unconscious attempt to seat his cock and digits as deeply as they would go. When he began again, his rhythm faster, his thrusts harder, she gave herself to him completely. With her submission, it wasn't long before she felt herself spiraling toward climax.

"Oh, God... oh, I'm-I'm going to come!"

"Come for me, Grace. I want to feel your ass grip my fingers and your cunt convulse around my cock." The sharp slap that landed on first one cheek and then the other, combined with his commands and his dual fucking, soon had her arching her back and her screams of pure pleasure filling the room. "God, you are incredible," he said, his movements stilling, and she imagined he was enjoying the very things he had demanded of her as she could feel her muscles spasming around him. She'd barely started to come down from her climax when he popped his fingers from her dark passage and grabbed her hips, pulling her up in order to pound into her with a force that had her seeing stars and climbing yet again the mountain from which she'd just taken flight.

He came only a second before she did, each calling out the other's name. She could feel his cock continuing to jerk as it emptied. His weight settled onto her as he bent to kiss her neck and his breath wafted into the shell of her ear as he whispered, "Someday very, very soon."

His promise no longer frightened her, even though she could swear she felt her anus twitch at his words. Turning her head up to allow him access to that sensitive area right beneath her ear, she whispered the only answer that she could give with honesty. "Yes, sir."

THE RINGING of Quentin's phone was the only thing that had him lifting his body from hers. It was a ringtone that he'd assigned to Brody. Pulling his phone from his pocket, he accepted the call.

"This better be fucking important."

"Sorry, I just wanted to catch you before you start class. I think I finally—"

"Wait... oh fuck! Hang on!" He pulled Grace up from the couch, her muffled protest informing him that she had come quite close to falling asleep again.

"Sugar, wake up," he said, looking at the time on his phone before tossing it onto the couch and pulling her to face him. "We've got to get to class."

"Class?"

"Grace... shit," Shaking his head, he gave one quick swat to her bottom that had her eyes going wide.

"Hey, I didn't cuss, you did!"

"Sorry, but we're late. Class starts in fifteen minutes."

That got her attention even more than that single swat. "Oh God, I've got to dress... oh, I've got to shower and change..." When she bent to reach for her clothes, he took her arm.

"No, you don't have time to dress, undress, shower, and dress again. You've got no more than ten minutes to be ready to go." He took a second to tuck his cock back into his jeans before swinging her up into his arms and going to the door.

"Quentin, I'm naked!" she protested.

"I'm very well aware of that fact," he quipped, giving her bare ass a pat before stepping into the hall and carrying her to the other side. Unlocking her door, he set her on her feet. "I'll be back in ten... make that nine minutes. Go!" He watched as she turned and fled across the room, taking a few precious moments to simply enjoy the view. Closing her door, he went back to his own apartment to get ready. It was only when he bent to toss her clothing onto the couch that he remembered the phone. *Jesus!*

"Okay, I'm back but make it fast."

"My, my, that was very—" Brody began.

"I swear, if you say one more word..."

"Easy, boy. I'm thrilled. Well, I am about you and

Grace. Not so thrilled to learn that we are both idiots."

Pressing the speaker button, Quentin set the phone on the bathroom counter as he peeled out of his clothes. "You've got one minute, then I'm hanging up."

"Okay, based on Grace identifying Brooks, I went back over the names of guests who were at the club that night, and discovered that while there wasn't a David Brooks, there was a Brooks Davidson. What are the chances that it's not the same person?"

"About zero," Quentin said, turning on the taps in the shower. "Son of a bitch. So even without a good photo, we now know the little weasel was there. I'll get with Jason after class and tell him—"

"I already did," Brody said. "He was going to go interview him in a little while. He said he'd come by the hospital tonight and I wanted to tell you so..."

"I'll be there," Quentin said. "I can leave class early if I have to but, fuck, I've really got to go. Good job, Brody."

"Go on, we'll talk later. At least you're not a total idiot—and, Quentin, I'm happy for you—give Grace my love as well."

"Thanks, I will." Quentin ended the call and stepped into the stall to take the fastest shower in history. He half expected to discover Grace begging for more time when he heard the click of the door opening before he reached it.

"Wow, you look amazing." She was wearing a black skirt and a white peasant blouse with lace around the scooped neckline and sleeves. Her heels were black, her stockings white. He immediately began to wonder what else lay beneath her clothing. When he dragged his eyes back to hers, it was to see them sparkling as she tossed her hair, which now lay in waves down her back. Forget being late for class, he suddenly wished she would state that she didn't feel the need to attend anymore. After all, she now had a Dom who was more than willing to give her quite personal lessons in anything she wished to know, and a daddy who'd tan her ass when she didn't take those lessons seriously. However, since she had indeed dressed to kill, he knew she had no intention of missing out on tonight's experience. Shit, he might need to rethink the agenda, as he didn't wish for another man to lay so much as a finger on her.

"Thank you, and may I say you look pretty amazing yourself, Master Quentin."

Damn the time. He bent to kiss her, taking her mouth hard until her arms wrapped around his neck, her lips opening to his demand for entrance and her body melting into his. By the time he pulled away, she was flushed and breathing hard. Satisfied that he'd taken yet another step toward staking his claim, he led her to the elevator.

"You go on down. I'll take the stairs." Before she could protest, the elevator arrived, and with a swat to her bottom that had her giving a little yelp, he encouraged her to step inside. "See you in just a few, sugar." When the doors closed, he adjusted his stiffening cock in his pants and then tromped down the stairs.

***

"HOLY SHIT, whatever model of *special friend* you have, I definitely want one," Gretchen said when Grace walked into the dining room. "My favorite toy must be definitely out of fashion or need stronger batteries."

Grace was about to play innocent when Starla spoke from one table away. "Don't be stupid, Gretchen. Anyone can tell that no piece of plastic, no matter how big or how powerful the vibration, put that smile on her face. Hell, *I'll* put a smile on your face if her friend was not only flesh and blood, but one I'm sure will be walking into the room any moment."

Not sure who was more shocked at Starla's audacity, she or Gretchen, Grace never got a chance to say a word before the door opened and the instructors entered. The only thought she had as all the women rose to their feet and assumed the position of attention was that at least all four men had entered together. Perhaps that would at least give Starla only a twenty-five percent chance of being correct.

Her eyes automatically went to Quentin. Gone was the little grin that always had her body responding. Gone was the soft gray color in his eyes. She couldn't help but notice that his jaw was tense, and looking at the other men, saw the same expression mirrored on Master Conner's face. The other two men seemed to be as calm as they always appeared, so whatever had transpired before the men walked into the room, it obviously concerned only Quentin and Conner.

"Good evening, ladies," Quentin said, turning from the other instructors and facing his pupils. "I am proud to see that most of you have returned. Two of your classmates have dropped out, which is unfortunate, but as we continue, there might be a few of you deciding to leave before Friday night." He instructed the women to come stand in a line and it was then that Grace realized that there were only seven women remaining. Not seeing Penny had her a little disappointed. From the little amount of conversation they'd shared, she'd not only known she'd enjoy getting to know the woman better, she had thought Penny was completely on board with what the class required of her. She didn't really know who else had chosen to leave but wondered how their departure would affect the rest of them. It wasn't long before she discovered the answer.

"Please kneel," Quentin instructed, and the line sank to the service position, far more gracefully than they had on that first evening. "Last night was but the first step in experiencing the actual reality of the interaction between a Dominant and a submissive. I understand that you might consider it an intense experience, but I assure you, from this point forward, every night will become even more so. Remember, you are free to leave at any time without censure or judgment. Giving yourself as a submissive takes a great deal of courage and requires placing trust in a Dominant.

"Before we go upstairs, let me explain what is on the agenda. You will be taught a new position and practice it here, though once in the club, you'll be required to remove your clothing." He paused and instructed all eyes to him. Only then did he continue. "All of your clothing. As you witnessed last evening, submissives dress in various attire. Some are totally nude, some are in lingerie, some are in body jewelry, some begin in clothing that is removed throughout the evening. I am not stating that you will always be completely naked within *Plaisir* or any other club where you might go to play. But it is imperative that you discover your comfort level now before you are in a situation where you don't have the safety or security that the classroom environment gives you."

He paused again and when he next spoke, Grace's question was answered.

"Even without our numbers dwindling, tonight is the point in our agenda where we switch it up a bit." Grace wondered if he was aware of the slight shuffling of bodies as his words became clear. As he continued, she realized that there was probably very little that he missed.

"As we discussed the very first evening, unless you are in a committed relationship with a single Dom, you can expect to be approached by number of Dominants on any given evening. It is just as important to become comfortable with that possibility as it is to become comfortable with your nakedness. Are there any questions?"

"What if we don't want to... I mean, what if someone wants us to do something that we aren't willing to do?"

"Miss Alton, let me assure you, it will always be your choice in a club environment. You are offering the gift of your submission when you play and, ladies, you must be comfortable with the person receiving that submission even if only for a short period of time. If you are not, for any reason, then by all means decline the invitation. And remember, the stoplight system is always in place. Even after you submit to a Dom, if you become uncomfortable, I'd hope you first attempt to communicate with your partner and resolve the issue. If it still is a problem, then, ladies, use the safewords. Does everyone remember what they are?"

A chorus of "Yes, sir," gave him the answer.

"Very good. From this point forward, my role will change."

Grace's pulse rate changed with that announcement. What exactly did that mean? She'd vaguely heard part of the phone conversation he'd had with Brody, even though she'd been almost comatose from the pleasure he'd given her. Was he leaving?

"Instead of giving individual instruction to a few, I will be moving among all of you as your lessons continue."

Okay, though she wasn't pleased to hear that, she

had to admit it was far better than thinking he was simply going to turn her over to another without at least being present. She didn't like her next thought as her head warred with her heart. Yes, they'd shared intensely intimate moments, several times, in fact. She'd not only addressed him as Daddy, she'd seen the pleasure in his eyes when she'd done so, but that didn't mean she should expect any special attention.

Daddy or Sir doesn't matter. The only relationship he's interested in is the one where you address him as Master... in this class. He doesn't make love, remember? He fucks. Telling that voice to shut the hell up, she almost smiled. Did cussing in your head count as being a naughty girl? Would he spank her for doing so? Or, she supposed, if she was nothing more than a convenient submissive who happened to be available not only in class but, shit, lived just down the hall, than his lecture on the consequences of cussing was really nothing more than rhetoric.

"Grace!" The sound of her name barely registered through her thoughts, and only when it was repeated did she realize it came not from the front of the room but from her side. It took another second for her to see that the line of women was no longer. Those not already out the door, were heading for it.

"Are you all right?" Gretchen asked.

"Oh... um, I'm fine. Just a little tired. Where is everyone going?"

"Master Quentin dismissed us to use the restroom before we learn the new position. I guess he didn't want anyone's bladder to be an excuse not to strip."

"I guess not," Grace said, following her friend to the door. Looking back, she saw that Quentin was looking toward her, and though her legs felt wobbly for the first time in days, she knew she couldn't blame it on her heels. No, she knew the exact source as she felt her heart ache, wondering how she'd managed to fall in love with a man who could have fulfilled her every desire if perhaps she'd met him before tragedy tore his heart apart. Still, her inability to keep this as just a fling wasn't his fault, and at the quirk of his eyebrow, his silent question as to her state, she managed to give him a small smile before leaving the room. Gretchen was waiting in the hall.

"You're not fine," she said quietly. "I didn't mean to offend you earlier. You just looked so, well, so freaking happy."

"You didn't offend me," Grace said, reaching out to give Gretchen a hug. "I am fine—it's just that, well, I'm wondering if I've really got it within me to be a submissive."

"Oh, please don't tell me you are going to quit. I-I count you as a friend and..." Gretchen paused as a couple of women passed them on the way back to class. Taking Grace's hand, she pulled her a bit further down the hall. "Listen, I don't give a shit what that Starla says. She is just jealous. Anyone with eyes can tell that you and Master Quentin have got some kind of connection." She didn't give Grace a chance to either confirm or deny. "It isn't anyone's business but for the two of you, but Grace, I've watched you every night. You are definitely a submissive."

"But what if I'm a woman who only wishes to submit to one person? I mean, that's not what I had intended when I started these classes, but..." Taking a deep breath, Grace again remembered that night at her door after her show when Quentin had offered to take her upstairs. No man who was interested in having her as his own sub, who wanted a committed relationship, would have made that offer—not if he didn't even care who scratched her itch. And yet, she honestly couldn't believe that what they had shared today, not just the amazing sex, but everything, had meant nothing. God, she was just so conflicted. Straightening, she shook her head. "You know what? It's not Quentin's fault. I practically threw myself at him and can't expect... well, I'm not going to ever know how I really feel for sure unless I continue."

Gretchen gave an excited squeal but then instantly calmed. "I won't deny that I'm glad you aren't quitting but, well, that's just the greedy part of me. I hope we can still be friends if it becomes clear to you that this isn't what you need or want."

Grace smiled. "I'd like that."

"Good, then we shall be," Gretchen said, her smile showing her sincerity. "And, well, since we'll be such good friends, perhaps you'll show me some of the fabulous jewelry you made."

"I'll not only show you, I'll make you something, if you want."

"Are you kidding me! Oh, God, that would be wonderful."

"Ladies, do you plan on rejoining your classmates, or are you quitting?"

Both women snapped their heads around to see Master Quentin standing just a few feet away. Grace wondered how long he'd been standing there but his expression gave nothing away.

"Sorry, sir," Gretchen said, reaching out to give Grace's hand a squeeze before moving back toward the class.

"Miss Kennedy?"

Quentin's voice had her stopping. "Yes, sir?"

"Would you please inform Master Trent that I will be a few minutes?"

"Yes, sir!" she said, her tone announcing that she would be delighted to do so. With a glance back at Grace, she smiled and then was soon out of sight.

18

"I-I'M GOING TO BE LATE," Grace said, though she didn't take a single step.

"Sugar, you are already late," Quentin said, approaching her until he was able to take her into his arms. He had been watching her since the moment he'd entered the room, and had seen the flush appear in her cheeks when he'd announced they'd be learning a new position and would be removing every stitch of their clothing. Her green eyes had shimmered and he'd known that, despite having climaxed several times in the past few hours, she was already becoming aroused at the thought. However, he'd watched the light dim in her emerald eyes when he'd made his last announcement.

After speaking to his staff, he'd followed the women out of the room and seen the two involved in what appeared to be an almost desperate conversation. Every instinct had told him that he was the cause of the trembling of Grace's body, which he could see even from several feet away. He hadn't heard every word, but he'd heard enough. Shit, how could he have not spoken to her before? Instead of sinking into her when he'd bent her over the couch's arm, he should have spent that time discussing how he felt. Then... well, even though they'd lost track of the time, he was the fucking lead instructor. Every woman in class would have waited, most likely chatting amongst themselves until he arrived. Instead, Grace had gone from bliss to what appeared to be the deepest abyss possible within what, ten fucking minutes?

"Grace, I was an idiot..."

"No!" she said, attempting to push away. "This is all my fault. You told me, and I... I swear, I tried not to, but... shit!" She wiped at her eyes and then yelped when his hand landed on her ass.

"Seems like my girl forgets her promises fairly quickly," he said, "or perhaps Daddy didn't give her bottom enough of a burn to impress the fact that cussing will cause her to be spanked."

He watched as the light in her eyes returned and then watched as it began to instantly dim.

"Don't. I can't—"

Quentin didn't give her a chance to state what she couldn't do. All he wanted was to tell her what he could do. What he had already done.

"Grace, forgive me. I never meant..." When she attempted to pull away again, he realized he was making an even bigger mess. Enough with this shit. Keeping hold of her hand, he pulled her toward the class.

"Quentin, I don't want..."

"Just a minute, sugar, please." Opening the door, he barked out Trent's name. The man came to the door immediately. "Go ahead and run the women through the first positions and then teach the next. They can practice in their clothing."

"Sure thing, boss," Trent said, not asking why, or when Quentin would return.

His class taken care of, it was now time to properly take care of Grace. He moved to the elevator, and when it opened, it was on their floor. Another minute and they were back in his apartment.

Only then did he release her hand but kept his arms around her as he took a seat on the couch and pulled her down onto his lap. When her mouth opened, he shook his head.

"I'm not through talking," he said, pleased to see a tiny spark of anger flare in her eyes. It was far better than seeing the blankness he'd seen earlier. "As I said, I was an idiot. Though I really thought I had no interest in a relationship, and was rude enough to make sure you understood that, I was not only wrong, I was a fool. Grace, in case you don't realize it, you have not only changed my mind, you've opened my heart. Yes, I did *fuck* you that first time, and then felt like an ass afterwards. What we shared today was not fucking..." When her eyes widened and her lips quirked, he shook his head. "Okay, it was fucking... but, hell, you know it was more than that." Suddenly he realized that it did indeed take two to enter a meaningful relationship. What if he'd misinterpreted the little he'd heard of her conversation with Gretchen? Well, now was the time to find out.

"At least, I hope to God that you know it meant more to me than just a... well, a quick fuck."

"I-I... it really was? I mean, to you?"

"God, yes. I've never felt this way before." Seeing the doubt in her expression as her tentative smile slid away and her head tilted in that questioning way, he continued. "I know that everyone thinks that Beth and I were... well, deeply in love. The truth is that while I thought I loved her, I also knew there was something missing, and to be honest, she knew it as well. I loved her for who she was but even if it makes me sound like the biggest bastard in the universe, I admit I was not *in love* with her. Though I finally understand that I wasn't responsible for what happened and I won't stop until we find who took her from this world, I can't let her death keep me from living any longer.

"I was here physically, but Grace, meeting you, talking with you, holding you and making love to you is what has really brought me home. I know that this whole submissive thing is new to you, but I also know that I've never felt the need to be someone's Dominant as well as their... well, their chosen partner, their..."

"Daddy?" Grace asked quietly, the light beginning to shine in her eyes again.

"Yes, their Daddy as well as the man they could perhaps love one day."

"Oh, Quentin, are you sure? I mean, this has been so fast and maybe... maybe you are simply coming back to life and feel this way because you've been alone for so long."

"I may have been alone but this isn't because of that. I'm not some teenager looking for a rebound, Grace. I'm a grown man, an experienced Dominant and I promise, this is nothing except what I stated. I'll let you in on a little secret." At her smile, he grinned and bent forward until his forehead rested against hers. "I know Doms are supposed to be stoic, strong, alpha males all the time but, right now, my heart is about to pound from my chest waiting to hear if the woman I'm falling in love with might be falling a bit in love with me as well."

Tears began to stream down her cheeks and his heart stopped pounding. Instead it simply seemed to stop. "Oh, sugar, please don't cry. It's—"

"I-I cry wh-when I'm too hap-happy to talk," she stuttered.

"Then let's not talk," he said, his heart beating again as he cupped her face and captured her mouth with his. The feel of her body relaxing into his, her tongue sliding against his own, was the most amazing feeling he'd ever experienced. He felt about a hundred pounds lighter as the sorrows of the past slipped away. His future was the brightest he'd ever be able to imagine simply because he'd met this wonderful woman. When he pulled back, she was no longer crying but smiling, and then she giggled as she ran a fingertip over her lips.

"Too hard?" he asked.

"Oh, no, sir, just right. I was just thinking that when I entered class tonight, Gretchen guessed that... well, that I might have just... um..."

"Come from being fucked?" he provided. At her blush, he chuckled. "Not to sound like an arrogant asshole, but I gotta admit, you were practically glowing, and I don't mean just your red little ass."

"Quentin!"

"That was a compliment, sugar."

"What-what are we going to do about class?"

"What do you want to do?" He knew what he'd prefer but this wasn't about his needs. It was about her having chosen to take the step into submission.

"You're not going to fail me, are you?"

"Hell, if I even tried that, I'd have the other men calling Brody regardless of the fact that I'm the boss. No, you are doing exceptionally well, and it is up to you what you want to do."

She snuggled into him for a few minutes before she sat up again. "There are only two more classes after tonight. I don't want you to be mad, but I'd like to finish..."

"I'm not going to be mad," he said, making a mental note to remind himself of that promise every time he felt his blood pressure increase, which he knew it would the moment anyone dared touch her.

Still, he forced himself to reassure her. "From what you've told me, this is your first entry into D/s or BDSM clubs. I won't keep you from exploring what brought you here in the first place." He paused and shook his head. All right, he was a selfish son-of-a-bitch, but he had to qualify that statement. "That is not to say that it will be easy for me to see you with someone else, but..."

Her fingertip on his lips had him quieting. "Thank you but I wasn't finished speaking," she said, throwing his earlier words back at him but doing so with a soft smile. "I meant that I'd like to finish tonight's class. Correct me if I'm wrong, but even with us being in a relationship, you aren't going to stop playing in the club, right? I mean, I know that Laurie and Brody still play, and Keith and Jessica do as well. So do you plan on playing—um, with me upstairs?"

"I plan on playing with you everywhere, but yes, I would definitely enjoy playing upstairs. After all, I did promise to make you come the next time I put you over that barrel you seem to love."

"I do love it," she admitted. "What I'm saying is that while it didn't take me but a second to be comfortable being naked in front of you, we were in this room and alone. I need to see if I can feel comfortable in a room full of strangers. I know my lingerie didn't cover all that much but, well, it did cover the important bits."

He chuckled and shook his head. "I hate to break it to you, sugar, but there were several important bits quite exposed when you were over that barrel."

"Oh! Um, I suppose so, but I think that stripping with the other students, facing that unknown together, would be the only way I wouldn't bolt for the nearest door. Does that make any sense?"

"It makes perfect sense," he said, bending to kiss the tip of her nose. "I can appreciate your desire to be with your friends." He sighed and knew he needed to wrap this up before he had a mutiny on his hands. "Can you appreciate the fact that if you see me looking a bit pissed, it isn't because of anything you need or are doing, but because I've realized that I'm just a jealous shit who will want to kick the crap out of anyone who touches what is mine?"

Her head tilted again as her lashes batted. "Really? Hmmm, from what Laurie said, I believed you to be a man who believed in not only sharing but in ensuring that his submissive wasn't denied the pleasures that said sharing could deliver."

"Well, well—so little Laurie didn't just teach you the Nadu position, did she?" At the shake of her head, he grinned. "I'm not stating that I will never share, nor that I don't want to show you exactly how different experiences can make a willing sub fly, but I only share with my closest friends, and only when you'd be comfortable doing so."

"Oh, I'm so glad," she said, her lashes stilling as she gave a deep sigh. "I'm not sure how I'm going to feel about that."

"Trust me, I have a feeling you're going to adore it, but only when the time is right. We'll take it a step at a time."

"Thank you, Quentin. I do trust you."

After kissing her deeply again, he forced himself to stand and set her onto her feet. "As much as I'd like to stay here, we've got to get back."

"I know, but first, may I use your bathroom? Gretchen and I never got a chance." At his nod, she ran down the hall. Her flight had him smiling. Since he and Brody had stated the women were not to be left alone, and since Laurie was conveniently pulling a double shift today, he knew that his guest bath wasn't the only room his Grace would be seeing for the first time. Nope, she would definitely be seeing his bedroom and, more importantly, be seeing that he had meant every word he'd confessed. He was hers, and he just prayed she wanted him to always be hers.

When she returned, he was adjusting his cock that always seemed to be uncomfortable when he even thought of her. Seeing her smile, he said, "Not funny," although he grinned as he did so.

"But very ego enhancing," she quipped, twisting sideways as if knowing his hand would be swatting at her backside. Instead, he waited until they had stepped onto the elevator before giving her that swat. She yelped and then giggled, shaking her head. "Are you going to be swatting me all the time?"

"Every chance I get," he confirmed. Once at the door to the classroom, she seemed to hesitate.

"Don't worry. I've got you."

She nodded, taking a deep breath as he opened the door.

Instead of releasing her hand, he led her into the

room proudly, instantly understanding that Conner was pissed. He led Grace to her normal position next to Gretchen and only then let her hand go, bending to press his lips to hers quickly.

"THANK GOD," Gretchen whispered from beside her.

Grace didn't speak but moved to the proper attention position, grateful that evidently her classmates had been instructed to keep their eyes up. Doing so allowed her to watch Quentin as he moved to speak to his staff, not missing the fact that Master Conner was not only speaking, he wasn't bothering to attempt to keep his conversation quiet.

"What the hell, Doucet? First you ditch the class and then Trent starts acting like he's the lead instructor, and to top it all off, you did so because what? You needed to have a private tête-à-tête with your little pet? That's bullshit!"

Grace felt her face heat but not in shame. She didn't care what Conner—or anyone, for that matter—thought. But she did care that this man was disrespecting her Dominant. When Conner's head turned toward her, she didn't drop her eyes nor make any moves at all, which seemed to tick him off further... until Quentin spoke.

"Don't you ever question my decisions again. The only time you may question my actions is if you are sure that they might negatively affect a student..."

"They have! Every woman here is affected when their instructor ditches them so he can..."

"Enough! Get yourself under control, or leave. Your choice, but make it now." Quentin didn't even bother to wait for Conner to make his choice. He turned his attention to the line of women.

"Ladies, I apologize. Yes, I am your instructor and yes, I am a Dominant, but I am also a man who has fallen in love with one of your classmates."

Grace felt her eyes fill at the public profession and the soft "oohs and ahhs" she could hear being muttered along the line. This time when Gretchen whispered, "Hot damn!" she whispered back, "Amen."

Quentin had given them a moment to digest his words. "That being said, Master Trent informed me that you have been instructed in the 'Present' position, and are ready to go forward. As I said earlier, normally we would be splitting you up under new instructors. However, I've decided to mix things up further. Instead of my making the assignments, I'm going to ask you to choose among Masters Trent, Sloan and..." Turning his head as if to ascertain if Conner was still in the room, he turned back to the women, "Master Conner. I will be moving among the groups. Tonight is a big night for you..." He didn't even bother to hide his grin when Gretchen's voice rang out.

"Not as big as for you, sir!"

"You're correct, Miss Kennedy, and thank you. However, I promise it shall be for all of you, as well. If at any time you need to ask questions or if you feel you can't continue, please don't hesitate to speak to any one of us. Tomorrow night, it will be our pleasure to host a dinner for you and open the floor for any questions before your first night as guest members of *Plaisir* on Friday. While you've begun your journey, there is so much more that only time and participation can teach you. I sincerely urge you to give thought to all you've learned, think about what you've experienced, and what you wish to experience." His eyes roamed the line and when they reached her, Grace saw the small nod of his head. as if reminding either himself or perhaps her that he was all right with her need to finish what she'd started.

"All right, ladies, please come forward and choose the Master you'd like to take you upstairs."

Gretchen grabbed Grace's hand. "I knew it! Oh, Grace, I am so freaking happy for you!"

"Thanks, I'm rather happy myself," Grace said.

"He's not only hot as hell, but when he said he was falling in love with you..."

"Ladies, need I remind you that you are still in class?" The two turned toward the voice and both realized that they were the only two remaining in what had been the line of women. They both also gave soft moans when it became clear that taking a moment of celebration had caused them to be the only ones left to be under Master Conner.

"I'm sorry, Master Conner..." Gretchen began, only to have him interrupting.

"As I've told you before, Miss Kennedy, I don't

wish to hear you speak. We'll discuss what happens to submissives who don't give Dominants even the most basic respect once we are upstairs."

Feeling Gretchen's grip squeezing her hand much tighter, Grace said, "Master Quentin said to mix it up, and Gretchen has already been with you."

"Let me remind you that despite the fact that you are fucking the teacher, you, Miss Hensley, are still nothing more than a wannabe submissive in this class. If Miss Kennedy isn't happy, perhaps she should have been paying attention instead of jumping about like some two-year-old, trying to suck up to the teacher's pet. And if she isn't prepared to pay the consequences for her actions, the door is right over there."

"It's all right," Gretchen said softly.

"No, Miss Kennedy, I'm afraid I disagree." The trio turned to see Quentin behind them. Grace instantly noted the vein pulsing in his neck. "Please go join Master Sloan's group and, Miss Hensley, if you'll join Master Trent's, please."

"Now wait a minute..."

Grace didn't wait to hear what Conner said next. She pulled Gretchen with her, only letting her hand go once they'd reached the other groups. That didn't keep her from turning to see Quentin shaking his head, nor from seeing Conner sending him a scathing look before storming from the room.

As if nothing untoward had happened, Quentin turned to address the class. "Last night you weren't required to sign in at the hostess desk. Tonight, and every time from now on, you will have to do so. With your completion of this class, you will have earned the status of guest members for six months without further charges. Remember, keep your eyes open and observe all that is going on around you, but also keep your attention on your instructor. Again, the only stupid questions are those left unasked." Grace noted he took the time to meet the gaze of every woman. "You are doing well, ladies, but it's time to take that next step. Any questions?"

"Yes, sir, I have one," Grace said, finally realizing the only thing that truly mattered.

"Yes, Miss Hensley?"

"What would the consequences be if I confessed I'd made a huge mistake when I told my Dominant that I needed to complete the class to make sure I was a true submissive?"

She heard a few of her fellow classmates giggle and yet the only person she was looking at was the incredible man standing before them all.

"Well, Miss Hensley, that's easy to answer," Quentin said stepping forward until he was right in front of her. "If you are positive that your Dominant can teach you all you wish to learn and provide you with the infinite possibilities you wish to experience, then, sugar, I'd say the consequences are that the two of us will explore together. Is that suitable?"

"Absolutely," Grace said, throwing herself into his opened arms and hearing cheers behind her.

"Master Trent and Master Sloan, I turn the class over to you tonight. Ladies, if you'll excuse us?"

Grace turned and looking at Gretchen, gave her a smile and said, "I'll see you tomorrow. Come early and we'll catch up, okay?"

"I'll be there, now go, girl!" Since that was about the best advice she could ever receive, Grace, her Dom by her side, did just that.

19

"ARE you sure you should leave the class? Master Conner left and, well, I don't mind waiting for you if you need—"

"What I need is you," Quentin said as they stepped off the elevator. "Trent and Sloan have it under control and besides, what's the point of being the boss unless you take advantage of the perks?" She felt a quiver run through her as he looked down on her, grateful to see the vein no longer pulsing.

Once inside his apartment, he said, "As beautiful as you look, I'm afraid you might cause a few cardiac arrests at the hospital. We'll go see Brody and find out what Detective Stewart discovered once we've changed."

Seeing her clothes from earlier neatly folded on his couch, she stepped away to reach for them. "It won't take me but a minute."

"I'm afraid that even with your Dom helping you,

it'll take a little longer than that, Miss Hensley," he said with his own grin. "Come here."

Returning to him, she saw that the soft gray of his eyes had turned smoky, and she felt as if tendrils of that smoke were wafting through her body, hardening her nipples and moistening her sex. As he reached for the hem of her blouse and began to draw it over her head, pausing to bend and kiss each hardened peak of her breasts through the satin of her bra, she instantly knew on a far more primitive level the truth of the adage: 'Where there is smoke, there is fire.' Her blouse was tossed onto the coffee table and was soon joined by her skirt.

"We've got enough time to have a private lesson. Stand at attention but with your arms at your sides."

She shivered and burned at the same time as his eyes raked up and down her body once she'd obeyed. Quentin ran his thumbs over the black satin and lace of her bra, teasing her nipples until she was afraid they'd poke through in desperation to feel his caress without any barrier, no matter how soft or silky their present containment was. In a state of bliss as he gently played, his fingers moving to trace the skin of her breasts that her bra didn't cover, she gave a startled yelp when he suddenly yanked the bra down, the straps tightening on her shoulders at the additional stretch required with the bra cups now beneath her breasts, the tighter fit forcing them to be displayed rather lewdly. And yet, when his head dropped and he began to retrace the path his fingers had taken, this time with his tongue, she felt her arousal ratchet up to a new level. She lifted her hand to run through his hair only to squeal when a sharp nip on her breast caused her to pause.

"A submissive who has been ordered into a position does not move without permission," he said, lifting his head for a moment to meet her eyes.

"Yes, sir." Her heart beat faster with the understanding that the teacher had not truly left the classroom, he'd simply changed its location. As his mouth returned to her breasts, a kiss delivered to the spot he'd just nipped, she felt a sense of wonder knowing that, while there were probably a thousand men who could teach such things as positions, protocol, or rules needed to begin to understand a BDSM club's environment, and millions could deliver a spanking or scratch an itch, she felt totally alive for the first time with only one man... this man...

"Eyes on me."

She hadn't realized she'd closed her eyes until his order. Opening them, she met his. "Don't move," he said softly. God, was it wrong to feel like she was almost being worshipped as his lips closed around a nipple, his tongue flicking rapidly across the puckered surface. Her question changed as his teeth closed and pulled lightly. How could he expect her not to move, not to squirm and not to put her hand on the back of his head and pull him closer? Still, other than issuing a soft moan and quivering, she didn't move, not even when he released her only to give her other nipple the same combination of exquisite pleasure combined with a sharp nip of pain.

"Good girl," he said, lifting his head and only then reaching behind her back to undo the clasp of her bra. Whereas she always just tossed it off, he drew it down her arms slowly, taking his time to watch her skin pebble into gooseflesh. "You've got the most delectable nipples. They are like raspberries, and when swollen, they become the prettiest dark pink, ready to be plucked and eaten."

Good lord, who said things like that? It appeared her Dom did, and once he'd added her bra to the growing pile, his fingers and thumbs closed around those raspberries and began to tug, twist and pull until she was breathing hard. He seemed to know exactly when she was about to give in to her almost desperate need to shift because his fingers released her nipples and began to slide down her sides, fingertips pebbling her skin with each featherlight stroke until they reached the lacy waistband of her panties. He kept his eyes locked on hers as he knelt and dragged her underwear down as slowly as he had her bra.

"Step out," he instructed, placing a hand on her in support as she obeyed, lifting one foot and then the other.

Forget pink, she knew her face turned scarlet as he lifted the black lace to his face and inhaled deeply. Oh, dear sweet mother of God, how could something so embarrassing be so erotic? When he tossed them aside then placed his hands on her upper thighs to give his next order to spread wider before pressing his tongue against her dripping sex, she began to wobble, her knees shaking as he licked up and down the seam of her sex as if he were some primal cat savoring a bowl of cream. He took her to the very edge and then pulled his tongue away. At the sight of him licking his lips free of her cream, her body was so primed that she almost climaxed. The soft mews she'd been uttering changed to form a single word.

"Please—"

"Naughty," he said with a grin that had her bottom twitching. "A sub at attention does not speak unless asked a question." He rose with a grace that defied the women he'd taught and took a step back, never dropping his gaze. "That's twice you've been naughty. One more, and I'm afraid you'll find it a bit difficult to sit tonight. Understood?"

When had swallowing become something she had to concentrate on in order to do? "Yes-yes, sir."

"Good. I wouldn't want you to feel you are behind in your class so, Grace, I'm going to teach you the position your classmates learned tonight. There are different terms given in various forms but for the submissives we reach, it is simply called 'Present'.

"Go ahead and assume the Nadu." After she had, he said, "Now, when told to 'present,' you'll lean forward and place your hands straight out and your cheek against the floor. You should always know where your Dom is and turn your face in that direction. Keep your hands crossed at the wrists, indicating your readiness to have them bound if your Dom so chooses. Go ahead."

Just seeing her move to follow his order, her face turned toward him, her legs still spread, and the bend pushing her ass up into the air, he felt his cock harden. He squatted down beside her, placing his palm on the small of her back. "Good. The position opens your body for both visual stimulation and preparation for being taken. You'll arch your back and lift your ass, keeping your legs widely spread. Do so now."

She did, and though she could see nothing but the black leather of his boots, she could easily imagine what she must look like. The waft of air across her exposed sex, its chill greater than the air she felt on any other part of her naked body, told her how wet she must be. Without thought, her teeth caught her lip as she felt a single finger move down the crack of her ass, pausing to give the tiniest press against the small orifice that he'd opened for the first time only an hour earlier. She gasped and yet didn't pull away as he continued his journey until he had skimmed the lips of her pussy, delving inside to twirl in her abundant juices.

"Do you understand how this position is one favored by a great many Doms?" he asked, removing his finger to circle the small bundle of nerves normally lying dormant in the concealment of its little hood.

"Y-yes, sir."

"You are so very beautiful," he said, giving her

clitoris a tap that had her hands fisting as she fought hard not to move, not to press herself back in an attempt to grind herself against his hand. "I can't tell you how honored I am that you have chosen me, Grace. I want to teach you everything you desire. And I admit that I'm not sure I could have kept myself from taking you if you'd assumed this position upstairs."

He rose, his hand abandoning her sex and leaving her on the edge of climax for the second time. "But we aren't upstairs, are we?"

"No-no, sir," she said softly, her pulse rate jumping as she saw that he was removing his boots, and her breathing almost stopping when she saw his pants dropping to the floor.

"Shh," he said, and only then did she realized she was whimpering. God, she wanted to lift her head so badly, to watch his body being revealed. When his black t-shirt hit the floor, she made a conscious decision. To hell with it, she'd been spanked before, and it was really a small price to pay in order to discover what ink he'd chosen to adorn his skin.

Intending to just lift her head enough to be able to look up, she gasped and was soon sitting back on her heels. The tip of the tattoo previously hidden by his shirtsleeve was only the tiniest part of the most incredible ink she'd ever seen. No color distracted the monochrome scheme of stark black shaded with lighter grays. The art was not only a feast for the eyes but seemed to draw her very soul into its wonder, and her fingers itched to reach up and trace every pattern, to dance from one to another as if following a labyrinth—but one for which there was no rush to escape. She'd known that he was ripped, but the defined muscles of his abdomen forced her to once again relearn how to swallow.

"Quentin, God, you are... are gorgeous!" When her eyes dropped lower, she sucked in her breath. Though he'd been inside her before, though she'd suckled him, the sight of his full erection, unrestricted or hidden by clothing, protruding from his groin, made her moan. "And, big... very, very big." She knew there would be a puddle beneath her hips when he crouched next to her, his cock a mere centimeter from her skin.

"And you, little one, are quite the naughty girl. Did you hear me giving you permission to release or change positions?"

She met his eyes, though took another moment to gaze at the tattoo before answering. "No, sir, but... well, I decided it was worth a spanking. I've been dying to know what you looked like bare and, yes, it was definitely worth a sore ass."

"Ah, sugar, I'm so glad you think so," he said, his finger reaching out to stroke her cheek. "But who said anything about a spanking?"

Surprised, she said, "You did."

"No, if you'll recall, I said that if you were naughty again, you'd find it difficult to sit."

"I know, that's what I just said—"

"Grace, I'm going to find great pleasure in teaching you that there are a thousand different ways to punish a naughty girl." His words had her mind spinning, the look in his eyes had her breath hitching and his soft kiss had her heart filling. When he pulled back, he said, "But first, a lesson in pleasure. Present," and as he stood, she obeyed.

QUENTIN MOVED but not behind her. Instead, he walked into his bedroom, returning a few minutes later to find Grace hadn't moved. He grinned, thinking that if her obedience, flushed face and glistening sex didn't prove she was a natural submissive, nothing would. He stepped behind her. "Arch your back more. I want your ass lifted high." She obeyed, and he knew he'd never seen a more beautiful sight as he knelt behind her, placing the objects he'd retrieved on the cloth he spread out.

He ran his palms across the hillocks of her bottom, massaging the skin, relishing her small moan as he reawakened the fire he'd built earlier even though the color had long disappeared from her pale flesh. His fingers continued to stroke and caress down her hips and upper thighs until he lifted one to cup the pouch of her sex in his palm. Grinning, he knew that he'd need very little of the lubricant he had brought back as she was providing a great deal of her own. Pushing two fingers into her caused her to moan deeply. Slow thrusts, just enough to tease but not to push her over the edge, had his fingers soaked and her beginning to move as if to help him in his finger fucking.

"Anxious, are we?" he asked, synching his movements so that the deep thrust and the slap against her ass were delivered as one.

"Ahh," she cried, her hips dropping a bit at the stroke and then instantly lifting at the next thrust.

"Ah, indeed," he said, pulling his fingers from her and spreading her buttocks with the hand that had just spanked her. "Or should I say, awe inspiring?" he asked, pressing his finger against her tightly puckered entrance and hearing her gasp. "Relax, Grace, I've got you." He took his time sinking his finger into her ass, pausing when it breached her sphincter, allowing her a moment to adjust before pushing forward. He thrust slowly and withdrew, time and time again until she had not only stopped clenching, she was making sounds of pleasure instead of little gasps of pain.

"Good girl," he said, pulling out only to add a second finger, again going slow at the greater stretch required of her for entry. His cock was twitching, silently demanding that it take the place of his fingers, and yet he was a patient man. She wasn't ready but, after tonight, she'd have taken a big step toward being prepared—though she wasn't yet aware of that fact. Once she was again making soft mews of pleasure, he began to scissor his fingers apart, stretching her opening, forcing the muscles to relax for his play.

Reaching for the first object, he lifted it, drawing it up the cleft of her ass, loving her little jerk as the cold glass met hotter flesh. "Care to guess what this is?"

"Um, I-I have no idea, sir, but it's cold!"

"I assure you, it won't be for long." Removing his fingers from her ass, he reached for the second object. Opening the top, he allowed a stream of lubricant to run down from the first sphere to the last, his fingers becoming slick as he made sure each anal bead was completely coated. Satisfied, he bent over her, allowing the string of glass balls to come into her view.

"Is that a... a necklace?"

Chuckling, he shook his head. "Beads, yes, but sugar, they don't go around your pretty neck." Pressing a finger into her ass, loving her soft moan, he said, "Care to guess where each of these will be going?"

"Oh my God, you're going to put those in... in my ass?"

"Every single one."

"You—you can't. They won't fit!"

"Shall we see?" He didn't wait for her to answer. Instead, he replaced his finger with the first bead on the string. She gasped at the difference in the feel of smooth glass pressing against her sphincter and the gave a moan as it easily slipped inside. "Count them as they enter your ass."

"One."

"Good girl."

"Two."

Another entered and was counted before her

small moan became deeper. "Oh... God, four. I can't..."

"You can," Quentin assured her, pressing the fifth against her anus. Each bead on the string was slightly larger than the previous, and this one was forcing her pucker to stretch wider and yet it still wasn't the largest. "It is so incredible watching your ass swallow each one."

She groaned and then gave a sharp yelp as her body did indeed accept the next invader. He slid a finger over her dripping sex. "Number?"

"Wh... what?"

He chuckled. "How many beads are you holding?"

"Um... four... five?"

"Maybe having two numbers both beginning with the same letter has you confused. Let me help you with that problem, shall I?" Her groan competed with his chuckle as the sixth bead began to press into her bottom. "What comes after five?"

"Sir... I feel..." The entry of the bead and his finger pressing in behind it to make sure it was deeply seated had her pausing. "Oh, God, I feel... so full."

"Not as full as you shall be," he assured her. "Ready for number seven?"

"Quentin, I... I can't!"

"Says the woman who never believed she'd take even one," he said. She not only managed to accept the seventh, she didn't miss a single count as he continued. "Last one," he said, rolling the tenth and largest bead against her opening. "Ask me for it," he commanded, once again bending over her, his lips at her ear. "Ask me to fill your ass completely."

Her breaths were coming in little pants, her eyes closed, quivering as his breath wafted over her ear. "Plea... please, sir... fill me..."

"Where?" he asked, giving her earlobe a nip.

"My... my ass, sir."

"My pleasure," he assured her, lifting off her body and watching with intense pleasure as he slowly pressed the last bead into her body, her passage now quite full, and yet he knew there were far larger things she'd learn to accept. Running his fingers through her sex, he wasn't surprised to find her dripping. "Shall I fill this, as well?"

"Ye... yes, fuck, yes!"

Positioning himself, he pressed into her and loved her squeal. She'd been tight before and with the string of beads buried in her ass, it took more effort to bury himself balls deep. He could feel the bumps of the spheres rubbing against his cock through the thin membrane in her body. As he began to thrust, she began to rock against him, her discomfort evidently not an issue as she was informing him within moments that she was going to climax.

"You'll soon learn that little girls who come without being given permission are considered naughty," he said, pulling almost completely from her.

"Oh, sweet Jesus, if that's true, I'm afraid my butt will always be sore."

"That may be but you are not to come until given permission, Grace."

"Please... I can't... I need—"

"You need to obey."

"I'm trying!"

Knowing that she was and that it would take additional training to achieve orgasm control, he took pity and began to thrust in long, slow strokes, making sure he was focused on her impending explosion rather than his own. "Good girl," he praised, giving the ring at the end of the beads a little tug, causing her to utter a groan that had his cock jerking. "I'm going to count to three and then, Grace, I want you to come for me. Ready?"

"God, yes, hurry!"

He chuckled. Yes, they had several more things to work on but, for now, it was time to reward her for her submission. Slipping an arm around her waist, he said, "One... two..." before pulling back until his cockhead was barely inside her slick channel. He then did three things simultaneously. Burying his cock as deeply as he could, he said the word *three* and pulled the string of beads from her ass in one smooth movement. The result was far more than he'd bargained for as she screamed and her body convulsed, her fluids spurting from her despite the presence of his cock in her pussy. Her contractions had the walls of her cunt clamping around his cock, the grip tighter than any he'd ever experienced as she continued to convulse.

"Shit," he groaned, his control lost and his seed jetting into her as he collapsed onto her back.

It was several minutes before her body stopped twitching, her pussy gradually loosening its vise-like grip on his shaft. Sitting back, he slipped from her and immediately pulled her to sit on his lap.

"Are you all right?"

"I-I think I died," she said, her eyes glazed as she looked up before collapsing against his chest.

"Ah, *la petite mort*," he said, kissing the top of her head. "Did you enjoy it?"

"Absolutely," she said, lifting her head, her cheeks flushing as if the admission were embarrassing. He kissed her again, the passion shared only moments earlier reflected in the crush of her mouth against his. It was several minutes before he gave her a final kiss and then watched her eyes widen when he ordered back into position.

"Shouldn't we be getting ready to go?"

"Not yet. There is the matter of learning what happens to subs who were warned to be good but then chose to be not only naughty, but deliberately naughty."

"I... I..."

"Yes?"

"Geeze, are you always going to be so single minded?"

Chuckling, he wrapped her in his arms. "Absolutely. I wouldn't want my girl to ever wonder what to expect from her Dom or her Daddy."

"So, this is another lesson on trust, isn't it?"

"Yes, Grace, it is exactly that." He saw her head bob and was pleased with her next words.

"Then, I have no more questions, sir, as I trust you with my very life."

He felt a wave of both responsibility and honor flood through him. "Thank you, my love."

A HALF HOUR LATER, after they'd enjoyed their first shower together, her face constantly flushing as his hands ran over her body but feeling on fire when his fingers played with the plug he'd seated inside her, Grace was giving him a look that had him grinning as he put the box of cookies Hannah had insisted he take to Brody and the nurses in the saddlebag of the Indian.

"Seriously? How can you expect me to ride on a motorcycle with this... this thing in my ass?"

"That thing is called a butt plug and, sugar, if you don't want it in your butt, then, my darling girl, don't be naughty."

"What's the world coming to when a girl can't compliment her man on how incredible she thinks his ink is?"

"The kind of world you wanted to explore, I suppose," he said, pulling the helmet onto her head and tightening the straps. "The kind of world where your Dominant won't hesitate to press beads up your ass for pleasure and your Daddy won't pause in placing a nice fat plug in your bottom to remind you to be a good girl. Now, hop on."

"You are a sadist," she mock-complained, carefully straddling the bike and slowly lowering herself as if expecting to be shooting up the moment her ass hit the seat. Instead, she only gave a small moan as the position and her body weight seemed to press the invader a little deeper inside.

"And you are adorable," he said, kissing her cheek before taking his place in front of her. She wrapped her arms around him and he wondered how long she could keep her butt lifted a bit before her legs tired. Deciding that as long as she hung on it didn't matter, he gave the bike gas and they roared out onto the street.

20

"SUGAR, YOU CAN WALK NORMALLY," Quentin said after helping her off the bike.

"That's easy for you to say," she muttered, accepting the smaller box of cookies. "I feel as if I'm sitting on a telephone pole."

"I assure you that analogy isn't even close to being true." He swatted her bottom, causing her to skip forward a step. "It will only become true once I've got my cock buried inside that gorgeous little backdoor of yours."

"Quentin!" she exclaimed before her eyes darted around the parking lot. "What if someone heard you?"

"Then they would know that you have a man who can't stop thinking about how much he wants you," he said, taking her hand and lifting it for a kiss before he began walking toward the hospital.

"Hmph, all they'd know was that same man has an awfully inflated opinion of himself," she said.

"Ah, you wound me," he said, pulling their linked hands to his chest to cover his heart. "But I'll remind you that you said that the first time I sink into your—"

"Quentin!"

He chuckled as she somehow managed to use both their hands to swat him. He would never tire of either loving her, sinking into her, or just plain teasing her.

After delivering the cookies to the nurses' station and hearing one state that she swore she'd already gained five pounds since Brody had been admitted, they stepped down the hall to his room. Pushing through the door, Quentin saw that Jason had yet to arrive but Laurie was seated on the bed beside her fiancé. Well, she was until she saw Grace, at which point she gave a screech, hopped up, and flew across the room.

Though he'd heard about it, he'd never actually witnessed two women clinging to each other and dancing around in circles like a pair of excited puppies, both talking over the other. He grinned as he shook his head. So much for her whining. If she could hop and dance so joyously, then that plug was definitely going to need to be retired and the next size up taking its place.

"So much for keeping your mouth shut," he said, approaching the bed.

"You can't expect me to keep secrets from my soon-to-be-wife, can you?" Brody said, grinning from ear to ear. "Besides, just one look at that stupid grin on your face and anyone can tell that you, my friend, are definitely hooked and not even squirming to slip off."

"What can I say?" Quentin asked as he gave the women another glance to find that while they were no longer spinning like little dervishes, they were standing with their heads together, their conversation appearing quite animated. "She's the most incredible thing that has ever entered my life." He shrugged sheepishly and then grinned. "Though I'm not guaranteeing that there will be anything left but cookie crumbs after that rather fetching dance."

"Cookies, hell, why didn't you say so! Grace Hensley, get your naughty little ass over here!"

Brody's semi-yell had both women looking up and Quentin almost strangled on his laugh when her eyes widened and she dropped a hand behind her as if afraid her jeans had somehow disappeared as well as her panties, to display the flange of the plug in her butt.

"Sugar, really?" he drawled, after he calmed a bit, motioning her forward. "Brody just meant he wants the cookies. I promise he had no idea your cute little ass is stretched around a naughty girl plug."

"Oh my God, Daddy!" was chorused with "Oh my God, Quentin!" as both women shouted the same words... except for the address. He accepted the two quick slaps at his arm as they joined him without complaint as well as the look of surprise and pleasure that passed between Laurie and Brody as he snagged Grace around her waist. Her cheeks flushed as if shocked she'd called him Daddy in the presence of others, but when he kissed her, she kissed him back without hesitation.

Laurie had the box open and Brody had his first cookie half eaten by the time Quentin pulled back.

"Like I said, hook, line and sinker," Brody said.

"Good grief, and I thought it was just Grace who talks with her mouth full," Quentin quipped, even as he snagged a cookie from the box and held it to her lips.

"I suppose I shouldn't, not if I eat like some little piggy," she said, though he'd seen her nostrils flare at the aroma of warm chocolate chips that had been generously added to the dough.

"Yes, you should," Quentin countered. "You're going to need your strength when I get you home, sugar."

"Promises, promises. A girl can't live on promises alone. Nope, she definitely needs chocolate," Laurie quipped, taking a cookie for herself only to find it plucked from her fingers by Brody. "Hey!"

He didn't respond but broke off a piece and beckoned with his fingers for her to come closer. When she bent forward and opened her mouth, she not only moaned with the first taste of chocolate but from the swat he'd delivered. "Are you insinuating that I haven't kept my promises? Brody asked.

"Absolutely not, sir. I'm just saying that women need chocolate," Laurie said, batting her lashes.

"Good, because I was about to promise that you'll be adding another set to that book you've been keeping. You know, the one that will take about six months to atone for at the rate you are going?"

"Hmmm, now where did I put that?"

"Oh, honey, I promise that if you don't know exactly where it is, I've been keeping the count as well."

Quentin had to laugh at the look on Laurie's face. She seemed to be wavering between making another joke and wondering if what he said could possibly be true. When she shrugged and bent forward further to press her lips against her Dom's, he knew that she didn't really care about the count at all.

The door opening had him looking toward it. "Am I interrupting?" Detective Stewart asked.

"Not at all," Quentin said. "Nurse Laurie just seemed to believe her patient needed a bit of mouth-to-mouth."

"Ah, think he'll survive?" Jason asked, striding into the room.

"He will if he isn't smothered first," Quentin said, lifting the box Laurie had left on the bed. "Cookie?"

"Don't mind if I do."

After he'd taken one, Quentin introduced him to Grace.

"It's a pleasure to meet you," Grace said.

"The pleasure is mine. In fact, I tried to tell you how very talented I believe you are but the gallery was swamped and my wife wasn't feeling well, so we had to leave before I could. I'm glad I'm able to do so now."

"Oh, I'm sorry to hear about your wife. Is she all right?"

"Yes, thank you. Instead of morning sickness, she gets nauseated in the evenings. But we both really enjoyed your work."

By this time, the couple on the bed had come up for air and Laurie had moved to stand. It was as if her moving was a signal for them to begin discussing what had brought them all together. Last bites of cookies were taken and the two women moved to the window seat; still close enough to be included in the conversation, yet allowing the men to see the computer that Brody was opening on the tray table.

"Maybe I should leave," Grace said softly.

"No," Quentin said, glancing over his shoulder. "There is no reason for you not to hear what's said." He didn't turn back until she gave him a nod, and tried not to let the fact that she was wiggling a bit on the seat as if to try to find a more comfortable position keep his focus off what he needed to do.

"You've got the floor, Jason," Quentin said, leaning against the wall next to the bed, his arms crossed over his chest as the detective took the only chair. "What did you learn about Brooks?"

The detective pulled a notepad from his pocket and flipped it open. "He hemmed and hawed but finally admitted that he was at the club that night. Seems he'd been waiting until there was an open night and thought it would make a great article. Prick stated that he was going to title it something about the real definition of the Big Easy. How the god-fearing citizens of New Orleans should know that it had yet another stain of depravity on its reputation with such a club as *Plaisir* operating only blocks away from the historic French Quarter."

"Prick is one word, total hypocrite is another," Brody said, "he's been trying to obtain membership into the club for years."

"Forget that, did he say who let him in?" Quentin asked.

"No, though he admitted he switched his name around and was gathering information for his article, he then started spouting his constitutional rights as a member of the press. Refusal to reveal his sources and all that shit. He stated that even if I arrested him, he would remain mute. When I said it would be a pleasure to test his resolve, he said he'd actually just waited until there was a large group, signed in as if he belonged, and no one had questioned it. Would that have been possible?"

"Hell. I'd love to swear it wouldn't, but we already know our security wasn't as tight back then and, yeah, I guess if some member used his ring to open the door and then more than one or two guests followed, Brooks could have gotten in," Brody admitted.

Jason shook his head. "I suppose it could have been worse. I have to give his boss credit. I asked why I'd never seen the article and he said that when he pitched the idea, his boss immediately nixed it. Seems like the man also believes in constitutional rights, though he meant the right to privacy. He also stated that he expected his reporters to do their basic research. Did you know that this city developed an entire community in the 1800s to pander to all types of vices, including those dealing with sex?"

"Yeah, Storyville was quite the place. You could pick up all sorts of things there, kickbacks if you were a city official, or a roll in the hay with the bonus of a sexual disease if you were a regular Joe," Quentin said.

"Anyway, he told Brooks that unless he could prove that there were illegal things going on at the club, he wasn't interested."

"Well, at least there's one intelligent man in the news business," Brody said.

"Evidently not too intelligent," Jason said. "After all, he did assign him to investigate Beth's disappearance and subsequent murder."

"Yeah, but he must have realized his mistake, because when Brooks started writing shit he had no evidence to prove, he was yanked when we informed him that we had every intention of suing for slander," Brody offered.

"Fuck," Quentin said, "I hate to admit it, but with his sleazy treatment of Grace, I really thought we might be on to something."

"Excuse me, I hate to interrupt, but I've got to get back," Laurie said, stepping in front of Quentin to bend and give Brody a kiss.

"Wait, I'll go out with you to get something to drink if that's all right?" Grace asked. When Quentin seemed to hesitate, she added, "I'm only going down the hall. I know talking makes you thirsty, and I'll be glad to bring all of you something back as well."

"I am a bit parched and am sick of water. A Coke would sure hit the spot," Brody said before Quentin responded.

"Of course. Quentin, Detective Stewart?"

"I'd like a Sprite if they have it, or a Coke if they don't," Jason said.

Quentin still hesitated but finally nodded. "Anything is fine, sugar, but hurry back."

"I'll be back in a jiffy." She stood on her tiptoes in order to press her lips to Quentin's cheek before she whispered, "Thanks for caring so much."

"Always, but a fat lot of good it did. It seems Brooks is just that, a sleaze."

"That doesn't matter," she said, cupping her palm against his cheek. "You'll always be my hero."

The women left together, though Quentin only had eyes for one as his heart skipped a beat. Brody was right, he already knew he was hooked for life. It took him a moment before he was able to pull himself back to the conversation.

"We're not giving up," Brody said. "What I haven't told you is that Peter Zinger called about an hour ago. He found Marti Ansell. Her full name is actually Morticia, and she is one smart lady. She just graduated from Tulane and has been accepted into the medical program. He says that she often made money for tuition working in various temporary positions, choosing the ones in clubs such as ours as the wages were significantly higher. Peter said that the only thing she remembered that struck her as being even the slightest bit odd was that for such a small building, there was not one but two elevators."

"Why would she even know there were two?" Quentin asked.

"Peter asked her what she meant. She said that she'd been instructed to keep her eyes on the elevator at the end of the hall, the one that members use that goes directly from the first floor to the club. She was to greet anyone who stepped off and to make sure they stopped at the desk to register any guests they had brought with them. It was late, and some people had already left when she said she was surprised to see the wall in front of the desk opening."

"That makes sense," Jason said. "I remember thinking that elevator was pretty well concealed, as there are no actual buttons or metal doors visible."

"Yeah, we didn't think there was any need to advertise that another elevator was available because it only operates for Quentin, myself, Laurie and, at the time, Beth."

"Are you saying she actually saw Beth?" Quentin asked.

"No, in fact, she states that even though there were a lot of women there that night, she was pretty positive she never saw Beth."

"Then who the hell was on the elevator?"

"According to Marti, no one."

"What? How can that be?"

"All I can think of is that someone either got on without being noticed, which I find hard to believe, or someone was already on either the first or second floor and, for some reason, sent the elevator back up and hit the wrong button. The only thing I know for sure is that it wasn't me or Laurie, as we went upstairs early to make sure everything was in place for the mixer and left early when we were sure the staff had everything under control. You had already left town, and we had that hospital fundraiser to attend," Brody said.

"Are you sure that someone can't just step on when one of you steps off?" Jason asked.

"Even if they did, they'd have to have one of our rings to operate it. It won't move unless the ring is first pressed into the indentation, which activates the elevator. Exactly like one of those special key cards in some hotels or office buildings that allow only the people registered or those working to access restricted floors. Quentin and I chose to use rings instead of cards as they aren't so easily left on a table," Brody explained.

"So with what you told me about the ring earlier, it had to be Beth's, though it didn't necessarily have to be her using it," Jason said.

"Yes. Have you gotten back anything from the lab on the ring?" Quentin asked.

"Just that there are no useful fingerprints, but we're still waiting on the other tests. If there is anything, we should know in a couple of days. I expedited the request."

"All right, and there's one more thing that Marti had to contribute," Brody said. "She was able to give

Peter Mike Farraday's current phone number. He's living in Baton Rouge now. His story is a bit less mysterious, but still important. It seems he quit because he overheard a conversation between two men that made him decide he'd rather leave than be fired."

"Are your employees prone to fearing they'll lose their jobs?" Jason asked, flipping another page over in his notepad to take additional notes.

"No, I wouldn't think so," Brody said. "We don't even have a large turnover, because we offer wages that a person can actually live on. It's always been our belief that happy employees keep our clients happy. Without contented clients, we'd have less income, so the least we could do was share that income fairly. In fact, I can't even remember the last person we fired, can you, Quentin?"

"No, but I came awfully damn close tonight."

"Shit, what did Conner do now?"

"Later, it doesn't have anything to do with this," Quentin said. "So what about Farraday?"

"Oh, right. He confessed that he'd lied on his application. You know we do our best to vet our employees, but evidently we were too trusting to question the recommendations the applicant puts down. Seems Farraday paid a few friends to pretend to have either employed him or worked with him before, and supplied them with the information he knew we'd want to hear. You know, how he is a great guy, can be trusted with everything from client confidentiality to money, blah blah blah; enough to answer whatever questions we might have before employing him. The truth is that he had not only been fired from the last club he'd worked in, which was located not in Louisiana at all but in Houston, but he'd also skipped town when learning that a warrant had been issued for his arrest."

"No wonder his name didn't come up in our system," Jason said, lifting his eyes from the pad. "Did Peter tell you why the warrant was issued?"

"Yeah. Seems that a woman wanted to make a formal complaint about a Dominant in the club. Mike supposedly talked her out of it, or at least he thought he had. He was trying to protect a friend of his, who had already been warned that if he messed with the rather loose rules of that particular club, he'd be banned. Anyway, the woman left, but went to the police the next day. When they came to the club to interview Mike, well, let's just say his boss blew a gasket. Loose rules or not, he was adamant about safe, sane, and consensual. Hearing that the woman was accusing one of his members of rape, and one of his employees of attempting to keep the rape hidden... well, the shit hit the fan. Mike was taken in for questioning and released, but failed to show up for court. I guess that's when he decided to split for greener pastures."

"That's not good, and though we would never have hired him if we'd known, I still don't see him as harming Beth. I mean, they might not have been close, but she never once said anything to me about being uncomfortable around him. Besides, according to our records, he didn't immediately split; he stayed until closing. If he'd had Beth with him at that point, the crowd would have been so thin that someone was bound to have seen her."

"He didn't," Brody said. "Marti said they hooked up when the club closed. When he said he was squatting with a friend, she took him back to her place and is willing to swear he didn't leave until Monday. She said they won't ever be serious but they do hook up occasionally."

"Okay, that might clear him of Beth's murder, but I'm still going to follow up on the arrest warrant," Jason said.

"I'd give that a day or two," Brody said. "Seems that he's really a good guy at heart. Told Peter he'd been sweating for two years and was going back to turn himself in. He also said to tell you that he was heartbroken when he heard about Beth."

Quentin nodded but didn't speak.

"Don't give up," Jason said.

"I'm not, but fuck, we're running out of suspects," Quentin said, his voice lower, as if exhausted.

"We just haven't turned over the right rock," Brody said. "I've instructed Peter to dig into every employee..."

He was interrupted by the sound of a phone ringing. Quentin pulled his from his pocket and seeing the name he'd only entered a few hours earlier, he looked around the room before pressing the button to answer.

"Grace, where are you?" The sound that came

from the phone was so shocking and so loud that he pulled it away from his ear. The rooster's crow chilled him to the bone, but hearing a scream of absolute terror threatened to shatter his soul. "Grace!" His own scream was met with the brief change of color stating the call had ended. Jason was on his feet but Quentin didn't seem to notice, attempting to push past him in order to get to the door.

"Quentin, wait!" Jason shouted.

"Fuck that, Conner has Grace."

"How do you know?" Brody yelled as Quentin wrenched the door open.

The last words they heard before he disappeared was, "Because he's telling me he's cock of the walk now."

JASON HAD his phone in his hand, dialing even as he stabbed at the call button for a nurse. He was barking orders into his phone when a nurse ran into the room.

"What's going on? We saw Quentin running like a bat out of hell—"

"Get whoever is head of security on the phone. Tell him to shut down the hospital. No one goes in or out."

"That will take more than a nurse," she said even as she made the call from the phone on Brody's side table.

"Just get him on the line," Jason snapped before

speaking to Brody. "What's Conner's full name and what does he look like?"

"Conner Matthews, Caucasian, six foot, blond, muscular, in his early thirties." As Jason took the receiver from the nurse, he put his own call on hold so he could speak to hospital security. Repeating the information Brody gave him, he added, "He's a suspect in the abduction of Grace Hensley. She's petite, probably no more than 5'2", long auburn hair, last seen wearing blue jeans, a green t-shirt, and black flats. I don't know what Matthews is wearing." He paused and his voice changed when he spoke again. "I know this place is huge, so the quicker you get your men on it, the faster we'll know if they are still here. Miss Hensley hasn't been gone longer than a half-hour or so. I've got officers on the way to help search." He gave the man his cell number, with instructions to let him know the moment he discovered anything.

"Oh, God," the nurse said. "What can I do to help?"

"Spread the word," Jason said. "Tell everyone you know that Grace has been taken. Let me know if you find anyone who has seen her." Nodding, the nurse left and Jason turned his attention back to Brody.

"All right, just in case he's managed to slip out already, what's his address?" Brody pulled the computer to him and quickly had Cullen's employee file open and recited the address. Jason barked more orders into his phone.

"Get officers over to *Plaisir* and send a car over to his address." He paused and shook his head. "Do you want to be the one who has to explain that you didn't think he'd be stupid enough to take his victim to his house, only to find out that was exactly where he took her? No? Then get a car over there now!"

Again, he consulted Brody. "What does he drive?"

"A blue Jeep." Looking at the file again, Brody gave him the Jeep's license plate number. After Jason passed that along with an order to issue an APB, Brody asked the detective to pass him his cell phone that was on the table and called the club.

"Look, I don't have all the details but I want you to shut the club down... hold on, Detective Stewart wants to talk to you." Handing him the phone, he said, "It's Trent Singleton."

"Mr. Singleton, do not allow anyone to leave. I've got men on their way to interview everyone." Jason paused and shook his head. "Fuck! All right, don't let anyone else leave, and make a list of anyone who has left already." Pausing to listen, he spoke again. "No, that's fine. Let them get dressed. We're not attempting to embarrass anyone. The dining room will be fine." He nodded and then said, "Thanks, I'll give you back to Brody."

The moment he did, Brody told Trent to take care of business and that he'd call back later. Ending his call, he said, "Fuck this leg! I can't do a fucking thing to help!"

"We've got a lot of people on it. I've got to go, but Brody, you can do something. You can pray."

21

GRACE TRIED NOT to make a sound as she slowly woke, her head aching and her thoughts fuzzy. Not to mention that whatever she'd been drugged with had her stomach roiling with nausea. Forcing herself to concentrate, she attempted to put the pieces of her memory back together.

The machine on the hospital's fifth floor held only healthy selections of beverages. She'd been walking back to the nurses' station to ask where she might find carbonated sodas when a nurse stepped out of a room and directed her to the cafeteria, and told her that if she got them out of the machines in the vending area instead of the actual cafeteria, it would be faster. Grace had thanked her and decided to take the stairs, since she planned on adding a chocolate bar to her own order.

By the time she'd reached the ground floor, her legs were shaking. It took her another few minutes to find the alcove that held a large variety of vending machines. She'd been bent over, taking the can of Sprite out of the machine's bay, when she felt a presence behind her. Before she could straighten up, she'd been pressed into the glass door of the machine, crying out as the shove pinned her wrist between the hard plastic of the bin's door. The next thing she felt was a prick in her neck and then... nothing.

Keeping her eyes closed, she tried to assess where she was. As her mind cleared further, she knew she wasn't in any room, as she could not only hear sounds of insects buzzing around her, the air was thick and humid, and the aromas of plant life were mixed with an almost briny scent, albeit one with an underlying layer of decay. Her stomach continued to churn, not helped by the almost indiscernible rocking she felt but couldn't place. Was she in a car moving with the windows down to allow the night air inside? Her body ached and felt cramped. Was the stiffness she felt a side effect of the drug? When she tried to flex her arms, she had to stifle a groan at the sharp pain the slight movement caused in her shoulders. Hearing a splash, she froze. Oh God, she wasn't in a car, the motion she felt was from the current pushing against some sort of boat. One low to the water, as droplets from whatever had caused the splash had landed on her cheek. When an owl hooted and a small squeal told of the bird's success in capturing his prey, she understood exactly where she was. She had been taken into the maze of channels that twisted and turned, doubling back or even disappearing with the seasons, like the venomous cottonmouths that called the dark bayous home.

The swamp offered so much, gave sustenance to those willing to work hard and learn how to pull a living from a place that was both beautiful and mysterious. A place where murky waters hid more than alligators... a primordial place where evil also roamed. A perfect place to make a person lose their soul to the devil as they slipped the evidence of their sins into the water and watched the water lilies part for only a brief moment, then merge again to cover a watery grave. Whatever the lilies failed to hide, the beasts lurking beneath would make sure it disappeared as they greedily accepted the gift of sustenance, becoming partners in keeping untold horrors from the sun's light.

A sudden bump almost had Grace opening her eyes, but it was the ungodly screech that had her biting back a whimper in an involuntary reflex of the need to locate the direction of the threat. Had she been wrong? Didn't roosters belong on farms? The question flew away when the sound of a woman screaming split the air. She lost her battle to remain a silent, unmoving observer when she heard her name being screamed with such a sound of despair that her heart stuttered. Quentin was a big man, a man who kept himself under control, a man who loved with a passion that promised to take her to heights she'd yet to imagine, and yet, she feared that not only would he blame himself for her disappearance, if her body was ever found, he might not survive. *Quentin, I am so sorry. I promise to fight. I promise to try to come back to you but if I don't... please, God, please don't give up on life... don't give up on love.*

"I know you're awake but I'll be happy to play it again. From the beginning, or just that last part?"

Not only did she not wish to hear what she now understood was a recording, she knew that if she had any chance at all, she needed to be ready for any opportunity to escape, no matter how small. Opening her eyes, Grace saw rough wood that rose to form the gunwales of a canoe... no, not a canoe... a pirogue. She'd seen them on television, always amazed to watch them slip through the waters without turning over, as they looked so very unstable. The bump she'd felt had been caused when whoever was paddling had turned toward the bank to beach the craft. She attempted to push herself up, but all that did was cause the pirogue to tilt toward the water. The laugh she heard had her wanting to twist around but she'd realized that the reason her shoulders were aching was because her hands were not only behind her back, her wrists had been bound.

"Be still. I've not yet dismissed you. You have more lessons to learn, Miss Hensley. And as I am the teacher, I will set the agenda."

She felt the boat rock harder and then lift as her abductor stepped out. Grace couldn't help but gasp as she was yanked up by her arm, her feet stumbling to find purchase as she was helped from the boat. The bank before her was a mass of the lush green kudzu vine that twisted around trunks and branches, draping like Spanish moss from tree to tree. When she was given a shove, she understood that she was expected to climb.

"I can't, not without my hands, it's too slippery."

"Pretend there is a twelve-foot gator behind you." As if to reinforce that suggestion, Grace heard a huge splash and began to crawl up the bank, sliding back only to push with her knees and feet until she'd gained the relative safety a few feet above the water. Sinking down onto her knees, she saw the twisted, knotty roots of huge trees that stuck up from the dirt like some sort of tangled mass of limbs attempting to decide in which direction to run.

"I believe you've had a long enough break. Rise to attention, Miss Hensley, class is resuming."

"Why are you doing this? I've never—" Grace cried out as she was backhanded, the stroke knocking her to the side, her stomach winning as she retched in the mass of leaves, her headache blooming back to pound like a drum in her skull. She didn't cry out again as she was hauled back into the kneeling position. She didn't flinch but she knew that if she were going to die in this place, a place that was created to be beautiful, a place that had been filled with God's bounty to provide sustenance to his people, a place that birthed men such as Quentin, then she wasn't going to go quietly into the night. Looking up, ignoring the pulsing in her cheek, she said, "Go to hell."

A second blow to her other cheek sent her to the

ground again, the coppery taste of blood filling her mouth as she bit her tongue.

"I can do this all night, Miss Hensley. Either we shall continue to test your pain tolerance, or you can choose to be a good little submissive and obey."

Again she was hauled back to kneel, her head reeling and her face already swelling. Spitting out the blood, enjoying the fact that it splattered on her attacker's feet, Grace knew that another blow might send her into oblivion... one from which she might never awaken. She had to survive long enough so that Quentin could find her. She couldn't fight if she was unconscious or... or dead. Bowing her head, she was ready to endure whatever was coming to gain every second of life that she could.

SEEING that the back gate of *Plaisir* had been opened, Quentin barely slowed as he turned into the drive and then swore as he swerved, almost colliding with a car that was pulling out as he was pulling in. Recognizing both the car and the face behind the wheel, he leapt from the bike. As it continued forward until it fell with a crash onto its side, he was already running toward the car.

Though the driver had already killed the ignition and opened the door, Quentin reached in and dragged him out, slamming him against the side of the Jeep.

"Where the hell is she?"

"What the fuck? Get your hands off me!"

"I swear to God, if you have harmed a single hair on her head, if you've left her to die like you did Beth, I won't need a gun. I'll kill you with my bare hands. Where the fuck is Grace?"

Conner Matthews shook his head. "How would I know?" The back of his head cracked against the frame of the Jeep when Quentin's fist landed.

"Don't lie to me! Where is she!"

"I swear, I don't know! You kicked me out of class and the last I heard, you and she left together."

Quentin's next blow never landed, as his arms were pinned against him and he was dragged back. His curse and struggles did nothing to relax the arms of steel. "Let me go! He has Grace!"

"Quentin, stop!" Sammy tightened his grip when Quentin continued to struggle to get free. "Son! Stop!"

Quentin stilled as he recognized Sammy's voice, but wasn't yet freed. "Matthews has been here all night," Sammy continued.

"No, he took Grace from the hospital..."

"No, son, he couldn't have. He only just left. Trent said Brody called with instructions to lock the club down and not let anyone leave. I'd just seen Matthews going out the back so I came out to see if I could stop him. The police don't want anyone to leave until they get here. I swear to you, he didn't take her."

Shrugging free only because Sammy allowed him to, Quentin shook his head, feeling sick. How could he have been so wrong?

"Just because he didn't take her, doesn't mean he's

not in on it. Where was he going if the police said to lock the club down? He's got a partner..."

Conner was smart enough not to move as he said, "Look, I didn't know about the lockdown or I wouldn't have left. I know you don't think much of me, but I swear, I'd never hurt a woman simply because you pissed me off."

Before Quentin could react, the flashing strobe lights of a car lit the yard as it pulled into the driveway and stopped. More lights flashed as additional cars arrived, policemen spilling out, all of whom quickly moved in different directions. Some entered the back of the club where Sloan was standing, holding the door open, some circled the house to go in the front. The only one Quentin was interested in was the detective who stepped from the first car, his gun drawn.

"Hands where I can see them!" Jason barked, and all three men raised their arms.

"It's not him," Quentin said, finally accepting the fact that Sammy wouldn't lie to him.

Jason nodded but continued toward them, instructing Conner to step away from the Jeep. Since the driver's door had been left open, the light making it easy to discern what was inside, Jason moved to the back of the Jeep, popping open the lift gate.

"What's in the duffel?"

Quentin felt his heart stop, imagining Grace unconscious or worse, unable to breathe in the confines of a thick canvas bag. He took a step toward Cullen, who instinctively ducked.

"It's my toy bag!"

"Open it," Jason said, motioning him forward and keeping the gun pointed in his direction. When Quentin attempted to follow, Jason shook his head. "Stand back." It took everything Quentin had to obey, his fists clenched at his sides.

Conner unzipped the bag, pulling it open to display various implements he used in his play. "Satisfied?" he asked, stepping back and turning toward Quentin. "I swear to you Doucet, I had nothing to do with Beth's murder, and nothing to do with Grace's disappearance."

"Let's take this inside," Jason said, holstering his gun. When Quentin hesitated, he said, "You can't just run off looking for her. We've got the hospital on lockdown and their head of security just called. They found the Cokes Grace had purchased on the floor downstairs and a wheelchair outside the emergency room." He paused and put his hand on Quentin's arm. "They also found a shoe, a black..."

"Ballet flat," Quentin said, his anguish at the news audible. "So whoever took her already has her out of the hospital, don't they?"

"It appears so, but I've got officers still searching. We need more information but I swear, not a soul will stop looking until we find her."

"Come inside, son," Sammy said. "Maybe someone knows something that will help."

Quentin nodded and, walking to his bike, he put it into gear as he didn't want it rolling when he lifted it. Since it had fallen onto its right side, he lowered the kickstand to keep it from falling on him as Sammy helped him get it upright. There was no smell of fumes or sheen of oil to indicate any of the fuel lines had been damaged in the fall. Quentin was grateful that he'd not only slowed to make the turn into the drive, he'd slowed further while swerving to avoid the Jeep. Once the Indian was stable, he turned and followed the other men inside.

Before the group made it down the hall and into the dining room, Quentin reached out and managed to grab Conner's arm before he could be stopped, though Jason had turned as well.

"Doucet, that's not going to help," Jason said, "let him go."

Instead of obeying, Quentin shoved him hard against the wall, pinning him with a forearm across his chest as he pulled a cellphone from his pocket.

"If you had nothing to do with Grace's abduction, then how in the fuck do you explain this?" He'd remembered that he'd instructed Grace on how to download the app necessary to enable her to record incoming calls. He'd wanted to have audio proof if Brooks called with additional threats, or simply to harass her. He'd made her practice answering, showing her that she needed to remember to press the number four button to begin the recording. He'd had the same capabilities for years, and it was an automatic response for him to record all calls, instantly able to stop the recording with a simple press of the same button.

Turning the speaker on, he held the phone up

and replayed the call. The significance of the godawful crowing sound was instantly acknowledged by the color draining from Conner's face. The woman's scream had him looking up into Quentin's face.

"That isn't me. God, I... shit, how could I have known—"

"Known what?" Jason said, stepping closer as Sammy did the same on the other side, effectively pinning the man between them even as Quentin removed his arm.

Conner shook his head. "Look, I fucked her but I—"

Quentin's roar had Conner ducking and Sammy grabbing him, this time barely able to keep the man he considered a son from committing murder.

"Not Grace! I never laid a finger on her! I was pissed, and so was she. We got together after class the other day. Had a few drinks and, well, one thing led to another and we wound up in bed together. Fuck, you even ruined that," Conner said, looking at Quentin. "All she kept doing was topping from the bottom, telling me that she didn't need some pussy, she needed some man strong enough to dominate her. I... I guess I told her to shut up, that subs need to keep their mouths shut and that she wasn't cock of the walk, I was."

"Who is she?"

Conner met his eyes and gave the answer.

Jason said, "Call Brody, he's got his laptop. Get her address..."

"I've got it," Quentin said, "it'll be in her folder..."

"That won't help," Conner said. "The one she gave is a townhouse on the square. We didn't go there. She actually laughed and said that she couldn't be free in some place where neighbors could hear what went on when she played."

"Fuck!" Quentin snarled, "Then where the hell did you go?"

"She has a place out in the swamp," Conner said, his face paling again when he met Quentin's glare. "It-it's right across from where... where Beth was found. I can show you." The moment the information left Conner's lips, Quentin ran for the door, ignoring Jason's call to wait.

───────

"THAT'S BETTER. Now, rise and stand at attention."

Grace did so, not caring that it took lurching to get to her feet. Gracefulness was the least of her concerns. Once up, though swaying a bit, she felt her attacker approach and her stomach almost heaved again at seeing the gleam of a butcher's knife. Her inadvertent whimper was met with a laugh as the knife was waved about.

"Don't fret, I just realized that something is not quite right. Your little proclamation of undying adoration for Master Quentin was made before class actually began, wasn't it, Miss Hensley?" When the knife stopped moving, now pointed directly at her stomach, Grace forced herself to answer.

"Yes."

"Yes, what!"

"Yes, ma'am."

"That's *yes, Mistress*, you stupid bitch. No wonder my Dom has to constantly remind you of the simplest rules."

Grace wanted to spit out that Quentin was not her Dom, but the knife was weaving about again. "Yes, Mistress."

"I suggest you don't move unless you're into the sight of your own blood." Grace held her breath as the long blade of the knife was slid inside her t-shirt, slicing through the thin fabric from her waist to her neck. It took a few more strokes to cut the shirt from her body, but only three to slice through the straps and front of her bra. Her skin pebbled instantly in the cool air and she managed to let out her breath and take another as the knife began to slice through her jeans. In moments, she was completely naked but for her one shoe.

"Tsk, tsk, are those the proper shoes... make that shoe, Miss Hensley?" Not waiting for a response, the woman continued. "I expressly remember you being instructed to wear heels. I suppose it's just another sign of why Quentin prefers me over you. It's time for you to learn how to properly submit. Take the 'Present' position."

Grace would never submit to this woman. She knew that doing so would put her at a distinct disadvantage. The woman was not only taller than she, but she'd seen how fit she was. If Grace had any chance, it would have to be while she was still on her feet.

"I haven't learned that position, Mistress. I knew I was not ever going to be as perfect a submissive as you and quit before I could embarrass myself any further, remember?"

Her statement, softly spoken, with respect bordering on faked awe, had the response she'd hoped for.

"That's right. My Dom failed you for your inability to serve."

"I was too clumsy," Grace said, "Not as graceful as you, Mistress. I was so horrid that I never got to see how a submissive is to offer herself properly."

"You are just like that other woman. Both of you think that this is nothing more than some kinky game."

"What other woman, Mistress?"

"The slut who tried to steal my Dom. Kept telling me she'd get me some help, like I was crazy. I didn't need her fucking help! All she had to do was go away, but she refused." A laugh that rose the hair on the back of Grace's neck rang through the swamp. She hated to listen, and yet knew the longer she could keep her talking, the more time Quentin had to find them.

"You're right. You can't be crazy... you have to be very smart. I mean, no one suspected you, no one could figure out how she was in the club and then just vanished."

"That's because she wasn't in the club. She was

right over there." A finger pointed toward the tangle of roots, and Grace felt a sadness flood through her. "She wouldn't give me her ring so that I could surprise Quentin so, well, I borrowed it, but he wasn't in the club or his apartment."

"But she had her ring when she was found," Grace said.

"Of course she did. I'm not a fucking thief! I said I borrowed it! I knew Quentin would give me my own."

Not a thief? Just a murderer! No, you're not crazy, you're completely insane, Grace thought to herself. She honestly didn't wish to hear any more, didn't want to think about the terror Beth must have felt with the horror of her impending death.

"Even in death she tried to screw with me! Quentin went away and I waited and waited. I knew he'd come back for me one day, and then you... you showed up, and he couldn't give me the attention he wanted because he kept having to correct you!"

The change in her voice had Grace's breath hitching. She was now ranting, her voice becoming shriller as the knife flashed back and forth. How did one talk down an insane person?

"I-I'm sorry—"

"Shut up! I'm sick of hearing you whine and beg. Get on your fucking knees!"

Instead, Grace bowed her head and bolted forward, putting every ounce of her strength into it and praying that God was with her as she rammed her head into the woman's midsection. The woman staggered backwards and then cried out as her foot caught on a root. Her arms flailed and the knife dropped away as she landed hard on her ass and Grace fell to her knees beside her.

Attempting to get the knife, Grace cried out as her hair was caught, and saw the knife being picked up. "You'll pay for that, bitch."

"Go to hell!" Grace said, twisting to kick whatever body part she could, her teeth sinking into flesh with the ferocity of a rabid animal. The woman howled and yet tightened her hold, pulling Grace's head back until she feared her neck would snap. When the silver blade of the knife was lifted and pressed against her throat, Grace didn't flinch, her eyes not on the woman or the blade. They were lifted toward the sky as the moonlight shimmered around an impossible figure and when she spoke, Grace felt peace in the face of death.

QUENTIN COULD HEAR the sirens behind him as he roared through the streets. Once he hit the highway, his speed increased until the motorcycle was nothing more than a blur. It was only with God's grace that he managed to weave in and out of traffic without losing control of the bike, and he was still flying when he hit the exit ramp. The sirens were fainter now and he knew they had taken another road. They could look all they wanted at the house, but his gut was telling him that not only was this the same person who had killed Beth, but that while she might like to scream in her own house, she wouldn't want to sully it with the screams of another woman.

Knowing how sound traveled in the swamp, he forced himself to slow and then to glide to a stop, climbing off the bike. It was dark but he never considered needing light. He'd been living in the swamp, tracking, hunting, and fishing his entire life. His boots barely made a sound as he made his way to a place he'd hoped he'd visited for the last time only a few days earlier. As he silently pushed through the growth, he could swear that he felt a presence beside him.

Hurry.

Not startled at the word that came from nowhere, he nodded and moved as fast as he could without giving away his own presence. It wasn't long before he heard sounds that didn't belong to the creatures of the night. Stepping out of the trees, he knew he had but seconds left before this deranged killer took another innocent life from the world.

Forcing himself to stand as still as possible, too far away to rush them with that knife at Grace's throat, he spoke in the sternest tone with the most absolute authority he could manage.

"Stand at attention!" Though the brunette's head lifted toward him, the knife didn't move.

"I expected so much more from you, Miss Wilson. I said stand at attention, and I suggest you do so immediately!"

He watched as Starla seemed to hesitate, and prayed that Grace wouldn't attempt to move. Taking a few slow steps forward, he said, "Don't make me sorry that I used you as an example, Miss Wilson. I'll be very disappointed. You are at the head of the class but if I must repeat myself again, I'm afraid that I'll have no choice but to fail you."

"No! Don't send me away!"

"That's your choice, but I won't wait long."

Starla looked down and shook her head. Quentin took another step, praying she wasn't silently stating that she wouldn't obey, and spoke again.

"What's that? You know your Dom can't hear you unless you speak. Are you asking to be let go?"

"No... no, sir," she said, finally releasing Grace's hair.

For God's sake, don't move, Grace, he prayed silently, keeping his eyes on the knife.

Starla wasn't graceful but she was moving away from Grace. When she backed into the root, she paused and then shook her head again, as if trying to remember what she was doing.

"Very good, Miss Wilson. Rise and prepare yourself for inspection." It was a command he'd not yet taught but one he was hoping that, as an experienced submissive, Starla would understand.

When Starla began to rise, Grace remained frozen, for which he was grateful. Finally, Starla was on her feet and lifting her arms in preparation of placing them behind her head. It seemed that it was only then that she began to come out of the submissive mode, her head turned toward the knife in her hand.

Quentin's heart stopped as her head swiveled toward him, the moonlight reflecting in her eyes. He had managed to get close, but not yet close enough to grab her.

"Your hands are to be empty, Miss Wilson. Drop it and place your hands behind your head."

Her head shook again and instead of keeping her eyes on him, she looked down to where Grace was still kneeling.

"No!" Starla screamed, lunging forward even as Quentin dove. The next second took a lifetime as he heard Grace scream, felt a searing heat in his back, and heard a gunshot. Rolling down the embankment, he kept Grace in his arms as they fell into the water.

"Quentin!" Grace screamed.

"I've got you," he said, staggering to get his feet under him, the abandoned pirogue offering him support as he pushed against it.

"You're hurt!"

"I'm all right," he assured her, and though his back felt like it was on fire, he tightened his grip around her. "Are you all right?"

"Yes, I knew you'd find me... I knew you'd come," she said, and only then broke into sobs.

"Shh, it's going to be all right," he said, his cheek pressed against her head, the water swirling at his waist. "Everything is going to be all right."

Lights began to bounce through the swamp until one found them. "Hang on," Sammy shouted, half walking, half sliding down the bank. "Give her to me," he said, opening his arms.

"Hell no," Quentin said.

"Fine, but may I suggest you get your ass out of the water, unless you think you can also wrestle an alligator, son."

Quentin didn't bother to respond but started toward the bank, noticing that lights were now aimed at the shore as if to either illuminate his path or to spot the reflection of a gator's eyes as it slid through the water toward its prey. Reaching the bank, he felt hands on his arms, Jason on one side and Sammy on the other. It took effort to pull him up as the mud was doing its best to suck his boots from his feet.

Eventually, between them, they pulled him from the swamp and helped steady him as he climbed the now very slick bank, the kudzu vines crushed into the mud and murk of the ground beneath them.

Once he was back in the clearing, his knees buckled and he sank to the ground but kept his love in his arms. A breeze sprang from nowhere and though he knew it should have chilled them as he held Grace, both of them dripping wet, instead it seemed to envelop them in warmth. Leaves swirled around their bodies, wisps of white moving fluidly against the black of the night.

"Beth," Grace said, "she's here."

"Yes."

Everyone and everything else dropped away as the couple experienced a moment neither would ever forget, a time where the horrors of the past were left behind and the path to the future was opened.

Love each other always.

Though the words were not spoken aloud, both Quentin and Grace murmured their promise and, with tears in their eyes, they thanked the woman whose life had been taken. Both lifted their eyes to the stars as the white mist gathered and caressed them for the last time before swirling away, seeming to dance with the joy of freedom to disappear and begin the greatest journey of all.

22

IT WASN'T until the next morning that Quentin woke. His eyelashes fluttered as if the effort was too much for them to open, and yet they did.

"Grace?"

"I'm here," she said, standing and then bending forward over the bed to gently stroke his forehead before brushing her lips across his skin. "How do you feel?"

"At the risk of sounding like a wuss, like hell."

"You'll never be a wuss, my love, but you have been in hell." She couldn't help the tears that fell on his face. "God, I was so scared I was going to lose you."

"Me? I was terrified that I'd lose you. Grace, I am so sorry—"

"Don't," she said, her hand squeezing his. "You saved my life. You almost died because of me."

He shook his head, moaning a little as he lifted his free hand with the IV needle stuck into his flesh.

"Don't you know that if I'd lost you, I wouldn't have survived?"

Grace didn't correct him as she felt the same way. He was the other half of her soul. When he tried to roll onto his back, she reached out to stop him. "Don't, you need to remain on your side, at least until the doctor comes in."

"Why? I want you to climb up here and let me hold you."

"Quentin, don't you remember? You were stabbed. They wouldn't even take the knife out until they had you in surgery."

"Fuck! So that's where the knife went."

She shook her head. "I knew you were tough, but honestly, who doesn't know when they've been stabbed?"

"Macho men who think their women will think less of them once they are discovered to be humans after all," Laurie offered as she breezed into the room. "Grace, I expressly remember you promising me that if I let you out of your bed, you'd sit in the chair and not move around."

"But he woke up and—"

"No excuses. You need to get off your leg."

"It doesn't hurt—"

"What's wrong with your leg?" Quentin asked, once again attempting to move.

"Listen up, folks. Until further notice, the only boss in this room is me! Grace, sit down before you fall, and Quentin Doucet, if you don't stop trying to squirm around, I'm going to find great pleasure in tying you into position!"

Grace and Quentin both gaped at her until Grace giggled. "Wow, you sound as bossy as my Dadd... I mean my Dom."

"You haven't even begun to see bossy," Laurie said, moving to help Grace back into the wheelchair she'd been sitting in at Quentin's bedside. "I love you and"—she grinned and gave Quentin a pointed look—"your *Daddy* dearly but after scaring the hell out of me and Brody, the least you can both do is follow my orders."

"I'm sorry," Grace said, "I was just so scared, too."

"I know, honey," Laurie said, moving the chair back so she could return the platform that her patient had lowered in order to move as close to the bed as possible. Lifting Grace's leg carefully, she soon had it elevated. "It was a miracle that I will continue to thank God for, but now that he's done his part, we must do ours. Okay?"

"Okay," Grace said. After kissing her cheek, Laurie turned her attention to Quentin. She checked all the monitors and grinned as she told him she needed to take his temperature.

"Hmm, now where did I put that big, thick thermometer? You know, the one that goes up a naughty patient's butt?"

"You even try that and I promise that once I get out of this bed, you'll not sit for a year!"

The women giggled and he grinned when she

also bent to give his cheek a kiss. "Welcome back, Quentin."

"Don't you mean welcome home?" he asked, remembering the conversation that seemed to have started his new life.

"Oh, I knew you were home from the moment you stepped into Brody's room. It just took you a while to realize it."

After making sure he was as comfortable as he could be, she promised that the doctor would be coming in soon. "Please don't try to move," she said. "Keep wiggling and you'll pop the stitches. You might have been unconscious when they were put in, but believe me, I can arrange for them to be replaced without the benefit of anesthesia by a green intern anxious to get experience."

"Yes, nurse, I promise to be a good boy."

"Oh, please, like I'm going to fall for that. That line never saves my ass when I yell it. Stop trying to suck up and just behave!"

Grace was having a hard time stifling her giggle as she listened to the interplay between the two.

"You know I love you, right?" Quentin said.

"I know, and I love you too, you big lug," Laurie said, bending to kiss his cheek again. "Now close your eyes and get some sleep."

She met Grace's gaze, and Grace quickly made a promise of her own. "I won't bother him but please let me stay."

"Only if you promise that until the doctor clears

him to move, the only thing you'll be holding is his hand."

"Laurie!" Grace said and then burst into giggles, her eyes and mind instantly going to a part of Quentin's anatomy that was definitely not attached to the ends of his arms. Laurie just winked as she swished out the door.

"Now that's a sound I love to hear," Quentin said, drawing her attention to his face, where his eyes were closing. She thought he'd already succumbed to the medicine she'd seen Laurie inject into his IV bag until he squeezed her hand and added, "Almost as much as I love the sound of you screaming my name when you come."

JASON VISITED, and it was a quiet conversation as he filled them in on what had happened. It had basically been Sammy who'd convinced him to change course and follow Quentin instead of the line of police cars headed toward Starla's shack.

"I've never seen anything like it," Jason said. "That giant of a man moved like a waif through the trees. He never hesitated... as if he knew exactly where you were."

Quentin nodded. "I have no doubt that he did."

"I really thought you were going to convince her to drop the knife," Jason said.

"So did I, until she seemed to realize she was holding it. God, I'll never forget the look in her eyes when she lunged at Grace." He paused and shook his head. "I was hoping to end it without another death, but I'll always thank God you were there."

"I am as well, but we weren't the only ones, were we? Beth was there as well, wasn't she?"

Looking at Grace and seeing her smile, he nodded again. "Yes, she told me to hurry, and Grace said she appeared to tell her that I was coming. She gave us her blessing—"

"And you gave her peace," Jason said, laying his hand on Quentin's shoulder.

GRACE WAS the first to be discharged, and yet she still spent every day at the hospital. Her sprained ankle didn't keep her from hobbling between Brody and Quentin's rooms, until Laurie pulled some strings and got the men moved into a room together. Though they were in a hospital, people passing their door often heard laughter and would smile, many taking the sound of hope with them as they either returned to their duties or visited their own loved ones confined within the hospital's walls.

After he'd been approved to move, Quentin began physical therapy. The knife had not only pierced his flesh, but with the roll down the bank, it had continued to slice through muscle, causing more damage. One day, Grace told him to take it easy, that there was plenty of time for him to heal. He'd grinned and stated that he wanted to make sure that when he left the hospital, he'd not only be healed, he'd be able to lift his arm higher than his shoulder.

"Why?"

"Oh, sugar, you really have to ask?" he said, slapping his uninjured left hand down onto his thigh.

"Oh, I see," she said, flushing as the sound made her bottom clench.

Another visit had Quentin pulling her onto his lap and her protesting that he was still recovering.

"Stop wiggling," he said, bending down to nuzzle her neck. "Or do I need to bend you over my knees? I might not yet be able to give you a proper spanking, but I'm sure I have enough strength to put a naughty plug up your bottom."

"Oh, God," she moaned, her face heating at the memory of that experience. Shocking herself, she then giggled. "You know, I never asked what the hospital staff thought when I was brought in wearing nothing but Detective Stewart's jacket and that plug."

"I'm sure they thought you were a very good submissive. I mean, sugar, you were kidnapped, beaten, and almost murdered, and yet you never lost it. That's pretty amazing."

She might have snuggled into his chest to hide her face as Brody chuckled from his bed, but secretly she was rather proud of herself.

ON THE DAY of his discharge, Quentin slid into the

passenger seat of his truck and grinned as Grace bounced on the seat, her small hands on the wheel.

"Do not get used to this," Quentin said, and when she rolled her eyes and turned the key, he groaned. "Really? Hard rock? Woman, you do not change a man's radio station."

"Hmm, perhaps I should just hop out and inform the doctor that you are far too grouchy to go home."

"Perhaps you should put the truck in gear and consider that all that physical therapy has ensured that when my palm begins to itch, I shall be able to scratch it quite successfully across your cute little ass."

They were met by a room full of people, all cheering and welcoming them home. Hannah gave Quentin a gentle hug and then squealed when he wrapped his arms around her and squeezed hard. "I won't break," he said, bending to give her cheek a kiss.

"Don't you ever scare Sammy like that again!" Hannah said, wiping her eyes.

"Yes, ma'am," Quentin said, releasing her and accepting a hug from Sammy.

"How are you doing, son?" the large man asked when he finally stepped away.

Pulling Grace into his side, Quentin's smile lit up his entire face. "I couldn't be better."

Sammy grinned, slapped Quentin on the back, hugged Grace, and announced that the spread he'd laid out was getting cold. The party was loud, the gumbo and Cajun dishes delicious, the sweet tea and beer flowing freely.

With a chuckle, Quentin pulled Grace to him, using one hand to tip her face up and the other to cup the nape of her neck. "Woman, you are definitely the sweetest thing in my life," he said, the tip of his tongue licking along her lips to remove the thick layer of powdered sugar left behind after the ginormous bite she'd just take of a beignet. Grace's giggle morphed into a moan of intense satisfaction as his mouth claimed hers. It was a few long moments before they broke apart, only to hear their friends breaking into hoots and catcalls yet again as they all celebrated the pure joy of being alive and together.

EPILOGUE

A Year Later...

THE SHOW WAS AN EVEN BIGGER success than Grace's first. Strains of soft jazz wafted through the large space, not from any sound system, but from the instruments that came to life in the hands of George Mathias. A larger than life canvas was displayed in the front window, where George's wife, the love of his life, showed the older woman sitting at her husband's feet, a hand on his knee, her face turned up, her lips curved in a soft smile as he played for an audience of one. *Rapture*, its title, was reflected on both of the couple's faces.

People moved about the gallery looking not only at Grace's art, but at her husband's. Jewelry was displayed beside exquisite leather pieces. The painting she'd done of Laurie was on one wall, the falls of the flogger Quentin had made for their wedding splayed across the mounds of her bottom, the expression on her face giving the painting its title: *Bliss*.

"I still can't believe that's me," Laurie said, her cheeks flushed as Brody chuckled.

"Believe it, honey, that is definitely my wife."

Grace accepted yet another hug and expression of thanks and then slipped away. There was another painting, and it was the only one she truly prayed that its owner would love as much as she. Turning a corner, she hesitated seeing Quentin standing before the canvas centered on the wall. He turned and smiled, holding out his hand and issuing the same words he'd uttered on that day.

"GRACE, COME," he said, holding out his hand.

"I'm not sure this will work," she said, not looking at him but at the array of tripods she'd set around the area.

"It won't matter," he assured her.

"It does matter. You said you wanted a gift of a painting for your wedding present. Let me set up one more camera. It will..."

Walking to her, Quentin took her into his arms before she could turn away. "Babe, you've given me the greatest gift of all... you, in the flesh." He tilted her face to his and lowered his mouth to within a centimeter of hers. "Flesh that I have promised to stripe, and flesh I promise to caress for the rest of our lives... beginning now."

His kiss had settled her, and his hands helping her undress had her trembling even before he led her to the St. Andrew's Cross. He'd fulfilled his promise one evening when he'd taken her upstairs and placed her over the barrel. She'd come not once, but twice as the flogger stroked every inch of her ass. It had been incredibly erotic and yet, for this painting she wished to give him, he'd chosen a different venue, and would use the gift he'd crafted for her. Once he'd buckled leather cuffs around her wrists and ankles and attached them to the chains, he stepped closer, running a finger along the gold of the collar he'd placed around her neck the day they'd wed. They'd worked together in its creation. He'd first crafted one of leather, and she'd recreated it in gold. The lock was hidden in the braided handle, the thin strip of leather depicted in gold encircling her throat signifying their mutual love of the medium and each other never out of their sight.

Quentin ran his fingers through her hair and down her body, circling her peaked nipples, dipping into her navel and stroking softly across her sex. She moaned and arched toward him, accepting his kiss with passion and the tremble of anticipation. Stepping away, he picked up not one but two single-tail whips, allowing the leather to unfurl from their coils, aware of her watching his every movement. He snapped one and then the other, the sharp sound followed by her almost desperate moan. He hadn't even started and yet he could see a glistening between her legs, a drop of her arousal sliding down her inner thigh.

"God, you are beautiful. Are you ready?"

───────

SHE THOUGHT he was the most magnificent thing she'd ever seen. Standing before her, she felt she could come from just watching the ink on his body undulate from the muscles he used to lift and snap the whips he'd crafted. He wore nothing but the black leather pants that fit him like a glove, molding around his cock that was testament to his arousal. He'd shut down all the lights in the room except those in this one corner. The room should have seemed cavernous with only two occupants, and yet it felt intimate and just perfect.

Looking at the man who had stolen not only her heart, but her soul, she smiled. "Yes, I'm ready, sir."

It had been the most incredible experience of her life. The whips had lifted and within his hands, had licked and kissed her flesh. The cracks had ended with her gasps and soft moans as they wrapped around her body, leaving evidence of their caress in small, raised wheals. It was a dance... it was a symphony... it was magical. From the first stroke, they both forgot the cameras, their only thoughts on each other, and when she arched for the last time, screaming his name as she convulsed, the music didn't stop... it was joined by his own cry as he released her, wrapping his body around her, holding her against him, whispering that he loved her.

THIS TIME it was Quentin who lifted a hand to wipe tears from his cheek as he stood before the painting hanging in the place of honor in the gallery. She hadn't allowed him to see the finished canvas before this moment. He'd been positive she'd choose one of the many photos of her on the frame, and yet he should have known that she'd had a different idea. Instead, she'd chosen one of the two of them, one that depicted him holding her close. One of her hands lay against the ink of his tattoo, the other circled his neck. His head was bowed and hers lifted as their eyes drank each other in. The leather coil of one of the whips he'd used lay against the small of her back, the tail caressing the curve of her ass. The black of his pants contrasted not only with her pale flesh but also with the red heels she was wearing.

While no person who ever laid eyes on the painting would doubt that the couple shown belonged to each other, only the two of them would fully understand the swirl of white that had been painted into the dark background.

Looking at the title, he smiled. "It's absolutely perfect," he said, and it was. He'd been lost in the darkness of despair until she'd entered his life. She was not only the first ray of light he'd known since Beth's death, she was his salvation. They'd gone through hell, and yet with God's grace, they'd found help in the deepest pit with softly spoken words of hope. No matter what came in the future, they knew they'd found heaven in their whispered words given that night in the swamp.

The script on the small brass plate simply read: *Promise.*

The End

ABOUT THE AUTHOR

Maggie Ryan is a USA TODAY bestselling author in Victorian/ Historical, Contemporary, Western, and Paranormal Romance. As a multi-published and Amazon Top 100 bestselling author, she brings you stories that are always sweet, extra spicy, and a little taboo. She writes about strong, stern alpha males and sassy, capable women who discover that life without a bit of fire isn't worth living. Maggie hopes you will curl up in your favorite chair and take the journey with her. Happy Reading!

Connect with Maggie on:
Website: http://www.authormaggieryan.com
Facebook: https://www.facebook.com/authormaggieryan/
Twitter @authorMRyan
Instagram: Instagram.com/Maggie.ryan.writes
Amazon: https://amazon.com/author/maggieryan
BookBub: bookbub.com/authors/maggie-ryan
Email: maggie.ryan.writes@gmail.com
Sign up for Maggie's Newsletter: http://www.subscribepage.com/z8j9x8

ALSO BY MAGGIE RYAN

Don't miss these exciting titles by Maggie Ryan

Please Daddy

Big Bad Daddy Wolffe

A Little Atonement

Daddy Says

Daddy Commands

Leather and Grace

Co-authored with Alta Hensley:

Bride to Keep

Kings & Sinners Series:

Maddox

Stryder

Anson

Black Light Series Stand Alone:

Suspended

Black Light Series Anthologies:

Roulette Redux – featuring my story SurrenderCelebrity Roulette – featuring my story Savor

Co-authored with Shanna Handel:

Shifter's Call Trilogy:

The Wolf's Demand

Her Alpha Mates

The Power of the Pack

Check out all Maggie Ryan books at Amazon: https://amazon.com/author/maggieryan

Made in the USA
Columbia, SC
28 June 2023

19625033R00204